MILLENNIUM

JOHN VARLEY

BERKLEY BOOKS, NEW YORK

MILLENNIUM

A Berkley Book / published by arrangement with
the author

PRINTING HISTORY
Berkley trade paperback edition / June 1983
Berkley edition / May 1985
Fourth printing / June 1986

ISBN: 0-425-09843-5

A BERKLEY BOOK ® TM 757,375
Berkley Books are published by The Berkley Publishing Group,
200 Madison Avenue, New York, NY 10016.
The name "BERKLEY" and the stylized "B" with design
are trademarks belonging to Berkley Publishing Corporation.

PRINTED IN THE UNITED STATES OF AMERICA

To the Moroccans:
Maurice,
Roger,
and one day,
Stefan.

Prologue

Testimony of Louise Baltimore

The DC-10 never had a chance. It was a fine aircraft, even though at that point in time it was still under a cloud of controversy resulting from incidents in Paris and Chicago. But when you lose that much wing you're no longer in a flying machine, you're in an aluminum rock. That's how the Ten came in: straight down and spiraling.

But the 747, as I was telling Wilbur Wright just the other day, ranks up there with the DC-3 Gooney Bird and the Fokker-Aerospatiale HST as one of the most reliable hunks of airframe ever designed. It's true that this one came out of the collision in better shape than the DC-10, and there is no doubt it was mortally wounded. But the grand old whale managed to pull up into straight and level flight and maintain it. Who knows what might have been possible if that mountain hadn't got in the way?

And it retained a surprising amount of structural integrity as it belly-flopped and rolled over—a maneuver no one at Boeing had envisioned in their design parameters. The proof of this could be seen in the state of the passengers: there were upwards of thirty bodies without a single limb detached. If it hadn't caught fire, there might even have been some faces intact.

I've always thought it would be a spectacular show to witness in your final seconds. Would you really rather die in bed?

Well, maybe so. One way of dying is probably much like any other.

1

"A Sound of Thunder"

Testimony of Bill Smith

My phone rang just before one o'clock on the morning of December 10.

I could leave it there, just say my phone rang, but it wouldn't convey the actual magnitude of the event.

I once spent seven hundred dollars for an alarm clock. It wasn't an alarm clock when I bought it and it was a lot more than that when I got through with it. The heart of the thing was a World War Two surplus air-raid siren. I added items here and there and, when I was through, it would have given the San Francisco earthquake stiff competition as a means of getting somebody out of bed.

Later, I connected my second telephone to this doomsday machine.

I got the second phone when I found myself jumping every time the first one rang. Only six people at the office knew the number of the new phone, and it solved two problems very neatly. I stopped twitching at the sound of telephone bells, and I never again was awakened by somebody who came to the house to tell me that the alarm had come in, I had been called and failed to answer, and I had been replaced on the go-team.

I'm one of those people who sleep like the dead. Always have; my mother used to tumble me out of bed to get me to school. Even in the Navy, while all around me were losing sleep thinking

3

about the flight deck in the morning, I could stack Z's all night and have to be rousted out by the C.O.

Also, I do drink a bit.

You know how it is. First it's just at parties. Then it's a couple at the end of the day. After the divorce I started drinking alone, because for the first time in my life I was having trouble getting to sleep. And I *know* that's one of the signs, but it's *miles* short of alcoholism.

But a pattern had developed of arriving late at the office and I figured I'd better do something about it before somebody higher up did. Tom Stanley recommended counseling, but I think my alarm clock worked just as well. There's always a way to work out your problems if you'll only take a look at them and then do what needs to be done.

For instance, when I found that three mornings in a row I had shut off my new alarm and gone back to sleep, I put the switch in the kitchen and tied it in to the coffee-maker. When you're up and have the coffee perking, it's too late to go back to sleep.

We all laughed about it at the office. Everybody thought it was cute. Okay, maybe rats running through a maze are cute, too. And maybe you're perfectly well adjusted, without a single gear that squeaks or spring that's wound too tight, and if so, I don't want to hear about it. Tell it to your analyst.

So my phone rang.

So I sat up, looked around, realized it was still dark and knew this wasn't the beginning of another routine day at the office. Then I grabbed the receiver before the phone could peel the second layer of paint off the walls.

I guess I took a while getting it to my ear. There had been a few drinks not too many hours before, and I'm not at my best when I wake up, even on a go-team call. I heard a hissing silence, then a hesitant voice.

"Mr. Smith?" It was the night-shift operator at the Board, a woman I'd never met.

"Yeah, you got him."

"Please hold for Mr. Petcher."

Then even the hiss was gone and I found myself in that

twentieth-century version of purgatory, "on hold," before I had a chance to protest.

Actually, I didn't mind. It gave me a chance to wake up. I yawned and scratched, put on my glasses, and peered at the chart tacked to the wall above the nightstand. There he was, C. Gordon Petcher, just below the chairman and the line that read "GO-TEAM MEMBERS—Notify the following for all catastrophic accidents." The chart is changed every Thursday at the end of the work day. The Chairman, Roger Ryan, is the only name that appears on every one. No matter what happens, at any time of the day, Ryan is the first to hear about it.

My own name was a little further down the list in the space marked "Aviation Duty Officer/IIC," followed by my beeper number and the number of my second home phone. "IIC," by the way, is not to be read as "two-C," but as "Investigator In Charge."

C. Gordon Petcher was the newest of the five members of the National Transportation Safety Board. As such, he was naturally a little suspect. Those of us hired for our expertise always wonder about new Board members, who are appointed for five-year terms. Each has to go through a trial period during which we decide if this one is to be trusted or endured.

"Sorry to keep you waiting, Bill."

"That's okay, Gordy." He wanted us to call him Gordy.

"I was just talking to Roger. We have a very bad one in California. Since it's so late and the accident is so big, we've decided not to wait for available transport. The JetStar is waiting for the go-team to assemble. I'm hoping it can take off within an hour. If you—"

"How big, Gordy? Chicago? Everglades? San Diego?"

He sounded apologetic. That can happen. Breaking really bad news, you can feel that somehow you're responsible for it.

"It could be bigger than Canary Islands," he said.

Part of me resented this new guy speaking to me in agency shorthand, while the rest of me was trying to digest an accident bigger than Tenerife.

Outsiders might think we're talking about places when we

mention Chicago, Paris, Everglades, and so forth. We're not. Chicago is a DC-10 losing an engine on take-off, killing all aboard. Everglades was an L-1011, a survivor crash, bellying into the swamp while the crew was troubleshooting a nose-gear light. San Diego was a big, grinning PSA 727 getting tangled up with a Cessna in Indian Country—the low elevations swarming with Navajos, Cherokees, and Piper Cubs. And Canary Islands...

In 1978, at the Tenerife Airport, Canary Islands, an unthinkable thing happened. A fully-fueled, loaded Boeing 747 began its take-off while another 747 was still on the runway ahead of it, invisible in thick fog. The two planes collided and burned on the ground, as if they'd been lumbering city buses in rush-hour traffic instead of sleek, lovely, sophisticated flying machines.

It was, or had been until I got the phone call, the worst disaster in the history of aviation.

"Where in California, Gordy?"

"Oakland. East of Oakland, in the hills."

"Who was involved?"

"A Pan Am 747 and a United DC-10."

"Mid-air?"

"Yes. Both planes fully loaded. I don't have any definite numbers yet—"

"Don't worry about it. I think I've got all I need right now. I'll meet you at the airport in about—"

"I'll be taking a morning flight out of Dulles," he said. "Mr. Ryan suggested I remain here a few more hours to coordinate the public affairs side of things while—"

"Sure, sure. Okay. See you around noon."

I was out of the house no more than twenty minutes after I hung up. In that time I had shaved, dressed, packed, and had a cup of coffee and a Swanson's breakfast of scrambled eggs and sausage. It was a source of some pride to me that I had never done it faster, even before the divorce.

The secret is preparation, establishing habits and never varying from them. You plan your moves, do what you can beforehand, and when the call comes in you're ready.

So I showered in the downstairs bath instead of the one by the master bedroom, because that took me through the kitchen where I could punch the pre-programmed button on the microwave and flip the switch on the Mr. Coffee, both of which had been loaded the night before, drunk or sober. Out of the shower, electric razor in hand, I ate standing up while I shaved, then carried the razor upstairs and tossed it into the suitcase, which already was full of underwear, shirts, pants, and toiletries. It was only at that point I had to make my first decisions of the day, based on where I was going. I have been sent on short notice to the Mojave Desert and to Mount Erebus, in Antarctica. Obviously you bring different clothes. The big yellow poncho was already packed; you *always* prepare for rain at a crash site. The Oakland hills in December presented no big challenges.

Close and lock the suitcase, pick up the stack of papers on the desk and shove them in the smaller case which held the items I always had ready for a go-team call: camera, lots of film, notebook, magnifying glass, flashlight and fresh batteries, tape recorder, cassettes, calculator, compass. Then down the stairs again, pour a second cup of coffee and carry everything through the door to the garage—left open the night before—hit the garage-door button with my elbow on the way out, kick the door shut and locked behind me, toss the suitcase and briefcase into the open trunk, hop in the car, back out, hit the button on the Genie garage-door picker-upper and watch to make sure it closes all the way.

Aside from picking a few items of clothes, it was all automatic. I didn't have to think again until I was on Connecticut Avenue, driving south. The house was all battened down because I kept it that way. Thank God I didn't have a dog. Anyway, Sam Horowitz next door would keep an eye on the place for me when he read about the crash in tomorrow's *Post*.

All in all, I felt I had adjusted pretty well to bachelor living.

I live out in Kensington, Maryland. The house is way too big for me, since the divorce, and it costs a lot to heat, but I can't seem to leave it. I could have moved into the city, but I hate apartment living.

I took the Beltway in to National. That time of night Connecticut Avenue is almost deserted, but the lights slow you down.

You'd think the Investigator In Charge of a National Transportation Safety Board Go-Team on his way to the biggest aviation disaster in history would have a red light he could mount on top of his car and just zip through the intersections. Sad to say, the D.C. police would take a dim view of that.

Most of the team lived in Virginia and would get to the airport before me, whatever route I took. But the plane wouldn't leave without me.

I hate National Airport. It's an affront to everything the NTSB stands for. A few years back, when the news of the Air Florida hitting the 14th Street bridge first came in, a couple of us hoped (but not out loud) we might finally be able to shut it down. It didn't turn out that way, but I still hoped.

As it was, National was just too damn convenient. To most Washingtonians, Dulles International might as well be in Dakota. As for Baltimore . . .

Even the Board bases its planes at National. We have a few, the biggest being a Lockheed JetStar that can take us anywhere in the continental U.S. without refueling. Normally we take commercial flights, but that doesn't always work. This time it was too early in the morning to find enough seats going west. There was also the possibility, if this really was as big as Gordy said, that a second team would follow us as soon as the sun came up. We might have to treat this as two crashes.

Everybody but George Sheppard was already there by the time I boarded the JetStar. Tom Stanley had been in contact with Gordy Petcher. While I stowed my gear Tom filled me in on the things Petcher either had not known or could not bring himself to tell me when we talked.

No survivors. We didn't have an exact count yet from either airline, but it was sure to be over six hundred dead.

It had happened at five thousand feet. The DC-10 had gone almost straight down. The 747 flew a little, but the end result was the same. The Ten was not far from a major highway; local police and fire units were at the scene. The Pan Am Boeing was up in the hills somewhere. Rescue workers had reached it, but the only word back was that there were no survivors.

Roger Keane, the head of the NTSB field office in Los Angeles, was still on his way to the Bay Area and should be landing soon. Roger had been in contact with the Contra Costa and Alameda County Sheriff's offices, advising them on crash site procedures.

"Who's running the show at LAX?" I asked.

"His name's Kevin Briley," said Tom. "I don't know him. Do you?"

"I think I shook his hand once. I'll feel better when Rog Keane gets to the site."

"Briley said he was told to grab the next flight to Oakland and meet us there. He'll be in L.A. a little bit longer, if you want to talk to him."

I glanced at my watch.

"In a minute. Where's George?"

"I don't know. He got the call. We tried him five minutes ago and there was no answer."

George Sheppard is the weather specialist. We could take off without him, since his presence at the crash site wasn't absolutely necessary.

And I was ready to go. More: I was aching to go, like a skittish race horse in the starting gate. I could feel it building all around me, and all around the nation. The interior of the JetStar was dark and calm, but from Washington to Los Angeles and Seattle, and soon all around the world, forces were gathering that would produce the goddamdest electronic circus anyone ever saw. The nation slept, but the wire services and the coaxial cables and synchronous satellites were humming with the news. A thousand reporters and editors were being roused from bed, booking flights to Oakland. A hundred government agencies were going to be involved before this thing was over. Foreign governments would send representatives. Everyone from Boeing and McDonnell-Douglas to the manufacturer of the smallest rivet in an airframe would be on edge, wondering if their factory had turned out the offending part or written the fatal directive, and they'd all want to be on hand to hear the bad news as it happened. By the time the sun came up in California a billion people would be clamoring for answers. How did this happen? Whose fault is it? What should be done about it?

And I was the guy who had to provide those answers. Every nerve in my body was crying out to get in the air, get there, and start looking.

I was about to order the take-off when a call came in from George, sparing me a decision that he'd surely have resented. He was having car trouble. He'd called a taxi, but suggested we'd better take off without him and he'd catch up later. I heaved a sigh of relief and told the pilot to get us out of here.

What's it like on your way to a major airline disaster? Fairly quiet, for the most part. During the first hour I made a few calls to Los Angeles, spoke briefly to Kevin Briley. I learned that Roger Keane had boarded a helicopter and was surely at the DC-10 site by now. Briley was about to leave to catch his own flight to Oakland, where he would meet me at the airport. I told him to set up security.

Then some of the others made calls to Seattle, Oakland, Schenectady, Denver, Los Angeles. Each of the go-team members would be forming his own team to look into one aspect of the crash, and each wanted to get the best possible people. Usually that was no problem. The grapevine operates quickly in a crash this size. Almost everyone we called had already heard; many were already on their way. These were people we knew and trusted.

But none of that took very long. After that first hour we were alone in the sky on the five-hour flight to Oakland. So what did we do?

Do you have any idea how much paper work is involved in an accident investigation? Each of us had half a dozen reports in progress. There were reports to read and reports to write, and endless items to review. My own briefcase bulged with pending work. I did some of it for an hour or so.

Finally I wasn't understanding what I was reading. I yawned, stretched, and looked around me. Half the team was asleep. That struck me as a fine idea. It was 4:30 in the morning, Eastern time, three hours earlier on the West Coast, and none of us were likely to get any sleep until well past midnight.

Across the aisle was Jerry Bannister, in charge of structures.

He's the oldest of us: a big man with a huge head and thick gray hair, an aeronautical engineer who got his start on the Douglas assembly line building Gooney Birds because the Army recruiter rejected him. He's deaf in one ear and wears a hearing aid in the other. Looking at him, you'd think he was the biggest mistake the Army ever made. I'd put him up against a platoon of German soldiers any day, even at age sixty. He's got one of those craggy faces and a pair of those giant hands that would make him look right at home in a machine shop. It's hard to picture him at a drawing board or putting a model through wind-tunnel tests, but that's what he's good at. After the war he put himself through college. He worked on the DC-6 and the DC-8, among many others. He was sound asleep, head back, mouth open. The guy is almost nerveless; nothing rattles him. He collects stamps, of all things. He's nutty about philately; once he starts talking about it it's impossible to shut him off.

Behind him, his bald head gleaming in the cone of light from overhead, was Craig Haubner, my systems specialist. He would spend the rest of the flight filling page after page of his yellow legal tablet, bounce off the plane and out to the crash site and spend all day and into the night poking and peering into the wreckage, and return to the temporary headquarters still neat, alert, and full of energy. It was impossible to like Haubner—he wasn't very good with people, and sometimes didn't even seem to be human—but we all respected him. His ability to examine a bit of charred wire or bent hydraulic tubing and tell exactly what happened to it is little short of the occult.

Then there was Eli Seibel, also awake, pawing through the matchbook covers, paper napkins, torn envelopes and crumpled papers he is pleased to call his working notes. I never complain to him about it, though I grit my teeth when I see him at work. Out of the chaos he manages to turn in very good work. He's overweight and allergic to just about everything and the only one of us without a pilot's license, but he's cheerful, popular with the secretaries at the office, and competent at his specialty, which is powerplants.

In the seats behind me was Tom Stanley, with his feet out in the aisle and the rest of him vainly trying to curl up and get comfortable. At twenty-seven, he's the youngest member of the team. He'd never been in the service—I suspected he'd have been a draft-dodger if he'd been old enough for Viet-Nam—and the only aviation-related job he'd held before coming to work for the Board was as an Air Traffic Controller. His family has a lot of money. He started out at Harvard, of all places, before switching to M.I.T., and his dad paid every penny. He lives in a house that's worth five times what mine would sell for. All in all, I could hardly imagine a biography more calculated to bring out hostility from the likes of old pros like Jerry, Craig . . . and myself. And that's pretty much how Haubner and Bannister felt about him. Eli Seibel tolerates him, and Levitsky more or less tolerates all of us.

But I get along with Tom quite well. If there was such a thing as a second-in-command of an NTSB investigation (which there is not), I would choose Tom Stanley for the post. As it is, I confer with him a lot.

The secret is probably his love of flying. He's been doing it since he was about eight, and I love flying so much myself that I can't find it in myself to resent the money that made it possible for him. I own a wonderful old Stearman biplane that swallows too much of my salary and probably will never be paid for. Tom owns a mint-condition Spitfire. And he lets me fly it. What can you say about a man like that?

Tom would be chairing two sub-groups in the investigation: Air Traffic Control and Operations. The other person who would wear two hats was asleep in the back of the plane. She was Carole Levitsky, in charge of Human Factors and Witnesses. She'd only been with the Board six months. This would be her second major crash. Originally a research psychologist with experience in forensics and industrial stress factors, she had managed to more or less win over us hard-technology types. I suspect she knew what made us all tick a lot better than we did ourselves; she had a way of looking at you that pretty soon had you thinking "I wonder what I *really* meant by that?" The one thing that still made us all nervous was a lingering suspicion that she spent as much time studying the effects of stress on us as she did on the pilots and ATC's who figured in the crashes we investigated. As I already mentioned, there were things about myself I'd just as soon keep away from a psychologist, and the rest of us were all fertile ground for job-stress syndrome as well. Carole is a small woman with short, dark hair and a rather plain face. She works well with the overwhelmingly male groups that assemble for an investigation.

There were three team members not present. George Sheppard would look into the weather as a factor leading up to the crash. Then there was Ed Parrish, who normally wasn't called up to the crash site since his function was Maintenance and Records. He'd be going to Seattle and Los Angeles, where the airframes were built, and to the Maintenance facilities of Pan Am and United, where he would pore through the mountains of papers filled out every time a commercial jet is worked on. And not even on the go-team list was Victor Thomkins, in charge of the Washington labs where the Cockpit Voice Recorders and Flight Data Recorders would be analyzed.

It was a good team. The only glaring absence was C. Gordon Petcher, who really should have been on the plane with us. Not that he was necessary; I was in charge, whether he was there or not. The field phase of the investigation was my responsibility. But it looked better to have a Board Member present to handle the press. I wondered why he'd elected to wait until morning to fly to the coast?

But I didn't wonder for long. I was asleep almost as soon as I leaned back in my seat.

I stepped off the plane, glassy-eyed, into the glare of television lights. They were at the foot of the stairs, crews from as far away as Portland and Santa Barbara. All the bright young men and women were holding mikes out toward us and asking stupid questions.

It's a ritual; the death-dance of our times. Television news is nothing without pictures, and it hardly matters what the pictures are so long as there's something to back up the narration. A plane crash presents them with special problems. What they'd have for their next newscast would be some indistinct night-shots of the crash sites—nothing more than twisted wreckage, with an intact wing or tail if they were lucky—some aerial shots of plowed-up ground that didn't look like much of anything, and shots of the people who flew in from Washington to sort it all out. Of those, a news editor would choose the shots with people in them, so there we were, shuffling between the plane and the helicopter, cameras before us and cameras behind us, wearing artificial smiles and saying nothing.

I got into the copter without even noticing who it belonged to. Inside was a man who stretched out his hand. I looked at it, then took it without any enthusiasm.

"Mr. Smith? I'm Kevin Briley. Roger Keane said I should take you out to the Mount Diablo site as soon as you got here."

"Okay, Briley," I said, shouting to be heard over the noise of the chopper. "One, I'm your boss right now, not Keane. Two, I said I wanted security here, and by that I meant keeping the press away from us until we had something to say. You fucked up on that. So three, you're staying right here. I want you to talk to whoever runs this airport, then look up Sarah Hacker from United and call somebody at Pan Am in New York and tell them what you need, which is some meeting space here in the terminal building, some hangar space somewhere to put what's left of those two aircraft, and a place to pen up these vultures and *keep them out of my hair.* Then get us some hotel rooms, rent a couple of cars...hell, Briley, talk to Sarah Hacker. She'll know what needs to be done. She's been through this before."

"I haven't, Mr. Smith." Briley managed to look belligerent and chagrined at the same time. "What should I tell the reporters? They want to know when they can expect a press conference."

"Tell them noon today. I doubt like hell there'll be one by then, but tell 'em anyway. And guess what? You get to catch the flak when it gets postponed." I grinned at him, and he managed a tired smile and shrug. Maybe he'd hate my guts, and maybe he'd get things done just to spite me. I didn't mind. He hopped out, and we closed the sliding door on the helicopter. Almost immediately the pilot started up. I looked around. It was a good old Huey, owned and operated by the U.S. Army. Hueys are great, but they tend to be drafty. The pilot wore a sergeant's stripes.

"How far apart are the two planes?" I asked him.

"About twenty miles, sir."

"Do you know which one Roger Keane is at? He's the guy from—"

"I know him, sir. I just took him to the one on Mount Diablo. He said I should bring you there."

"That's fine. What's it like? On the ground."

"Muddy. It stopped raining about a half hour ago. The trucks are having a lot of trouble getting to it. There's nothing up there but fire trails."

When I found out the DC-10 was not too far out of the route to the 747 crash site, I told the sergeant to detour and fly over it. It wasn't hard to find.

The DC-10 had made an impact about half a mile north of Interstate 580, not far from Livermore. In what looked to be open fields, hundreds of red and blue lights flashed. Some flame was visible, but the fuel had by then burnt itself out and the damp ground wasn't going to present any problems. All the pinpoints of light were more or less centered on a dark, circular area.

Obviously, I had known what to expect, but some part of me is still surprised, still asks the stupid question. I was out here to see a plane crash, but *where was the plane*?

The pilot brought us down lower, nervously eyeing the myriad lights of other aircraft hovering, landing, or taking off from the vicinity. Still, there was no plane. There were spotlights down there. All they showed was churned up ground and a meaningless confetti of small, shapeless objects, nothing that looked bigger than a hubcap or a car door.

I got a bad feeling looking down at it. Part of it was because it was an unusual site; generally the imprint is a long, messy streak. There will be some recognizable objects strewn along the way, some of them quite large, like engine cowlings, big hunks of wing, part of a fuselage. The mark Flight 35 had left on the ground looked very much like what a bullet would make hitting thick glass: a crater and rays of disturbance.

Flight 35 had literally splashed into the ground.

2

" 'All You Zombies—' "

Testimony of Louise Baltimore

Tell everything, he said.

Fine, but where do I start? The order of events is, at best, a convenient fiction. Seen from another vantage point, things happened very differently. I can hear the universe laughing at me as I try to envision a beginning. However, even us highly evolved mutant-type critters from the seventeenth dimension are, when you get down to it, time-binding apes who live in the eternal Now. No matter how many knots I tie in my lifeline I still move down it the old-fashioned way, in only one direction, taking it one subjective second at a time.

Seen from that perspective, the story begins like this:

I was jerked awake by the silent alarm vibrating my skull. It won't shut off until you sit up, so I did.

Mornings had been getting both better and worse than they used to be. Better because I didn't have that many of them left and valued each new one more. Worse because it was harder to get out of bed.

It would have been easier if I'd allowed myself to sleep plugged in. But you start doing that and before you know it you're plugged into more things than you want, so I didn't. Instead I kept the revitalizer console on the other side of the room and forced myself to make that long walk every morning.

Ten meters.

This time I made the last two meters on my hands and knees. I sat on the floor and plugged the circulator tube into my navel.

That almost makes the walk worth it. I'd been feeling like I'd shrunk inside my skinsuit. Then the go-juice reached my heart and I practically exploded. I could feel the tingling spread down my limbs. The sludge I use for blood was being replaced with something that's half fluorocarbons and half mountain dew. I guarantee it'll get the sleepy dust out of your eyes.

I said, "Listen up, motherfucker."

And the Big Computer answered, "What the hell do you want?"

No toadying servomannerisms for me. When I accessed, I wanted to feel like I was talking to something at least as nasty as I was. Everybody I know likes to have the BC simper at them like a receptionist or baritone its words like a wide-screen Jehovah. Not me. The BC obliges by seeming to barely tolerate me.

"Why'd you get me out of bed? You owe me three hours' sleep."

"A problem has come up in connection with an operation in progress. Since you are Chief of Snatch Team Operations, someone at the Gate had the foolish notion you could be of help straightening it out. No doubt he was wrong, judging—"

"Shut up. How bad?"

"Terrible."

"How soon . . . how much time do I have?"

"In the philosophical or the practical sense? You have no time. You should have been there half an hour ago."

If it had said fifteen minutes ago I think I might have made it.

I pulled on a pair of ersatz twentieth-century jeans. I stopped in the bathroom long enough to buzz my teeth clean and choose some hair (blonde, this time) and see if my face was on straight. Say five seconds for the teeth and hair, and six seconds at the mirror. That was an extravagant waste of time, but I like mirrors. They lie so fetchingly these days. *You beautiful fraud, you.* I grinned at myself. It would most likely be the last chance I had to grin all day.

Then I was out the door, bowling over Sherman the houseboy on the way out. He spilled his breakfast tray.

I ran barefoot down the hall, fell down the drop tube, hurried to the slidewalk and ran on that, too, pushing the more sedate drones out of my way. I reached the speedcaps and got into one. I punched in the code for the Gate, sank into the padding and took a deep breath, then me and the capsule arched out over the city like a high pop fly to centerfield.

Faster than that I cannot hurry. I relaxed and watched the buildings slide by beneath me, not really giving it my attention. It wasn't until then that I remembered this was the day. One of my messages was coming due at the Post Office.

I looked at my Lady Bulova and frowned. There were still several hours before I could open the time capsule. Which meant it was not likely to have a bearing on *this* crisis, whatever it was. We seldom see a crisis at the Gate that isn't resolved within two or three hours.

Which meant I could expect *another* crisis before the day was out.

Sometimes I wonder why I get up.

My capsule was fielded by the retarder rings. When I decapsulated I hurried into the Gate complex and down the corridor to Operations. The gnomes sat there in the blue and green light from their consoles, which filled up a huge horseshoe gallery overlooking the activity on the floor beneath them. Operations was glassed in, insulating it from the sounds of the things happening below.

God, how I hate the gnomes. Every time I went to Operations I could smell their putrefaction. It was nonsense, of course; I was smelling my own fear. In another year or so I'd be behind a console. I'd be *built in* to a console, with all my guts on the outside and nothing left of my body but the Big Lie. I'm twenty percent fake, myself. They're more like eighty percent.

To hell with them.

I got a few withering looks. They don't care much for walkies, either.

There was something new behind the Operations Controller's

console. It was Lawrence Calcutta-Benares. Yesterday he'd been in the deputy's chair, and five years before he'd been my team leader. There was no point in asking what had become of Marybeth Metz. Time flies.

I said, "What's up?"

"We had an indication of a twonky developing," he said, with deplorable grammar. A twonky used to mean some anachronistic object left behind during a snatch, but lately people had begun using the word to refer to the paradox situation that object tended to generate.

"Sorry to wake you," he said. "Still, we thought you should be notified." It's a shame how a good team leader can degenerate into a slackbrain. I should have had the whole situation by then, and there he sat, trying to draw me into a fuggin' conversation.

"Shortly after the twonky alarm, one of your girls lost her stunner on the plane."

"Lawrence, are you going to dribble this story out over the next three days, or are you going to tell it to me and let me *do* something about it?" *Stop doddering, you ancient bag of shit.*

I didn't have to say that last part aloud. He got it. I could see his so-called face icing over. The poor bastard just wanted to talk. He thought he was still my friend. Well, boo-hoo. This was his first day dealing directly with walkies, and it was about time he learned how we felt about each other. I didn't take this job to win the Miss Congeniality award.

He became all business, which is just what I had intended.

"The snatch is to 1955 Arizona. A Lockheed Constellation. It still has about twenty minutes, 55time, and then it's going to lose most of its right wing. All the team is still aboard. They're looking for the gun and trying to finish the snatch at the same time. Indications from the scanners are still inconclusive. We can't tell if you'll find it. It might be possible."

I thought briefly of the period jokes inherent in losing one's right wing over Arizona, then shoved it out of my mind.

"Give me the bridge, then," I said. "I'm going back."

He didn't argue, though he might have. It's a breach of temporal security to send somebody back who's not replacing somebody else. I suspect he wouldn't have minded if I rode it down and bought myself a piece of Arizona real estate. For whatever reason, he gave the order. One of his scurvy underlings played with his buttons and the bridge moved out over the sorting floor. I slammed through the door and out onto it, ten meters above the shouts and screams and curses of the passengers who'd already come through from 1955. They would be the first-class people. There is a special indignant quality to their shouts. They had paid the extra fee, and now *this*. I shall write my congressman, Cecily, really I shall.

I paused at the end of the bridge where it touched the narrow strip of floor that ended in the uptime side of the Gate. I always do. I've gone through the damn thing a thousand times, but it's not something one ever does lightly. Down below me, somebody was demanding to speak to the stewardess. No kidding. He really was.

The poor fellow thought he had problems.

In the twentieth century people used to jump out of airplanes with silk canopies folded into packs on their backs. The canopies were called parachutes, and what they did was—theoretically— open up and retard one's fall to the ground. They did this for fun. It was called skydiving, aptly enough.

Trying to understand how somebody who could expect to live seventy *years* would take that sort of chance—with a body the contemporary medicine men could heal only imperfectly or not at all—how, in spite of that, they could take that first step out the door of the plane, helped me some in dealing with the trip through the Gate. Not that I ever understood why those people jumped: 20ths don't have the brains of a sow, that's well known. But even *they* didn't actually enjoy it. What they did was sublimate the universal fear of falling into another part of the brain: the part that laughs. Laughter is an interrupted defense mechanism. They'd interrupt their fear of falling so well they could pretend to themselves that jumping out of an airplane was fun.

With all that, I'm convinced that even the most experienced of them had to hesitate at the door. They might have done it so many times they no longer noticed it, but it was there.

It's the same way with me. Nobody watching would have seen me break stride as I came to the end of the bridge and stepped into the Gate. But that moment of gut-clutching fear was there.

The trip through the Gate is different every time. It is instantaneous, and it's plenty of time to go insane. It is a zone of simultaneity where I become, for a time too short to measure or remember and too long to endure, all things that have ever been. I encounter myself in the Gate. I create myself, then create the universe and emerge into my creation. I fall downtime to the beginning of the universe and then bounce back to a time elsewhen. That time turns out to be the dead past, come alive again, re-animated for me and the snatch team.

I could devote a billion words to the experience of stepping through the Gate and not come close to the actuality.

At the same time, what happened is that I stepped through. Simple. One foot in the dead future, the other in the living past (with my ass on the line: one cheek in the land of the Brooklyn Dodgers and the other in the Last Age—or my face in the fifties and my fanny in Tomorrowland).

Those two feet of mine were connected by legs. Yet they were some thousands of miles apart in space and billions of years apart in time.

One of the feet was not even my own, but that's neither here nor there.

I shall simply say I stepped through. It should be taken to mean I went through a terrifying ordeal that I had become used to, to the point that I managed to convince myself it was routine.

I stepped through the Gate.

I emerged in the lavatory of the Lockheed Constellation in 1955, and immediately had to duck as two members of the snatch team threw a screaming woman over my head. Her scream cut off when her head went through the Gate. It would finish in the far future, and by then it would probably be a dilly. The situation was simply not going to make sense to the poor dear. *Greetings! Your descendants are proud to welcome you to Utopia!*

I stepped out of the lav as two more snatchers dragged a bulky man in a torn gray suit toward the door. He struggled feebly; probably stunned at low power. It didn't take long to see not much was going right with this snatch. For one thing, the passengers were rebelling.

Of course, we expect hysteria, eventually. No snatch is going to come off without some screaming and the involuntary release of a few pints of urine. If I got snatched, I'd probably piss, too.

But it struck me that the mayhem stage of this snatch had arrived ahead of schedule. There were still too many conscious goats against a handful of snatchers.

It was easy to distinguish the snatch team members from the goats. The snatchers were all dressed like stewardesses. In 1955, on this airline, that meant pert little caps and skirts reaching halfway between knees and ankles and precarious, high-heeled shoes.

They also wore blood-red lipstick. They looked like vampires.

1955. I had to take their word for it. When you've been to as many times as I have the styles blur. They *all* look weird. But I had no reason to doubt the date. Outside, down below us in the world, cars were sprouting tail fins. Chuck Berry was recording *Maybellene*. Phil Silvers and Ed Sullivan were on the vidscreens, which were being called television sets. Nashua would win the Preakness this year, and the Brooklyn Dodgers would win the World Series. I could have been a rich woman in 1955 if I could have found a way to get a bet down. Tomorrow's newspapers, for instance: *Constellation Crashes In Arizona Desert . . .*

Wanna bet?

But this little section of 1955 was not a healthy place to be. Even without the chaos the snatch operation had become, this airplane did not have much flying time left.

I shook my head to clear it. Sometimes that works. I get vague for a few seconds after a trip through the Gate. I forced myself to concentrate on what needed doing this second, and the next, and the next . . .

Jane Birmingham was hurrying down the aisle. I snagged her arm. Things were falling apart around her and I guess the last thing she needed was to have the boss show up to joggle her elbow.

"It's a mess back there," she said, gesturing to the curtain separating first-class from tourist. I heard shouts and the sounds of a struggle.

"We were shorthanded when we went in on them," Jane was

still explaining. "Pinky discovered her gun was missing not too long after we took off. We tried to locate it quietly; didn't work. I had to start the snatch. I let Pinky look while we started caulking the folks up front." She looked away from me, then dragged her eyes back. "I know I shouldn't have done that, but—"

I waved it away.

"We'll sort it out later," I said.

"I don't know what went wrong from there. Shorthanded, I guess. Plus, we were all on edge. When we faced them down a fight got going. Kate's down and out. Some big bastard got past—"

"Never mind. Toss her out with the goats."

There was no way to tell for sure what started the brawl. I'd been on snatches where the goats got out of hand. It's a surreal experience, pointing a weapon at a twentieth-century native and telling him what you're going to make him do. Some 20ths have no more sense of survival than a stalk of broccoli. They'll walk right into a gun. They don't believe death can happen to them, especially the young ones.

Then there are their odd political ideas. They are often obsessed with the explanation they "deserve," the things they have a "right" to, the decent treatment we "owe" them.

Very weird stuff. Me, I'll do anything somebody with a gun tells me to do, and say please and thank you. And kill him instantly if he gives me a chance.

"How many are still awake back there?" I asked.

"When I left, maybe twenty."

"Get 'em to work, quick. Where's Pinky?"

"Tearing up the seats in tourist."

I followed her back. Things had quieted a little. There were maybe a dozen passengers still awake, forty or fifty snoozing in uncomfortable positions. Lilly Rangoon and another woman whose name I couldn't recall were facing the conscious ones, who huddled in the back of the plane. I could smell their fear. The two snatchers were facing them, one on each side of the aisle, stunners held in two hands and steadied on seat backs.

"Okay, folks," Lilly bawled in a voice like a drill sergeant. "I want you to shut the fuck up. Calm down and *listen*! *You*, shithead, pipe down before I cram my foot up your ass sideways. Is that your wife, mister? You got two seconds to shut her fucking mouth before I blow you both away. One . . . that's better.

"*Now.* These people are not injured. They're alive. Look at 'em and you'll see they're breathing. They can even hear us. But I can *kill* with this weapon, and I promise you I'll snuff the first son of a bitch that gets out of line.

"You are in *great danger.*

"You will all *die* if you do not do *exactly as I say.*

"Each of you grab the nearest unconscious person and drag him toward the front of the plane. When you get there, the stewardess will tell you what to do. You have no time to waste. If you move too slowly, I'll show you what else I can do with this weapon."

She got them moving, with a few more shouts and obscenities. That's one of the main things we study when we bone up on a culture: what words will shock the hell out of 'em. In the twentieth century, it was mostly intercourse and excrement.

The other ability of the stunner that Lilly hinted at is to function rather like a cattle prod, but at a distance. It hurts but does not incapacitate. It works best when aimed at the soft, sensitive flesh between the legs—even better when delivered from behind. Lilly prodded a couple of them and they got the idea real fast, for 20ths.

I heard all this going on in the background. What I was doing was ripping up the seats in the front rows of tourist section. Pinky was across the aisle from me, doing the same thing. I don't think she was aware she was crying. She worked steadily, monomaniacally.

She was rational. She was doing her job.

She was also scared spitless.

"You're sure it's on the plane?" I called across the aisle.

"I'm sure. I saw it in my purse after I got on."

She had to think that, since there was nothing to be done if it was on the ground in whatever city this flight had come from. But she was probably right. My people seldom fall apart during an operation, not even if things have become hopeless. If she said she saw it after she got on the plane, then she saw it. Which meant we could find it.

While we looked, the conscious goats were busy dragging the sleeping goats to the front of the plane. When they got there somebody was directing them to toss their loads through the Gate and go back for more. It quickly became a routine. They huffed and they puffed, but there's hardly anything stronger than a 20th. They abuse their bodies, drink, smoke too much, don't exercise, let the flab build up, and they think they're worn out after they've licked a postage stamp. But they've got muscles like horses—and the brains to match. It's amazing the physical feats they can do if we push them hard enough.

There was one guy pulling his share of the load, and I swear he must have been fifty years old.

Jesus! *Fifty!*

The plane was soon emptied. As each walker carried his last body to the Gate he was shoved through himself. Then there was only the snatch team. Even the pilots had been caulked this time. We really hate to do that, and we usually can't. One of my people was flying now. If she didn't do exactly what the pilot would have done the plane would come down miles from where it ought to. However, this one was on autopilot and would remain so until the explosion in the engine. There was not going to be anything the pilot could have done (if you can thrash your way through that thicket of verb tenses) to alter anything once that wing fell off.

Which was fortunate. There is one more trick I can use on a flight where the cockpit crew becomes aware of the snatch before it's finished, but I *really* hate to use it.

We could bring in a man from my Very Special Team. (I'm speaking 20th Amerenglish; "man" includes "woman," or so it says in my *Strunk and White*.) This would be a man with a bomb in his head to insure no teeth survived for identification. A man who was willing to fly an airplane into the ground.

Did I hear someone say flight recorder? Ah, yes. Those people up front *do* chatter when they get into trouble. There is an interesting solution to that problem. Uptime, it was already being prepared, had been set in motion as soon as the cockpit crew came through and we knew it might have to be used. It was an elegant solution. More than a little puzzling, but elegant.

With our time scanners we can look anywhere, anytime. (Well, almost.) That's how we knew this plane would go down. We scanned newspaper stories and found accounts of the crash. It might have been nice to look inside the plane and see how the operation was going to go off, but unfortunately we can't look into any place or time where we've been, or will be. (Time travel is tough on verb tenses.) So we couldn't know we'd have to take the pilot. But we could now scan ahead to the investigation afterward. (See what I mean about verb tenses? This was happening *now*—if that word retains any meaning—uptime, in the future. They were scanning events a couple days in the '55 future: my future, at the moment.)

At that investigation the tape from the cockpit recorder would be played. So we'd make a recording of that recording, put it on a self-destructing tape player, like the ones on *Mission: Impossible*, and leave that in the cockpit where it would play into the original recorder.

Paradox!

Because of what we were doing now or had already done, those words would never be spoken by the man whose voice everyone would hear. They would have been/will be/had been merely recorded from the recording itself, which had never been made, because of what we were doing or had already done.

Look at this sequence hard enough and you realize that cause and effect become a joke. Any rational theory of the universe must be shitcanned.

Well, I shitcanned all my rational theories a long time ago. You may hold on to whatever makes you happy.

I was getting nowhere with my search for the missing stunner. I looked up, saw we were the only ones left, and yelled.

"Hey! All you zombies!" When I had their attention I went on. "Everybody keep looking. Tear this plane apart. Don't rest until the wimps start arriving, and don't even rest then. I'm going uptime to see what I can do from there."

I hurried to the front of the plane and . . . stepped through.

And landed on my ass at the bottom of the sorting floor.

I saw instantly what had happened and started yelling bloody murder. That did me no good. *Every* goat through the Gate comes through yelling bloody murder.

At the uptime end of the Gate is a complex series of cushioned, frictionless ramps. They're designed to catch people who are unconscious or out of their minds with fear and shuffle them off very quickly before the next goat comes through. Sometimes this process breaks bones, but seldom important ones. Time is of the essence. We can't be too fussy.

But the system is designed to sort snatch team personnel from the goats: goats to the prep room and then the holding pen and then the deep freeze, snatchers to a well-deserved rest. We all carry a radio squealer on snatch runs. The sorter listens for that squeal. I knew where my squealer was: back in the ready-room.

So I got a chance to see how the other half lives. I could have done without it.

There was no way to get a grip on anything (that's why they call it frictionless). I slid through a series of chutes and onto a flat surface coated with a sheet of plastic that clung to my skin. It all happened so fast I never did understand the sequence. At some point mechanical hands removed my pants and I found myself wrapped in a tight cocoon of clear plastic. I was straitjacketed, arms at my sides, feet together.

I was tumbled in a blue light. It was frightening, even to me, and I knew what was happening. My body was being studied in minute detail, from the bones outward. The process took about two seconds. I was catalogued out to eighty decimal places and the Big Computer began thumbing through its card file of wimps, looking for the best match. That took about a picosecond. Miles away, a morgue drawer would be springing open in the wimp vaults. My slumbering double would then come rushing toward the prep room, pulling twenty gees of acceleration at the beginning and end of her trip. Twenty gees is a lot—enough to cause brain damage if sustained for any time, but that would be carrying coals to Newcastle. Compared to a wimp, a carrot is a mental giant.

I knew the process was fast, but I'd never seen it. I was dumped on a slab no more than fifteen seconds after coming through the Gate. The wimp arrived five seconds later and was slapped onto the slab next to me. I was still being probed and prodded by mechanical examiners. When the human customizing team arrived everything would be in readiness.

The plastic wrapping was permeable. I could breathe through it, but there was no hope of talking. So I lay there, simmering. I could turn my head just enough to see the wimp. The likeness was very good: my vegetable twin sister. Of course, her left leg was real and mine wasn't. I wondered how the BC would cope with that.

I found out.

A mechanical leg came down from an overhead conveyor and was deposited beside the sleeping wimp. Surely that would indicate something to the human operating team, which I was beginning to think would never arrive.

But they did, and they gave me unwanted insight into why goats are so jumpy after going through customization.

There were five in the team. I knew one of them to speak to, though not well. He looked right through me.

They prodded me and turned me. They referred to the computer screen, consulted hastily, and apparently decided to pass the problem of the artificial leg on to others. All they were supposed to do was make the wimp look enough like me to fool FBI investigators in 1955. I was just a piece of meat wrapped up like a frozen steak in a supermarket.

The team worked damn well together. Nobody got in anyone else's way, everything needed was always at hand. Literally. They would reach without looking, and it would be there.

They were *fast*. They sliced that wimp's leg off and kicked it aside the instant it hit the floor. Meanwhile someone was extracting all the wimp's teeth and plugging in new ones that would look just like mine. They hooked up the artificial leg, slashed the wimp here and there in the places where my skinsuit shows scars. They peeled the skin away from her face and began building it from beneath, then closed it again and applied the forced regenerators. It healed without a scar.

But there were scars they wanted the wimp to have. The only way to make those is with a timepress field. When everybody was ready they plugged feedlines from big nutrient tanks into the wimp, connected her ureter and anus to evacuator lines, and jumped back.

The blue glow of the Gate surrounded the wimp. It began to breathe so fast the chest was a blur. Its hair and fingernails grew visibly. It used nutrient fluid so fast that it had to be pumped in, and it emitted urine in a pulsed, pressurized stream that hissed into a tank on the floor. In ten seconds it grew six months older. The scars healed normally.

Then they pulled my jeans onto the wimp, inserted a funnel into its mouth and were about to pump it full of half-digested airline food when one of the workers looked at my face.

I mean she *really* looked at it. She had looked right at me several times before but nothing had registered.

Her eyes grew wide.

When she managed to make them realize who it was they were duplicating, the whole team helped me peel out of the plastic skin.

Things got a little hazy for a time.

I remember looking down at the sleeping face that looked just like mine. Then they were pulling me away from it. There was a stout aluminum bar in my hands and a rip in the palm of my skinsuit from thumb to index finger. I had wrenched the bar loose from one of the examining machines.

And I had sure made a mess of that wimp.

I regret that. I really do. The thing had been wearing my jeans, and I never did get all the blood out of them.

The head of the wimp-building team trailed me all the way to the door.

He kept trying to apologize and I kept ignoring him. If there was blame, it was mostly mine, but I didn't want to say that. Like plugging into life-support equipment, I view apologizing as a dangerous vice that can take over your whole life if you give in to it. Inside, I was whipping myself severely for pulling a tyro stunt like leaving my squealer in the ready-room. Outside, I trust, I was at work and the man's apologies simply got in my way.

I had wasted five whole minutes in there. I would never know if those minutes were the margin between life and death for Pinky.

I wasted fifteen more seconds just getting through the door.

There were no procedures for it. The whole goat-sorting operation was designed to prevent anybody getting through easily. But with a few quiet, totally sincere death threats, I managed it. I raced up to Operations, told Lawrence to put every available operative on the search for Pinky's stunner in the city from which the flight had originated—which I learned was Houston—got him to extend the bridge again, and . . . stepped . . . through the Gate.

It was a shambles.

They had looked just about every place it was possible to look, and they had not been gentle. The aisle was knee-deep in torn seat cushions. The carpet was ripped up. The contents of the galley were strewn from nose to tail of the plane. Tiny bottles of booze clinked underfoot.

To make everything worse, the customized wimps began arriving.

So much time had already been wasted that we had to hurry getting them placed. We seated a few and strapped them in, but most we just threw. We had our portapaks on full power, and we were *strong*. Instead of just enriched blood, adrenalin, and vitamins—the wake-up mixture—we were now getting an insane brew of hyperdrenalin, methedrine, Essence of Hysteria, TNT, and Kickapoo Joyjuice. We picked up those half-corpses and tossed them around like beanbags. I could have torn sheet metal with my eyebrows.

Three-quarters of the wimps had been through the process I had recently seen firsthand. They looked exactly like the people they were replacing. To save time, the other quarter came pre-mutilated. Most were hideously burned. Some were still smoking.

One is supposed to say the smell of charred human flesh is revolting. It's not, actually. It smells pretty good.

Most of the wimps were still breathing. They'd existed an average of thirty years in the wimp tanks, kept alive by machines, exercised mechanically to keep the muscle tone. Theoretically they didn't have the brains to breathe, but the fact is they were too dumb to stop. Most would still be breathing when they hit the ground.

It didn't take long to get them all through. When we were

done we still had three minutes and forty seconds. I sent one of the team back to the future to see if anyone had located the stunner in Houston. The rest of us kept looking for it on the plane. The messenger returned with the expected bad news, and now we had two minutes and twenty seconds.

Pinky had calmed down, if you could call it that. She was no longer crying. I believe she was paralyzed with terror. I found Lilly Rangoon, the squad leader, and pulled her aside.

"I don't know Pinky well," I said. "What does she have in the way of twonkies?"

"Nothing. She's clean." Lilly looked away from me.

That's a rarity. We were talking about such things as artificial legs, kidneys, eyes—medical implants of any kind that were too advanced for 1955. Pinky was a healthy girl. She would be a great loss to the teams, if for no other reason than that.

At the same time, her lack of medical anachronisms made Lilly's job a little easier. It would have fallen to Lilly to cut those items out and bring them back with us.

"Thirty seconds," someone called out.

"There's a minute leeway," I said. "We'll have to go on the click. You stay long enough to get her skinsuit and—"

"*Shut your freaking mouth*! I know my job. Now get out of my aircraft."

Nobody talks to me like that. Nobody. I looked into her eyes. If looks could freeze I'd have been a one-legged popsicle.

"Right," I said. "See you in fifty thousand years."

I hurried to the front, where everyone was hanging back, away from the Gate. Nobody wanted to go. Neither did I. It would have been a lot easier to ride it in.

I looked back and saw Pinky hand something floppy to Lilly. I knew it was Pinky, though it didn't look like her, because there was no one else it could be. The floppy thing was her skinsuit. She was no longer a sexy stewardess; without her disguise she was a terrified, naked little girl.

Lilly gave her a salute which Pinky did not have the will to return, and sprinted toward me.

"Start walking through, or I start kicking ass," I said.

They did. I turned to Lilly.

"How old was she?" I asked.

"Pinky? She was twelve."

I didn't make the rule. I'm not trying to absolve myself by saying that. I think it's a good rule. If we didn't have it, I'd write it myself.

No hardware gets left behind. The penalty for carelessness is death. You bring it back, or you stay with it.

We couldn't always work it the way we did with Pinky. That was the *best* way. It could be done because this flight would hit so hard and burn so fiercely that no one would expect to recover more than fifty percent of the bodies in any form at all. If they got ten identifiable corpses it would be miraculous, so one girl who shouldn't be there would never be noticed.

Even so, Lilly's last act before leaving the plane was to grab a wimp of about Pinky's body mass and toss it back into the future. The balance is critical.

The worst way? If we'd had to bring Pinky back with us for temporal reasons, Lilly would have stood her up against the wall and shot her. And then, possibly, have shot herself. I had a team leader do that once.

Nobody ever said it was easy duty.

I came through the right way this time. I still didn't have my squealer, but Operations knew that now, and knew nobody but snatchers would come through the Gate until they closed it for good. Which they were preparing to do.

We all fetched up at the padded Team Recovery Area. Medics were waiting all around us, like crash trucks at an airport. We all made hand signals that we were okay except one girl who wanted a stretcher.

It's traditional just to lie there for five or ten minutes. Our portapaks had automatically returned to normal operation when we passed through the Gate, so our hysterical strength was fading fast. Behind it was the exhaustion the drugs had masked, both physical and mental.

But I had to get up.

"Reward time," I said, as I grabbed Lilly's weapon and

headed for the door to Operations. "One hour at full power. Set 'em up, girls."

"See you in intensive care, Louise," one of them called out, twisting the dial on the portapak strapped to her wrist.

"Tell my dear mom I died grinning," yelled another.

I ran into Operations and confronted Lawrence. He was going through his checklist preparatory to shutting power to the Gate.

"One of my people is still on that plane," I told him. "I want you to keep the Gate focused on it until it actually touches the desert."

"Out of the question, Louise."

"One of my people is still on that plane, Larry. If she manages to find her weapon she can still come back."

"Do you *realize* the problems we have keeping the Gate tuned in on a plane that's flying *straight and level*? Do you have any inkling of how that problem squares and cubes in complexity when it starts to twist and turn on the way down? It can't be done."

There are three settings on a stunner. The first puts you to sleep. The second delivers pain. I let him see me set Lilly's gun on the third notch. I put the muzzle to his temple.

"One of my people is still on that plane, Larry. I have now said that three times."

He managed to bring the Gate to the falling plane twice, once for two seconds, then again for almost five. Pinky didn't come through.

What the hell. I had to try.

I sat on the floor beside Larry's console and watched him supervise the powerdown operation. I asked him if he had any smokes, and he tossed me a pack of Lucky Strike Green. I lit three of them.

When he was through, I reversed the stunner and handed it to him.

"For me?" he said. He took it, hefted it in his hand.

"Do whatever you want with it," I said.

He aimed it at my forehead. I took another drag, and waited. He used the barrel to brush hair away from my eyes, then tossed the weapon to me.

"You don't really care right now," he said.

"No. I really don't."

"That would take all the fun out of it." He folded his arms and leaned back. Well, not really. He didn't exactly have a chair; he was more or less built into it.

His eyes lit up.

"I'll wait till things are going great for you. The next time I see you smile, you've had it."

Tricky bastard. I did smile, but he didn't ask for the gun.

"Larry, I'm sorry."

He looked at me. We'd been lovers for a while, before he fell apart too much to get around under his own power. He knew my feelings on apologies.

"Okay. My fault, too. Tempers run a bit high during a snatch."

"Don't they, though."

"Forgotten?"

"Until the next time," I said.

"Naturally."

I looked at him and felt a deep regret for what had once been. No, let's get brutally honest here. For what I would one day become. One day real soon now.

Larry had elected to acknowledge his gnomehood all the way. Most of the gnomes at the other consoles looked like anyone else except they had thick bunches of cables running from their backs. Those cables ran into their chairs and down into hundreds of bulky machines in the basement.

Larry hadn't seen any use in living on a leash. If he couldn't leave the building, what was the point of phoney legs? So Larry's chair was part of Larry. It had no back. He sort of grew from it, planted there on the floor in front of his console. He looked like a bizarre chess piece.

From the waist up he looked like a normal human being. I knew most of that was a lie, too. Even when I'd known him he had only one real arm. His face had been hit-and-miss the one time

I'd seen it without the skinsuit: nose gone, lips eaten away, only one ear. I didn't know which diseases he had. One doesn't ask. I didn't know which parts of him were actually organic; probably not much more than the brain. One doesn't ask that, either.

Nobody but me and my doctor and Sherman know which of my organs and limbs are my own, and I'm happy to keep it that way. I must care, or I wouldn't live in this lying skinsuit pretending to be a film star from the year 2034. That's right: the me everybody knows is patterned, down to the last birthmark, on a glamor queen we snatched from a terrorist explosion.

It struck me, sitting there with him in a rare moment of quiet, that when I could no longer carry all my prostheses I would do well to emulate Larry. Then the time for attractive lies would be over. Then it would be time to face, finally, what I am, what all of us here in the glorious future really are.

The Last Age.

I got up and wandered from the Operations room. I found some clothes and got dressed, had breakfast from machines in the Snatch Team Ready-Room, and just sat for a while. I realized the day was still young.

So far it had been pretty typical.

3

"Let's Go to Golgotha"

Testimony of Bill Smith

The chopper pilot told me Roger Keane had already spent three hours at the DC-10 site.

I wasn't quite sure what to do. We had two big planes separated by twenty miles, and seven people to begin the investigation. What I saw below me was unpromising. In the absence of any better guidelines, I turned to my team and polled them.

"I'd like to get out here," Eli said. He'd been looking down at what might have been one of the engine cowlings, and I could see he was eager to get his hands on it. "I mean, what's the difference? We'll see them both eventually so I might as well start here."

"I'll get off, too," Carole said. "It's close enough to those farmhouses that I might get some useful eyewitness accounts. Isn't the other one up on top of a mountain?"

"Yes, ma'am," the pilot said. "Mount Diablo. I doubt anyone was close when it came down."

Craig and Jerry said they'd just as soon start here, too, which left me and Tom Stanley.

"Keep your eyes open for the recorders," I told Craig as he was getting out. The pilot heard me.

"You mean the black boxes?" he asked. "They already got those. I flew 'em back to Oakland an hour ago."

I nodded at him, and jerked my thumb into the air. How the Flight Data Recorder and Cockpit Voice Recorder got nicknamed black boxes has always been a minor mystery to me. For one thing, they're usually red. To me, a "black box" has always been some esoteric gizmo that does something mysterious. The CVR's and FDR's were perfectly straightforward devices. Anybody who could run a car stereo could understand them.

It looked like the 747 had flown a little after the collision. It had plowed a long furrow up the side of the mountain.

Tom and I reconstructed it from the air, hovering over a site that was not nearly so crowded as the other, and which had much more to tell us.

The plane had come in on its belly. The impact had demolished the nose, and probably cracked the fuselage. It had bounced, then bellied down again, and this time the fuselage broke into four distinct sections, each of which had rolled end over end. There were big hunks of wing to be seen. The engines had been stripped away and were not visible from the air. But the cockpit seemed almost intact, though blackened by fire. That's the thing that makes the 747 unique among commercial airliners; instead of being perched out at the nose—"first to the scene of the accident," as the pilots like to say—the flight crew of a 747 sit high atop everything and well back.

The other large piece we saw was the broken-off vertical stabilizer, still attached to the rear section of the fuselage. That looked good for the flight recorders. I thought I could see a group of people working around it, and asked the pilot if he could set us down there. He said it was too risky, and took us to the assembly area, where a dozen fire trucks and police cars and a handful of ambulances had begun to gather.

It's not like Mount Diablo was really remote. If a single plane had come down there it would already have been crawling with workers. But the other plane had come down in full view of the freeway and had quickly drawn off the lion's share of the available rescue workers. As soon as it was determined there were no survivors from the 747 and thus no real hurry, Roger Keane had decided to concentrate the clean-up at the more accessible site.

Before we were even out from beneath the helicopter rotor a big guy in a yellow raincoat was coming toward us with his hand out.

"Bill Smith?" he said, and grabbed my hand. "Chuck Willis, CHP. Mister Keane's over at the tail section. He told me to bring you up as soon as you got here."

I had time to recall that CHP meant California Highway Patrol, and to attempt to introduce Tom Stanley, but the guy was already off. We followed, and I glanced back to see yellow body bags being loaded into the helicopter we had just left. I didn't envy the pilot his trip back to town. The whole place smelled of jet fuel and charred meat.

We were halfway to the tail section when Tom said, "Excuse me," turned aside, and threw up.

I stopped and waited for him. In a moment, Willis of the CHP noticed he was no longer being followed, and he stopped, too, and looked back at us impatiently.

The funny thing was, I didn't feel queasy until Tom got sick. I never could stand to see someone vomit. I had forgotten that about Tom. I'd been to some bad ones with him—small planes, but with really awful corpses. Most of the time he'd been okay, but once or twice he'd lost it.

What can I say? We had been walking through plowed-up ground with the main wreckage still ahead of us, but there had been many bodies, or parts of bodies. I honestly hadn't seen them. I'd gone around them. Thinking back, I recalled actually stepping over one. But at the time, it was as if they didn't exist. It was an ability I'd developed. We were here to look at wreckage, at wire and metal and so forth, so my mind simply ignored the human wreckage.

"You okay?" I asked.

"Sure," he said, straightening up. And I knew from past experience that he would be. Well, if a guy's got to throw up, so what? It didn't matter to me.

I could tell Willis didn't think much of it, though. I decided that if he told us he'd seen worse on the California highways, I'd sock him.

He didn't say anything. Pretty soon I could see why.

The place was crawling with people in various uniforms. Most of them were firemen and police and paramedics from towns in the area, men who thought they were used to seeing violent death. They were finding out how wrong they were. Some of them would be going to psychiatrists for years because of the things they saw that night. There's a syndrome associated with working at the site of an airliner crash and seeing things your mind doesn't want to deal with. It can hit very hard at professional people who think they're ready for anything, who have an image of themselves as tough and experienced. They just aren't ready for the *scale* of the thing.

I saw several firemen stumbling around like sleepwalkers. One guy in a CHP uniform was sitting down, crying like a child. He'd probably come out of it okay. It was the guys who held it in, who played it tough to the end, that would eventually need help.

At least we didn't have any zombies around. I saw some at San Diego, where the plane came down in the middle of a neighborhood. There was no way to keep people away at first, and some really sick cases were drawn to the site before the police could get it cleared. Some of them picked up pieces of bodies for souvenirs, if you can believe that. I didn't want to, but a guy at PSA swore to me it was true. He said a cop came within an inch of shooting one of these guys who was making off with somebody's leg.

And why should it be such a surprise? Nothing draws a crowd like a big disaster. If a freeway smash-up was fun, an airplane crash ought to be a hundred times as much fun.

Crashes are like tornadoes. They play ugly tricks. I've seen severed heads, unmarked, hanging from tree branches at eye level. Sometimes there are hands clasping each other, a man's and a woman's, or a woman's and a child's. Just the hands, still hanging on when the rest of the bodies have been thrown elsewhere.

I looked where Tom had been looking when he had finally turned green. There was a woman's arm, cut off pretty neatly. The trick the crash had played with this arm was to arrange it on the ground, palm up, fingers curling as if beckoning. There was a wedding ring on one finger. It would have been a sexy gesture in another context, and I guess that's what got Tom.

It was going to get me in a minute if I didn't look away, so I did.

* * *

Roger Keane's the perfect man to head the Los Angeles office of the NTSB. He looks a little like Cary Grant in his younger days, with just a touch of silver in his hair, and he buys his suits in Beverly Hills. He's not a guy to get his hands dirty, so I wasn't surprised to find him back by the spotlight, supervising the crew who had clambered up the precarious tail section with cutting torches to get at the flight recorders. He had his hands thrust deep in the pockets of his trench coat, the collar turned up, and an unlit cigar clenched in his teeth. I got the impression that the biggest annoyance he faced in that landscape of carnage was the fact that he didn't dare light his cigar with all the kerosene fumes still in the air.

He greeted me and Tom, and a few moments were passed in polite pleasantries. You'd be surprised how much they can help. I suspect I could carry off a reasonable imitation of polite conversation in the middle of a battlefield.

When that was done he took us off for a guided tour. There was a proprietary air about him. This had been his site, for better or worse, and until we were filled in on what he'd found out it still was, in a sense. This is not to say he was delighted with what he'd found. He was grimfaced, like the rest of us, probably taking it harder because he didn't see it as often.

So we trudged through the devastation like solemn tourists, stopping every once in a while to puzzle out what some of the larger chunks were all about.

The only really important thing for me here were the CVR and the FDR. The famous black boxes. Eventually we got back to the tail section. We were just in time to see the Cockpit Voice Recorder lifted free and handed carefully down to someone on the ground. Roger looked happy.

I was, too, but the other one is more important.

The Flight Data Recorder, in the newer aircraft, is one hell of a piece of equipment. The old ones recorded just six variables, things like airspeed, compass heading, and altitude. The readings were inscribed by needles on rolls of metal foil. This 747 had one of the newer FDR's that recorded forty different things on magnetic tape. It would tell us everything from flap settings to engine rpm's and temperatures. The new FDR's were a big improvement except for one thing. They were not quite as tough as the old metal-foil machines.

Tom and I stuck around until the workers came up with the second flight recorder, and we lugged them out ourselves. Roger didn't offer to help, but I didn't expect him to. The chopper came back and returned us to the other crash site.

The sun was coming up by the time we got back to the airport.

This time we went in the back door and airport security managed to keep the press away from us. We were shown to the rooms the Oakland Airport had made available to us. There was a small one for the top brass—me and my people—a medium-sized one for the nightly meetings when all the people we'd gathered to investigate the crash got together to exchange findings and compare notes, and a big one, for press conferences. I didn't give a damn about the latter. Presumably C. Gordon Petcher would be here before long and that was his job. It was his photogenic mug everybody would see on their television sets at six o'clock, not my bleary and unshaven one.

I checked out the facilities, got introduced to liaison people from United, Pan Am, and the airport management, and once again met Kevin Briley. He seemed a lot happier than the last time I ran into him. He dropped a couple of keys into my hand.

"This is to your car, and this is to your hotel room," he said. "The car is at the Hertz lot, and the room is at the Holiday Inn about a mile from here. You go out the airport access road—"

"Hell, I can find a Holiday Inn, Briley," I said. "They don't exactly hide them. You did good. Sorry I jumped on you so hard."

He looked at his watch.

"It's 7:15. I told the reporters you'd be talking to them at noon."

"Me? Hell that's not my job. Where's Gordy?"

He obviously didn't know who I was talking about.

"C. Gordon Petcher." Still a blank. "Member of the Board. You know, the National Transportation Safety—"

"Oh, of course. Of course." He rubbed his forehead and I

thought he swayed slightly. I realized the guy was at least as tired as I was. Probably more tired; I'd had a few hours sleep at home, and a few on the plane. The crash had happened at 9:11 P.M., his time, so he'd certainly been awake all night.

"He called," Briley said. "He won't be in until later this evening. He said you should handle the noon press briefing."

"He said . . . the hell I will. I've got a fucking *job* to do, Briley. I don't have time to smile pretty for the fucking cameras." I realized I was yelling at the poor stooge again, when I ought to be yelling at Petcher. "Sorry. Listen, you get him on the phone and tell him he'd better get out here. When we start the hearing phase, he's the big cheese. Technically, he's in charge of the whole damn thing, but he doesn't know shit about airplanes and he's *aware* of his ignorance and he knows damn well that without me and my boys to feed him the stuff we find out he's going to look like a fool . . . so for all practical purposes *I'm* in charge here for the next couple of weeks. And that means he will do his job, which is to suffer the gentlemen of the goddam press gracefully. It's all he's good for anyway."

Briley watched me for a while, wondering, I guess, if I'd get violent.

"Are you sure you wouldn't rather tell him yourself?"

I grinned at him. "I'd love to," I said, "but I'll have to pass it up. I've got to deal with him day-to-day in Washington, and you're safe out here on the coast. Now where are they stacking the scrap iron?"

"United has a hangar at the north side of the field. They're bringing everything out there."

"And the Pan Am?"

"They're renting space from United. Both planes will be brought there."

"Good. That'll be handy. What about the bodies?"

"Pardon me?"

"The corpses. Where are they putting the corpses?"

I think I'd upset him again. He looked nervous, anyway.

"Uh, I presume they're taking them somewhere . . . but I—"

"It's okay. You can't do everything. I'll find out where they are." I patted him on the back and advised him to get some sleep, then looked around for Tom. He was talking to somebody I thought I recognized. I went over there.

Tom was about to introduce us, when I remembered the guy's name.

"Ian Carpenter, right? Air Traffic Controllers' Union?"

He looked pained at the word "union"—they're a new group, and still pretty sensitive and quite aware that they rated just below Senators and Congress-critters in public esteem. That was a damn shame, in my book, where Air Traffic Controllers rate a bit higher than pilots—who are almost as clannish and self-protective as cops and doctors—and a damn sight higher than union-busting Presidents.

"Association, please," he said, trying to make a joke out of it. "And you're Bill Smith. I've heard of you."

"Yeah? Who was handling those two planes when they hit?"

He grimaced. "You want to know what I heard about you? I heard you get right to the point. Okay. His name is Donald Janz. And before you ask, he isn't a trainee, but he's not what I'd call a veteran, either."

We looked each other over. Maybe he knew what I was thinking; I had a pretty good idea what was going through his head. He didn't want this crash pinned on the ATC's, and he was afraid I'd see them as an easy target. It's no secret that the Board has been unhappy about the state of Air Traffic Control for some time now. It's been years since the mass firings, and the country's network of air routes still wasn't back to normal. No matter what you may have heard, we're still training people to fill the spots left vacant by the PATCO strike, and there ain't no ATC University. They learn on the job, and these days they get shoved into the hotseat a lot quicker than they used to.

"Where's Janz?"

"He's at home, and he's under sedation. Naturally, he's very upset. I think I heard him talking about finding a lawyer."

"Naturally. Can you have him here in two hours?"

"Is that an order?"

"I can't give you orders, Carpenter. I'm asking you. He can bring his lawyer if he wants to. But you know I'll have to talk to him sooner or later. And you know how rumors get started. If your boy isn't at fault—and somehow, looking at you, I get the feeling you don't think he is—isn't it better to let me hear his story now?"

Tom had been trying to catch my eye, so I glanced over at him and he picked up the spiel without a pause.

"Ian, we're ninety-nine percent sure the problem wasn't with the planes. Weather seems unlikely. You been listening to the talk around here. You know what's been said. It's pilot error, controller error . . . or computer error. If you get your man in here, it could go a long way toward getting us off on the right foot."

Carpenter had glanced up at the mention of computer error; something was smouldering inside the man, but I didn't know what it was. He looked back at his shoes, still undecided.

"The press is going to want some answers, Carpenter. If they don't get at least a hint soon, they'll start to speculate. You know where that's going to lead."

He glared at me, but I don't think I was really the target of his anger.

"All right. I'll have him here in two hours."

He turned on his heel and marched away. I looked at Tom.

"What was that all about?"

"He told me the air traffic computer was out when the planes hit. It was the third overload that day."

"No shit."

It was too early to tell if it was a break, but it was the first thing I'd heard so far that interested me.

"What the hell time is it, anyway?" I asked Tom.

"I've got oh-seven-hundred."

"Is that East Coast, or West Coast? You want to go out to the hangar, see what they've got going out there?"

Tom knew me, I guess. Maybe I'm obvious.

"How about finding a bar first?"

Bars are never hard to find around big airports, and California isn't a state that's too stuffy about the hours. There was no trouble finding a drink at seven in the morning.

I ordered a double scotch on the rocks and Tom had Perrier or sarsaparilla, or whatever it is non-drinkers drink. Whatever it was, it bubbled like the dickens and gave me a headache just to watch it.

"What else did you learn while I was stuck with Mister Briley?"

"Not a lot. Mostly that Carpenter's going to make a case that his men are working too many hours, and the computers are too old, and they can't be expected to make the switchover when the computer goes out."

"We've heard that before."

"And the Board said the hours weren't too long."

"I wasn't on that particular investigation. I read the report."

Tom didn't say anything. He knew my opinion about that report. I think he shared it, though it's not something I'd ever ask him. I've got enough seniority to shoot off my mouth every once in a while if I think somebody's pulling a fast one. I don't expect him to join my subversive opinions, at least not publicly.

"Okay. When did the computer go down?"

"About the worst possible moment, according to Carpenter. Janz was handling something like nineteen planes. The computer shuts down, he's faced with a soft display and he's got about ten seconds to match blip A with blip A prime. Two of those blips were jets he was about ready to hand over to Oakland approach control. He couldn't figure out which was which, and he told each of them exactly the wrong thing. He thought he was steering them *away* from a collision. What he was doing was guiding them toward each other."

I could see it in my head. Trouble is, it's a hard thing to explain unless you've actually been in an Air Region Traffic Control Center when the computer goes down. I'm sorry to say that I've seen it happen many times.

One minute you're looking at a sharp, clear circular screen with a lot of lines and a lot of dots on it. Each dot is labeled with several rows of numbers. It may baffle you if you've never seen it before, but to a trained ATC those numbers identify each aircraft and tell a lot about them. Things like altitude, air speed, transponder I.D. number. The picture is generated by a computer, which updates the screen once every couple of seconds. You can play with it, adjust it so each plane leaves a little trail of successively dimmer blips, so you know where the plane has been and have some idea of where it's going, just by looking. You can tell the computer to erase extraneous stuff and just let you deal with a problem situation. You've got a little cursor you can move across the screen to touch a particular aircraft, and talk to the pilot. If two planes get into a situation, the computer will see it before you do and ring a bell to let you know you'd better turn them away from each other.

Then the computer overloads. It shuts down.

You know what happens then?

The screen falls from a vertical to a horizontal position. There's a good reason for that: the blips you see are no longer labeled. You have to get out little plastic chips called shrimp boats, which you label with a grease pencil and lay beside each blip. When the blip moves, you move the shrimp boat. The screen resolution goes to hell. It's like you're not even looking at the same scene. It's as if you'd dropped out of the computer age back to the infancy of radar, like they had to work with in World War Two.

As if that weren't enough, the blips you see on the new, long-wave display may not be in the same positions as they were before. The uncorrected radar-reflection imaging is nothing like the computer-corrected display. Where you had tasteful little hatch marks to indicate clouds—all carefully labeled for altitude—now you've got a horrendous splotch of white noise that isn't anywhere near where you thought it would be.

If it happens during an off-hour, the controllers simply groan and break out the shrimp boats. If it happens during a rush—and in an ARTCC like Oakland-San Francisco, with three commercial and three military and God-knows-how-many private airfields it's usually a rush—there are two or three minutes of desperate silence as the ATC's figure out who's who and try to remember where everybody was and if anybody was approaching what they call a "situation."

I'm not a big fan of euphemisms, but situation was a good one. What we have here, folks, is a situation where six hundred people are about to be spread all over a mountain like a family-sized can of tomato paste.

"What do you think?" I asked Tom.

"It's too early. You know that." Still, he kept looking at me, and he knew I was asking for an off-the-record call. He gave it to me.

"I think it's going to be tough. We've got a guy who's almost a trainee, and a computer built in 1968. That's practically the stone age, these days. But some folks are going to say Janz should have been able to cope. Everybody else does."

"Yeah. Let's get out to the hangar."

The bar had tinted-glass windows, so I didn't know what a glorious day it was until we got out on the field and looked around. It was one of those days that make my fingers itch to hold onto the stick of my Stearman and head up into the old wild blue yonder. The air was crisp and clear with hardly any wind at all. There were sailboats out in the Bay even this early in the morning. Even the big, ugly old Oakland-San Francisco Bay Bridge looked good against the blue sky, and beyond it was the prettiest city in America. In the other direction I could see the Berkeley and Oakland hills.

We used Tom's car and headed out across the field. The hangar wasn't hard to find. Just follow the stream of trucks with piles of Hefty bags in the back.

The rest of the team was there before us, except Eli Seibel who had gone to examine the DC-10's left engine, which had come down about five miles from the main wreckage. When we got inside I was amazed at the amount of wreckage they'd already hauled away from the Livermore site.

"United's in a big hurry to get it cleaned up," Jerry told me. "It was all we could do to keep them from carting away the biggest pieces before we had a chance to document their positions." He showed me a rough sketch map he'd made, meticulously noting the location of everything bigger than a suitcase.

I understood how the folks at United must feel. The Livermore site was damn public. No airline likes to have hordes of rubberneckers hanging around looking at their failures. They'd got a crew of hundreds of scavengers together and by now the site was just about picked clean.

The inside of the hangar was a mess. All the big pieces were stacked at one side, and then there were tons and tons of plastic trash bags full of the smaller stuff, most of it coated with mud. Now parts of the 747 were starting to arrive as well, and room had to be made for them.

It all had to be sorted.

It wasn't my job, but it gave me a headache anyway, just looking at it. I began to feel that two double scotches at seven in the morning wasn't the brightest idea I ever had. There were some headache pills in the pocket of my coat. I looked around for a water fountain, then saw a girl carrying a tray full of cups of coffee. She looked a little lost, walking slowly by the mounds of trash bags. She kept looking at her watch, like she had to be somewhere soon.

"I could use some of that coffee," I said.

She turned around and smiled. Or at least, she started to smile. She got about halfway there and the expression froze on her face.

It was a weird moment. It couldn't have lasted more than half a second, yet it felt like an hour. So many emotions played over her face in that little bit of time that at first I thought I must be imagining it. Later, I wasn't so sure.

She was a beautiful woman. She'd looked younger from behind. When she turned and I saw her eyes, for a moment I thought she was a hundred years old. But that was ridiculous. Thirty, maybe; no more than that. She had the kind of striking, hurting beauty that makes it hard to breathe if you're fifteen or sixteen and never been kissed. I was a hell of a lot older than that, but I felt it just the same.

Then she turned and started to walk away.

"Hey," I yelled after her. "What about that coffee?"

She just walked faster. By the time she reached the hangar doors she was running.

"You always have that effect on women?"

I turned, and saw it was Tom.

"Did you see that?"

"Yeah. What's your secret? Oil of polecat? Is your fly open?"

He was laughing, so I did, too, but I didn't feel anything was funny.

It went beyond any feelings of rejection; I honestly wasn't bothered by that. Her reaction was so overdrawn, so ludicrous. I mean, I ain't Robert Redford but I don't have a face to frighten little girls, and I don't smell any worse than anybody else who'd been tramping through the mud all night.

What bothered me was the feeling that, far from being lost, she was *looking* for something lost.

And she'd found it.

4

The Time Machine

Testimony of Louise Baltimore

I had been putting off going to the Post Office to take a look at my time capsule, but I knew if I waited much longer the BC was going to remind me. So I finished the pack of Luckies and took the tube to the "Federal Building."

The Fed is the oldest building in the city. It's a relic of the forty-fifth century, and has stood up to more nuclear explosions than the Honduras Canal. Civilizations rise and fall, wars swirl around its ugly perimeters and choke the air above it, and the Fed just sits there, massive and dour. It's shaped like a pyramid, pretty much like the one Cheops built, but you could have used the Pharaoh's tomb as one brick if you were building the Fed.

Not that anybody could, these days. It's made out of something nobody knows how to fabricate anymore. We're not even sure it's a human artifact.

We use the Fed to house the vault somebody nicknamed the "Post Office" many years ago, no doubt because the vault is clogged with packages that are not delivered for years or centuries.

The Post Office is one of those weird side-effects of time travel. It proves once more that paradoxes are possible, though only strictly limited ones. A woman had died today because it was necessary to avert most types of paradoxes, but the ones the universe permits are literally handed to us.

On the day I was born, my mother knew there were three messages waiting for me in the Post Office. It must have been a comfort to her: she knew I'd live to open them. At least I hope it helped. She died bringing me into the world.

I know it was a comfort to me. The date on the first one was better than a life-insurance policy. I would live long enough to open that one, and the second one as well. They were all found about three hundred years ago, quite close together.

A time capsule is a block of very tough metal about the size of a brick. If you shake it, it rattles. That's because there's another piece of metal in a hollow inside the brick. The second piece is thin and flat. On the outside of the brick is a name and a date: "For ——————. Do not open until ——————."

We find these capsules from time to time. Usually they are dredged up from the ocean depths. Dating techniques establish just how long they've been there—usually around a hundred thousand years. When we find them, we store them away in the vault at the Fed, under safeguards as stringent as the BC can devise. Under no circumstances has one ever been opened before its time. I don't know precisely what would happen if we did, and I don't want to find out. Time travel is so dangerous it makes H-bombs seem like perfectly safe gifts for children and imbeciles. I mean, what's the worst that can happen with a nuclear weapon? A few million people die: trivial. With time travel we can destroy the whole universe, or so the theory goes. No one has been anxious to test it.

When the time capsule is opened a message is discovered. It is often a very queer message. My first capsule bore today's date, to the hour, minute, and second. The second one was dated not too long after the first. The third . . .

Having *three* messages waiting for me had made me something of a celebrity. Nobody had ever received three before. However, I wouldn't recommend it if you're the nervous type. My third time capsule had been alarming people for three centuries. It alarmed me, too. It was the only one ever discovered without a specific date.

On the outside it said:

FOR LOUISE BALTIMORE, DO NOT OPEN UNTIL THE LAST DAY.

What the hell is the Last Day? It was both pretty definite and achingly cryptic.

I had to assume I'd know it when I saw it.

"Listen up, motherfucker."

"Yeah, I hear you. Right on time. I'll give it to you on the click, of course."

"Of course," I said. "What time would that be, precisely?"

"Two or three minutes."

I'm sure the BC gave me that "precise" answer just to annoy me. So with all the annoyances in my life, I need a machine thumbing its nose at me?

Apparently so. I tried having it kowtow and hated it even worse.

I'm just not a big fan of machinery.

The brick was sitting there across the room, on a transparent table. It looked like I could just walk over and grab it, but I knew better. I'd have been immobilized three times before I got within twenty meters, and killed if I got within five. When the BC says on the click it means precisely that.

There were a few other people in the Post Office with me. Some of them were people I knew. Keeping me company, I guess. And there was Hildy Johnstown, the "newsman," with his felt hat and his worn press pass sticking out of the hat brim. He puts out a paper with a circulation of around a thousand—actually pastes it up and prints it with ink on paper. The last gasp of a once-proud profession. Today, who gives a shit? News is, by definition, bad news.

I wondered if he'd get a story. Sometimes the messages say it's okay to tell others. Sometimes it says keep this under your hat. Sometimes it doesn't say anything, and you have to decide for yourself. Time would tell.

On the click, the BC caused the brick to be opened. It made some noise. I confess to a slight case of nerves as I crossed the room and pulled up a chair. I picked up the tablet and looked at the message.

It was in my handwriting. I had expected that; they almost always are.

It said:

*There are good restaurants in Jack London Square. Go
north on the freeway and follow the signs.*

*The Council will give in if you do not push them too
hard.*

*Tell them the mission is vital. I don't know if it is, but
tell them anyway.*

Don't fuck him unless you want to.

Tell him about the kid. She's only a wimp.

It was written in 20th Amerenglish. I read it through four
times to be sure I had it all, and my jaw got tighter with each
second I had to look at it. Finally, I stood up and backed away.

"Blow it to hell," I said.

"You got it," said the BC. The metal glowed white, whiter,
whitest, and began to evaporate. I turned before the process was
complete and strode from the room. I felt eyetracks all over me,
but nobody said anything, not even Hildy.

I held on all the way back across town and right up until my
apartment door slammed behind me. Then I fell down on the floor.
I don't know what happened then. Whatever it was, it got my face
wet and left me exhausted. Sherman carried me to bed and stroked
me gently for a while, then left me alone. That fucking machine is
the best friend I ever had.

I was not telling *anybody* about the kid. If the universe had to
be destroyed because of that, so be it.

Sherman coaxed me out of it.

He's the only machine I've ever had any use for. At one time
I scorned robots like Sherman. I thought they were only good for
jaded femmedrones looking for a thrill. I used the pronoun "it"
when referring to them, called them walking vibrators or humanoid dildos.

I stopped doing that after I got Sherman. He is definitely a
male robot. One glance between his legs could leave no possible
doubt of that.

He let me . . . weep. *That's* the word I was looking for. I have
cried before, but it usually comes from fury and I remain rigidly in

control as the tears drip down my cheeks. I had never been helpless like this. Not even on the day she died.

If Sherman was surprised, he never let on. He stroked me, let me curl up in his arms. He could never make up for the mothering I missed and we both knew that, but goddam it, he was the next best thing. I could no longer handle the idea of a real human man. I hadn't been with one for years.

Sherman's attentions grew more meaningful. I didn't think I wanted to fuck, but he would know that better than I. His fingertips are lie detectors. He can read my feelings as though they were punched on my skin in Braille. Presently he pushed me onto my back and entered me.

I fell into a dream state. He fucked me for three hours, from late morning to early afternoon. (Made love? Don't make me laugh. I know when the merely ludicrous turns into the psychotic. I am well aware that, technically, what I did that afternoon was masturbate with the world's smartest solid-state life-size inflatable rubber novelty.)

I had very little to do with it. That's my custom with Sherman, the Lord of Latex; I just lie there and he ravishes me.

What the hell else should I do? He can't feel a thing. He's an extremely complex series of programmed responses. He feeds off my responses and always does the right thing at the right time. He's a *machine*. I might as well worry about satisfying a pop-up toaster.

Sherman has no face.

He's a competent therapist, and he told me directly what that means in psychological terms. It is a very common female fantasy to be roundly and thoroughly fucked by a faceless stranger. At first glance, it looks like a rape fantasy. It most emphatically is not. Rape is not sex for a woman, and it has very little to do with sex for a man.

Sherman does not ask me what I want. He doesn't ask me when I want to screw; he knows. He simply takes me.

And I am so totally in control of the experience that I don't even have to tell him what to do. Each step he takes is perfectly in tune with what my body is telling him I want.

He is a reasonable facsimile of the perfect lover.

When I first got him he had a face. I couldn't stand it. I choose when and where to tell myself lies, and the lie his face told—I am a real man, with real emotions—was not one I wanted to hear. So I had him rebuilt with a head round and smooth as an egg. Like all the rest of his skin, it feels just like the real thing. As does my own "skin."

Sometimes he pastes pictures of faces over the front of his head and we pretend he's performing as some famous figure from the past would have. I've fucked my way through several history books.

Bizarre? All right. But it depends on what neighborhood you live in. I won't say it was as good as making love with a real man. I won't say it was worse, either. There was no emotional component. Sometimes I missed that; then I would think of Lawrence, and take Sherman to bed and practically wear him out. Sherman was a *lot* safer.

My reasons for this preference were complex and incompletely understood. Part of it was simple. There were plenty of opportunities to get hurt without going out searching for love.

Another part of it was deep down, and Sherman-the-therapist had to dig it out in many sessions. I was terrified of a real penis. It could make me pregnant and if I was pregnant I'd have another kid and be hurt again.

Part of it was lies. The ones I told myself, and the ones others told me.

It is impossible in my neck of the woods to tell if the fellow you're bedding down with has real equipment or a clever imitation. Harsh, but true. The chances were excellent that his cock was no more real than Sherman's. Then again, he might still have the genitals he was born with.

The whole idea of skinsuits is that *you can't tell*. And you certainly can't ask.

And I had to know.

Don't misunderstand. I didn't want the real thing. I wanted a prosthesis. Safer. So if I'm looking for a man who actually remains male only on the genetic level, why not settle for Sherman?

* * *

Cold, cold.

I know it's cold. But I never promised this would be pretty. Nobody ever told me my life would be anything but nasty, brutish, and very short, and I never expected anything else.

You take what you get, and you run with it.

Like this:

When Sherman had brought me to the place he calculated it was best for me to be that afternoon, he stopped fucking me. He prepared a light lunch and brought it to me in bed. I got out of my skinsuit and he massaged me while I ate.

We talked of this and that. As he massaged, he was examining me for new medical developments. About every second week he finds one. That day he didn't.

Maybe I've given the impression that the real me looks like something dredged out of a sewage canal after a three-month swim.

It's not that bad. Really. I don't have any unpleasant smells. My skin is deathly white but it's intact. My genitals are my own. I suppose the kindest adjective for my face would be emaciated, but I couldn't use it to crack mirrors. The false leg is not the result of disease; it was an accident. I don't miss it. The prosthetic works better, and feels the same.

The hands are my worst feature. Those, and my remaining foot. It's called para-leprosy. It's not contagious. It's passed down mother-to-child, locked in the genes. One day soon those hands will have to go.

I had lost all my hair when I was nine. I hardly remembered it.

The critical problems were all inside. Various organs were in advanced states of disrepair. Many were gone, replaced by artificial ones. It was a toss-up which would be the next to go. Some we can replace with self-contained, life-sized imitations. Some require a roomful of machinery if they go rotten.

And what's it to you, bug-fucker? For a twenty-seven-year-old woman in my place and time, I was the picture of robust health.

You don't think we were running these snatches because we

liked the exercise, do you? You must have grasped by now that they were the desperate solution to a terminal problem. If you saw me without my skinsuit, you'd understand the problem instantly.

But no one but Sherman ever will.

When he was through massaging me I redressed my grievances. I should insert a grateful little plug here for those wonderful folks who brought us the skinsuit. Cut it: it bleeds. Stroke it: it responds just like the skin you used to have or takes the place of the skin it's covering. You're never aware you're wearing it. You can't *feel* it; you feel *with* it. It's semi-alive itself, and it works in some kind of symbiotic relationship with whatever's left of one's body.

A handy thing about it is that it's a great deal more malleable than real skin. It can be reset to new features if the need arises. In the snatch teams, it often does.

I put some clothes over the skinsuit and stepped out of the apartment.

I live on about the eightieth or ninetieth floor of a residence complex. I never actually counted; the lift tubes worry about where to take me. The building is about half full.

I paused at the balcony and looked down at the masses of drones milling about on the atrium floor.

Oh, my people. So lovely and so useless.

Call me Morlock.

At about the turn of the twentieth century a man named Herbert George Wells wrote a book. He knew nothing about time travel, had never heard of the Gate; his book was largely social commentary.

But his hero traveled into the future. There he found two societies: the Eloi and the Morlocks.

We call them drones and . . . what? Those of us who worked called each other zombies, or hardasses, or morons. Morlocks was good enough for me. In Wells' book the Eloi were lovely and useless, but they had a lot of fun. The Morlocks were brutish and worked down in the crankcase of society.

You can't have everything; this metaphor has run out of

steam. In our case, both the drones and the workers were lovely on the outside and rotten at the core. But we zombies worked and the drones didn't.

I have never really blamed them. Honest.

There are several possible responses to a hopeless situation:

Despair and lethargy.

Eat-drink-and-be-merry.

Suicide.

And mine, which was to grasp at the last straw of hope time travel offered. About one citizen in a thousand chose to emulate me.

Suicide was popular. In the springtime you didn't dare walk the streets for fear of being squashed by a falling body. They jumped singly, in pairs, in great giggling parties. The Skydivers at the End of Time.

But the favorite anodyne was to live it up. I can't think of any cogent reason why that choice was not the best. For them, that is. If I could do it, I'd have been a grease spot on the pavement a long time ago.

The trouble is that grease spot would not be doing anything to change the world that had killed my child. I could not prove that my work was any more effective, but at least there was a chance of it.

Nobody forces anyone to work. If they don't want to, we wouldn't have them anyhow. I can't imagine stepping through the Gate toward some long-ago catastrophe with a draftee at my side.

There are some fringe benefits of working. Extra drug and nutrient rations, personal robot servants, black market tobacco . . . I guess that about sums it up. Oh, yeah. As a worker, I can kill anybody I want to if they get in my way while I'm working on a Gate project. The BC protects the civil rights of drones only where it concerns other drones. I can snuff them with impunity, can go amok, if I want to, and lay waste to thousands and the BC will never upbraid me for it.

I usually don't. Though sometimes in the mornings, on the sidewalks . . .

If I kill another worker I'd better have a damn good reason. But I can do it if I think I can talk my way out of it.

That may be the biggest difference between my world and the thousands of years of human civilization that have preceded it. We don't have a government to speak of. The BC takes care of running things. We are the Anarchy at the End of Time. An odd thing for somebody with the title of Chief of Snatch Team Operations to say, maybe. But I simply took the job when it became vacant. If anybody wanted it bad enough I'd give it to them.

One day nobody will want it, and we can shut down the Gate.

There was another snatch scheduled for that afternoon. It had been on the agenda for three days. In that time the Operations gnomes had been setting up the details, choosing the teams, plotting the strategy. We don't usually have that much time; I've been on snatches that got off in twenty minutes, total.

But on this one I'd be leading personally. Again, I didn't pick myself. The BC did that, based on the fact that I was the closest body match to a stewardess who would be alone in her hotel room from the night before the ill-fated flight until shortly before she boarded the plane. That can be a handy way to start an operation. We call it a joker run, and I was to be the joker.

The name of this stewardess (flight attendant, actually, since the snatch was not going to 1955 but to the liberated '80s) was Mary Sondergard. She worked for Pan American World Airways.

It meant I'd be spending a night in New York, all by myself. I didn't mind. New York in the '80s is not a bad place. If you can't make it there, you can't make it anywhere.

There was a large team assembled for the snatch. This was to be a mid-air collision. Two large jets were going to tangle in the air and our job, as usual, was to get the passengers off before they hit the ground.

I assembled everyone in the ready-room and examined their disguises. Each was made up to look like a flight attendant on one of the planes, so they fell into two groups according to company uniform. There was Lilly Rangoon and her sister Adelaide, Mandy Djakarta, Ralph Boston, Charity Capetown, William Paris-Frankfurt, and Cristabel Parkersburg, plus several others I didn't know well. It looked like a good team to me.

And it felt good not to be rushing. Cristabel pointed out to me after I briefed them that my speech was rather jumbled and full of words that were antique in 1980 America. That can happen. Among ourselves we talk a polyglot with elements as varied as thirteenth-century Chinese and fortieth-century Gab. Before a snatch we try to limit ourselves to the target language, but it can get messy. I have the fragments of a thousand tongues in my head. Sometimes the cross-chatter is awful.

So I took a booster shot of 20th Amerenglish and hoped for the best. In no time, my head was buzzing with vocabulary and idiom. It doesn't always go smoothly. Once I caught an alliteration bug from a defective language pill and spent weeks babbling my Babylonian and scattering silly syllables in my Swedish until people could hardly live with me.

I . . . stepped through the Gate and saw instantly there had been a mistake.

We'd tried to catch Ms. Sondergard in the bathroom, preferably in the tub. You're never more helpless than when you're naked, prone, and up to your neck in water. She was in there, all right, but instead of stepping inside with her I had materialized stepping *out* of the bathroom.

I'm sure the BC would have a long, technical explanation for it; for my money, the silly son of an abacus must have reversed a sign.

But it was a pretty problem. I couldn't go in after Sondergard, even though I could see her there in the tub, because I'd simply step back through the Gate and into the future. However, the Gate has only one side (one of the *least* odd things about it). From where she sat she could not see the Gate, though she was looking right through it. This was as it should be, since from her side the Gate was not there. If she stepped through she'd only travel into the bedroom.

So I caught her eye, wiggled my fingers at her, grinned, and stepped aside. She could no longer see me. I waited.

It sounded like she churned most of the water out of the tub. She had seen something . . . or at least she *thought* she had seen . . .

"What the hell?" Her voice was not pleasant when she was scared. "Who the hell...is somebody...Hey!" I was taking mental notes. The voice is the trickiest thing to get right, and I'd have to imitate it for a while. Now if only she wasn't a screamer.

I figured she'd have to come out and see what was going on, scared or not. I was right. She hurried out of the bathroom, passing right through the Gate as if it wasn't there—which it wasn't, from her side. She had a towel wrapped around her.

"Jesus Christ! What are you doing in my—" Words fail you at a time like that. She knew she ought to say something, but it would sound so silly. How about, *Excuse me, haven't I seen you in the mirror*?

I put on my best Pan American smile and held out my hand.

"Pardon the intrusion. I can explain everything. You see, I'm—" I hit her on the side of the head and she staggered and went down hard. Her towel fell to the floor.

"—working my way through college." She started to get up, so I caught her under the chin with my knee.

I knelt and checked her pulse, and rubbed my knuckles on the carpet. Heads are surprisingly hard. You can hurt yourself hitting them. She'd be okay, but I had loosened some front teeth with my knee.

I was supposed to shove her through the Gate, but I had to pause. Lord, to look like that with no skinsuit, no prosthetics. She nearly broke my heart.

I grabbed her under the knees and wrestled her to the Gate. She was a sack of limp noodles. Somebody reached through, grabbed her wet feet, and pulled. *So long, love! How'd you like to go on a long voyage*?

Then there was not much to do. I sat on the edge of her bed for a while, letting the excitement die away, then kicked off my shoes and took her purse from the table beside the bed. I poked through it. There was an open pack of Virginia Slims and one still in cellophane. I lit four of them, took a deep drag, and leaned back on the bed.

It's rare to have free time on a snatch. Here it was only eight o'clock in the evening. Sondergard's flight didn't leave until tomorrow evening. I was suddenly struck with very un-Chief-like thoughts. Just outside my room was the Big Apple, and I was in the mood to make applesauce.

I pulled the drapes and looked out. I estimated I was on the third and top floor of one of those long, new (in the '80s) airport motels, the kind whose signs seem to blur together: the Thunderhilton Regency Inn. I couldn't spot the airport itself, wasn't really sure if I was near La Guardia or Idlewild (sorry; JFK). Some sort of shopping center was spread out below me. The parking lot was crowded with Christmas shoppers. Across the way was a disco.

I watched the couples coming and going and tried to fight off the blues. It would have been nice to go over there and dance the goddam night away. Hell, I'd have settled for pushing a cart through the aisles of the big barn of an A&P.

As a younger woman I would have done it. As Chief of Snatch Team Operations it was out of the question. There were strict security regulations against that sort of thing. Risks had to be minimized, and a one-legged para-leper be-bopping to the Bee Gees just didn't qualify as a risk that needed to be taken. What if I got hit by a car while crossing the parking lot? What if I was driven mad by the muzak Christmas carols in the A&P? Whether I lived, died, or stayed sane was not ultimately important to the Gate Project, but letting some doctor from the '80s get a look at my bionic leg was.

So I pulled the curtain.

I picked up the phone and ordered a big meal from room service, then discovered Sondergard had almost no cash. She had lots of plastic, but signing her name on the check was not something I was prepared to do. So I went to my own purse and dug out the wad I'd brought with me. I checked the dates on a couple of bills—ultra-cautious, I guess, but it never hurts to be sure—and even went so far as to rub one with my thumb to be sure the ink was dry.

They'd fool the Treasury Department, no doubt of that.

I sat on the bed and read the *Gideon Bible* until the food came. That Gideon sure had a weird sense of humor. Try "The Book of Genesis."

The book was bogging down in a lot of begats when the bellhop arrived. Along with a rare steak I'd asked for a six-pack of Budweiser and a carton of Camels. I lit a couple of the cigarettes, turned on the television set, and ate the steak. The meat was bland, as twentieth-century food always is. I looked through the closet, but mothballs were no longer a common item in hotels, so I wolfed it down as it was.

Then I took a warm bath and stretched out on the bed, wiggling my bare toes in front of the TV screen.

Who needs disco? I was having a wonderful time, I realized. It was nice to be completely alone. I watched the news and the Johnny Carson show. The late movie was *The Candidate*, with Robert Redford. I could eat that guy alive. I'd been in love with him since they showed *Butch Cassidy and the Sundance Kid* on one of the flights I was snatching.

All I can say is he better watch what planes he gets on. If I ever get my hands on him, Sherman goes on the junk heap.

I slept late. I can't remember how long it had been since I'd done that.

The television kept me company through the afternoon, until it was time to dress, call a taxi, and get to the airport. It was a beautiful day. The freeway was blanketed in a thick fog of hydrocarbons. The air was so rich I smoked the Camels one at a time.

I was aware that I was surely the only person in New York that day who was enjoying the air, but that made it even better. *Suffer, you healthy bastards!*

I deliberately arrived as late as I safely could. When I got there, the other flight attendants were boarding. I was able to keep the chatter to a minimum; since some of the others knew Sondergard I had to be careful. I pleaded a hangover, and that went over well. Apparently it wasn't out of character.

For the early part of the flight I kept away from the others by working my tail off, keeping too busy tending to passengers to spend time jawing with the rest of the crew. That got me some odd looks—I was realizing Sondergard had not exactly been the Pride of Pan Am—but it didn't matter. As the flight went on I replaced the stews one by one as the Gate appeared and then vanished in the mid-ship lavatories.

That's an easy trick. There's an indicator on my wristwatch. It senses the presence of the Gate. When my wrist tingled I'd simply go to the lavatory, open the door, and call for one of the flight attendants.

"Look at this," I'd say, with a disgusted expression. They were invariably eager to see what new atrocity the passengers had worked on their domain. (Flight attendants are almost as contemptuous of the goats as I am.) When she was in position I'd plant my boot on her fanny and she'd be through before she could draw a breath. Her replacement would arrive almost as quickly.

We started the old thinning gambit when the dinner trays had been cleared.

There are many ways to go about a snatch. Thinning them first is something we do when we can. The in-flight movies often help with that. While the cabin is darkened people don't notice as much as they would otherwise. We could take this one or that one and, in most cases, they never would be missed. From the moment the last stew was replaced there was a team member stationed at all times in the lavatory corridor in the center of the 747. When circumstances permitted we'd see to it that a passenger who got up to piss didn't actually get to do it for fifty thousand years.

Each snatch is unique, each presents different problems.

On this one we were clearing two jumbo jets simultaneously. That's good—numbers usually are—and bad, since the Gate can appear at only one location during any moment of time. That meant it had to be shuttled back and forth between the two planes.

Both these flights were transcontinental. That sounds like an advantage, but it usually isn't. We can't take the people out during the first hour and let the plane fly empty across the country, hoping the pilot never leaves the cockpit.

In this case, the 747 was going to remain marginally airworthy after the collision. That meant the real pilot had to stay with it to the end. It was just too dicey to take him and replace him with one of our people—even a kamikaze. There was too much chance the plane would come down in a place history had already shown us it would *not* come down.

With the DC-10 we had a lot more leeway. If it came to it, we could take the cockpit crew and simply follow instructions from Air Traffic Control, since that's what was going to cause this crash.

The thinning was going well. We still had two hours to fly, and we'd taken forty or fifty out of the 747. The plane had departed with almost every seat full. One would think people would begin to notice empty seats, but the fact is it takes them a long time to realize what's happening. Part of that is because we pick the candidates for thinning very carefully. We would not take a child without its mother, for instance. Mommy would come looking. But taking a mother and her crying infant is perfect. The other passengers may notice on some level that the crying has stopped, but they *never* try to find out why. That's the sort of good fortune you just don't question.

In the same way, we were alert for people most dissatisfied with the sardine-can seating arrangements, such as anybody sitting next to a tall person, or three unrelated men sitting in a row, especially if they were trying to work. If that middle fellow got up to get a drink or visit the rest room he was unlikely to come back. I'd never heard anybody complain about that, either.

But the biggest thing we had working in our favor was the unimaginable nature of what we were doing. I'd see someone looking troubled, walking the aisles. Maybe he'd noticed all the seats were filled when we took off, and now there were all these gaps. What gives? But logic is on our side. The guy *knows* nobody has stepped outside for a smoke. Thus, logic proves everyone is still aboard; ergo, they must be in some other part of the plane. Nobody ever gets farther than that, not even if we take half the passengers.

I concluded things were going smoothly and decided to take a look at the other plane, the DC-10. So the next time the Gate appeared I . . . stepped through into the future, changed into a United uniform while Operations shifted its focus to the other plane, and . . . stepped onto United Flight 35.

Another advantage to jumbo jets: nobody notices a new flight attendant.

Since the hazard was less on this flight, the team was being even more aggressive. They were summoning passengers to the rear of the plane on one pretext or another, never to return. I surveyed the situation with approval, and signalled to Ralph Boston. He followed me into the galley.

"How's it going?" I asked him.

"Easy. We plan to start the final operation in another couple minutes."

"What's the local time?"

"There's twenty minutes left."

That can be disconcerting. When I'd left the 747 it still had three hours to go, which meant it was somewhere over the midwest. This plane was already in California, two and a half hours later. It's enough to give you a headache.

But why not work it that way? Why, for instance, should the people uptime wait twenty-four hours while I watch the Carson show in a New York motel room?

They had not, of course. As soon as the Gate vanished in my motel room Operations had reset it for the lavatory of the 747 the next day. What had happened, from Lawrence's viewpoint, is that I'd stepped through, Sondergard had come out, the Gate had flickered, and out came the first flight attendant I pushed into the lavatory the next day.

It takes some getting used to.

"Something wrong?" Ralph asked. I glanced at him. Ralph was *not* impersonating a male flight attendant this trip. His skinsuit made him a perfect copy of a very black, very female person whose name he probably did not even know. Ralph is small, and has been with my teams a long time. Over a year.

"No. We might as well get going. Should I stay here, or go back to the other plane?"

"Lilly's alone in first-class. You could help her out up there."

So I did. Technically, of course, I'm in command, but Ralph was the DC-10 team leader, and Cristabel was in charge on the

747. On a snatch like this one I find it best to let my team leaders lead.

The first-class operation went smoothly. We used the standard "coffee-tea-or-milk" gambit, relying on our speed and their inertia. I leaned over the first two seats on the left, smiling big.

"Are you enjoying your flight?"

Pop, pop. Two squeezes on the trigger, close to the head and out of sight of the rest of the goats.

Next row.

"Hi, folks. I'm Louise. Fly me."

Pop, pop.

We were close to the rear of the cabin before anybody tumbled to anything. Finally, a few people were standing up and looking at us curiously. I glanced at Lilly, she nodded, and we plugged the rest of them rapid-fire. All of the first-class cabin was now peacefully asleep, which meant none of them could help us pull sleepers through the Gate. It's completely unfair, but there's no solution for it. Another benefit of your first-class ticket, air travelers!

We hurried back to tourist, which is always a bigger problem. They hadn't started putting people to bed yet. Ralph was still working the thinning con, and as I watched, he leaned over a man in an aisle seat and asked if the man would please come with her (him) for a moment.

The guy stood up and Ralph's back exploded. Something hit me hard in the right shoulder. I spun around on my heel, starting into a crouch.

I noticed a fine film of red on my hands and arms.

I thought: hijacker, the guy's a hijacker.

And: But why did he wait so long?

And: Hijackers were rare in the 1980s.

And: Was that a bullet that hit my shoulder? Is Ralph dead?

And: The goddam motherfucker is a *hijacker*!

It seemed I had all the time in the world.

What actually happened was the bullet hit my shoulder and I turned with it and brought my left arm up and thumbed the selector switch to OBLITERATE and crouched as I came around and took careful aim and blew him apart.

His upper torso and head lifted away from the rest of his body. It leaped into the air and landed six rows back, in the aisle. His left arm landed in somebody's lap, and his right, still holding his gun, just dropped. His legs and groin fell over backwards.

Okay. I could have stunned him.

Better for him that I didn't. If I'd taken him through the Gate with me alive, I'd have fried his balls for breakfast.

There's little point in describing the pandemonium that followed. I'd have a hard time doing it, even if it was worth describing; I was sitting in the aisle during most of it, looking at blood.

The crew had to stun just about everybody. The only bright spot was the number we'd managed to shuffle through during the thinning phase. The rest would have to go through on our backs.

When Lilly finally knelt beside me she thought I was hurt more than I actually was. She acted as if I might break if she touched me.

"Most of this is Ralph's blood," I told her, hoping it was so. "I guess it's a good thing I stopped the bullet. It could have punctured the fuselage."

"That's one way of looking at it, I guess. We had to take the cockpit crew, Louise. They heard the ruckus."

"That's okay. We're still in business. Let's get them through."

I started to get up. On the count of three: *one*, and a *two*, and . . .

Not that time.

"We can't move them yet," Lilly said. I didn't care for the alarmed expression on her face when I had tried to rise. Well, I'd show her. "We're stacking them by the lavatory," she went on. "But the Gate is with the 747 right now."

"Where's Ralph?"

"Dead."

"Don't leave him here. Take him back with us."

"Of course. I'd have to anyway; he's mostly prosthetics."

I managed to get to my feet and that felt a little better. This didn't have to be a disaster, I kept telling myself. One dead, one wounded; we were still all right. But I was beginning to appreciate the drawbacks in snatching two planes at once. I like to have the Gate *there*, ready to use, all during the operation.

We couldn't. The most limiting factor about the Gate is the Temporal Law that states it can only appear once in any specific time. Once, and once *only*.

If we send the Gate back to—for instance—December 7, 1941, from six to nine in the morning on the island of Oahu, we can snatch most of the crew of the Battleship *Arizona*, but then those three hours are closed to us forever. If something interesting is happening during those same hours in China, or in Amsterdam, or even on Mars, it's just too damn bad. We can't even see the events of those hours in the time scanners.

This results in another paradox. The timestream is littered with these blank areas. Most of them were the result of snatches we'd done, or time-traveling done by people who came before us. But some were the result of trips yet to be taken. In other words, in a few years or a few days somebody would decide it was worth our effort to go to those times, at a location we didn't know yet. Because we *would* take that trip, that stretch of time was closed to scanning.

The phenomenon was known as Temporal Censorship. We couldn't look back and see ourselves and thus find out what we would do. We could know a blank area existed and that nobody had yet visited that time, but we couldn't know *why* somebody would decide to go there.

If you think all this makes sense to me, you're giving me too much credit. I simply take the rules as they are handed to me and do the best I can.

My right arm was useless. I can't say it hurt much by then. It simply wasn't there. So I ignored it and pulled the goats by winding the fingers of my left hand into their hair—a trick known in the trade as Excedrin Headache number one million B.C.

Finally the Gate appeared and we practically shoveled them through. It took three minutes, tops. As soon as that was done the Gate vanished again. It came back on almost instantly and the wimps started to pour through.

No more than five percent of these had faces. Flight 35 was

going to hit so goddam hard there was little point in expending our best work on them. A lot of them came through in sacks, just bundles of burnt body parts which we scattered through the plane.

I guess I passed out. All I know for sure is somebody pushed me through the Gate and, for once, I didn't recall the trip. I sat there on the floor and the medical teams started to lift me onto a stretcher, but I waved them away. Something was bothering me. I saw Lilly step through.

"Who got Ralph's stunner?" I yelled.

Lilly looked at me oddly, then turned around. But she didn't get anywhere; the rest of the team came tumbling out behind her and she was sent sprawling on the floor not far from me.

"I thought you got it," she said.

"I didn't get it," I said.

"Get what?"

"Ralph? Did somebody say Ralph? He's dead."

"Where's his stunner?"

I was already up and running for the Gate. I had no idea how much time there was on the other side before the crash, but it didn't matter. Even if it was seconds I had to go back.

A warning horn sounded. I glanced up, thought I could see Lawrence frantically waving his hands behind the glassed-in Operations section overhead. I turned back and screamed something, but Lilly was already through.

Or at least she was half through.

An odd thing happened to her. Leaning forward, she was into the Gate with her head and shoulders, almost to the waist.

And the Gate shut down.

We had discussed what might happen in a case like that, but we didn't know because nobody had tried it. The theory was unclear. It seemed certain that a body half-way through the Gate would not simply be cut in half. The process was much more complex than that. When passing through the Gate one is never actually in two pieces. The integrity of the body is preserved through a dimension we can't sense.

Lilly did not get cut in half. She just vanished. As she did, the building shook as if from an explosion. Alarms began sounding.

I was picked up and put on a stretcher. I could see frantic activity in Operations. Then I passed out.

I was brought up to date as the doctors fixed my shoulder.

The explosion I heard had resulted from Lilly's body overloading the power system that supplied the Gate with the awesome amount of energy it consumes. It would be inoperative for two days while repairs were made.

What happened to Lilly?

I don't even like to think about it. When we pass through the Gate we enter a region that is in many ways beyond the reach of human senses, yet in other ways impinges on our minds unpredictably. Some people emerge from a trip through the Gate as screaming animals, and they never get better. We lose five percent of the goats that way, and a fair number of snatch team novices.

Whatever that region was, Lilly was in it, and she'd never get out.

5

Famous Last Words

Testimony of Bill Smith

I never did find out who got the temporary morgue set up. Briley hadn't had the stomach for it, but apparently Rog Keane had somebody on his staff that had dealt with the problem before. When we got there it was already a going concern.

Personally, I think it would be much neater and sweeter, more compassionate all around, just to dig a big hole where the plane went down and shovel them all in and put up a big stone with everybody's name carved on it. But nobody's ever going to buy that idea. The next of kin all want a particular body in a specific grave.

In some crashes, we can accommodate them. In the worst ones, there's just no way, but they have to find that out for themselves. All that's left of uncle Charlie would fit into a plastic sandwich bag.

What are you going to do? Show them a severed hand and ask if that wedding ring looks familiar? Most of them don't even have faces.

This morgue was in a high school gym. The parking lot was full of cars belonging to relatives, and one news truck from a local television station.

"Easy, Bill," Tom said, and guided me gently away from the camera crew. "You don't want to wind up on the six o'clock news. Not *that* way."

"I hope there's a hell, Tom. And when those guys get there, I hope the devil's waiting to shove a camera in their faces and ask them what they feel like."

"Sure, Bill, sure."

It was a relief to get inside the gym with the corpses.

There were maybe seventy or eighty of them. What I mean is, that's how many long, narrow body bags were arranged in neat ranks. Against the far wall were many, many more bags with no shape at all. An FBI team had arrived from Washington. They'd already taken prints from the reasonably intact bodies, and now were at work on whatever fingers they could find. Later, jaws would be examined for dental work, though you'd be surprised how few people get identified that way.

We were introduced to the Oakland Special-Agent-in-Charge, or SAC, as they like to be called. We already knew the boys from the Washington fingerprint team. The FBI inherited this messy job simply because they have more fingerprints on file than everybody else put together. If you read their literature you might think they get about a ninety-nine percent match of names with carcasses. The plain fact is that, after a couple weeks, a lot of next of kin would be told there was just no way to find even a piece of their dead relative, and there would be a lot of memorial services in a lot of chapels. A lot of burned meat would go wherever such things end up for quiet disposal. I'd never asked where that was. Doctors and morticians should have some secrets.

We met the Contra Costa and Alameda County coroners, the heads of paramedic and fire department teams, and quite a few doctors. It was a busy place.

I've been to crashes where they were just letting relatives wander through the morgue lifting up the corners of blankets. There's no way you can make it pretty or easy to stomach, but there are limits. Here, they were mostly going by personal effects. In a separate room they had lines of tables covered with burnt clothing and jewelry, all tagged as to which corpse it had been taken from. A lot of people were looking through this stuff.

Tom and I were looking for Freddie Powers, the agent who had called us to the morgue in the first place. We spotted him on the far side of the property room. He's more or less your standard Texas blond-headed collegiate G-man, tall and conservatively dressed.

"Hello, Bill. Tom. Got something over here you might like to see." Not too long ago he'd have said "Howdy." They say you can't take the Texas out of the boy, but Freddie was working on it. His drawl was practically gone.

"Bill Smith, Tom Stanley, this is Jeff Brindle." Brindle was a short, curly-haired intern in his late twenties, dressed in a bloody smock. He had a quick smile and slightly buck teeth.

"Jeff put all this together and brought it to my attention," Freddie went on. I thought he was looking a little uncomfortable. Strictly speaking, he was here to put names on stiffs; maybe he was afraid he was encroaching into my territory. Or maybe it was something else.

"Actually, I don't know if it means a damn thing, but it sure as hell is funny," Brindle contributed. He glanced at Freddie. "You want me to show them?"

"I wish somebody would," I said.

Freddie nodded, and picked up a man's wristwatch. It was a Timex on an expansion band. The band was stained with dried blood and the crystal was cracked, but you could see the second hand still moving.

"Takes a licking and keeps on ticking," Freddie drawled. I looked up at him. With Freddie, when the drawl gets thick, the kicker is on the way. I looked back down at the watch. It read 10:45 and some seconds. I glanced at my own watch and saw that it was actually a couple seconds shy of 10 A.M.

"I've got ten and about eighteen seconds," Tom said.

Freddie beckoned me a few feet down the table, where he'd arranged about twenty watches. I leaned over and examined them.

Several things could be seen at once. They were all working, though some had completely lost the glass. They all showed the same time—10:45. There was something else about the group, but it eluded me for a moment.

"They're all mechanical," Tom put in. Of course, that was it.

Freddie didn't say anything. He just led me to a second group of watches.

There were a lot more of these, though I could see down the table that the bulk of the weird exhibit was still to come. I sighed, and looked down.

Again, all mechanical. None of them were working. Some were so badly melted they might have been scraped off a Salvador Dali painting. But of the ones that were still readable, none had a time later than ten o'clock. The great bulk of them read 9:56, exactly.

"The planes hit the ground at 9:11," Freddie said.

"And eleven and forty-five is fifty-six. They're forty-five minutes fast, like the others. What else have you got?"

He seemed to realize I was getting impatient, because he hurried through the next part.

"These four here, also mechanical, are reading 1:45. Still running. And over here we've got a dozen stopped mechanicals that all read 12:56."

"These people hadn't set their watches back to Pacific time yet," Tom suggested.

"That's the way I read it."

I thought it over. I couldn't think of anything real intelligent to say, but I had to try something.

"Are these from one plane, or both?"

"Both. Most from the 747—I doubt we'll ever find all of them from the DC-10. But those we *did* get from the DC-10 agree with the rest."

It was Tom who finally put into words what we'd all been wondering.

"Who sets their watch forty-five minutes ahead?"

I sure couldn't think up a good reason, much less explain why two planeloads of people would all get the same brilliant idea.

"Thanks, Freddie," I said, starting away from him. "I don't know what it means yet, but we'll sure look into it."

Freddie was looking a little guilty.

"That's not quite all, Bill," he said. I should have realized. He led me further down the table, to where a large number of digital watches were arranged. They all had blank or broken or melted faces.

"Maybe the old-fashioned stuff's the best," Freddie said. "At least the gear-and-mainspring equipment came through better than these things did. But we did get a couple of survivors. Like this one.''

He held out an undamaged Seiko and I glanced at it. It had constant day/date display, and a second indicator silently flicking out the numbers in its inscrutable digital way. The time read 3:14, December the 11th.

''This one's really screwed up,'' I said. ''It's not even close to the others.''

''You're telling me,'' Freddie said. ''It's 'cause it's counting in a way I'd call a little odd. Take another look.''

I did, and this time I really looked at the seconds.

Forty, thirty-nine, thirty-eight, thirty-seven . . .

I plunked it down on the table.

''Goddam it, Freddie, every crash I ever saw plays crazy tricks, one way or another. All those watches reading forty-five minutes fast, now that's something I'll buy as having a bearing on the crash. Or at least it *might*. But one watch that's gone haywire and is running backwards . . . shit.''

Freddie sighed.

''I'd agree with you, pal, but for a couple of things. One of them is that I've had some electronics training and I couldn't figure out what would make one of these go backwards. I mean, anything that would knock it that far out of kilter would destroy the whole chip, you know what I mean?''

I didn't, but these days nobody likes to admit they're ignorant about any part of computer science, else you start looking like an old biplane fogey. So I shrugged.

''You said a couple of things. What's the others?''

He just held out his hand and let me look. There were three other digital watches there. All of them read 3:13, and all were counting backwards.

Donald Janz was in terrible shape. He looked like there was more Valium than blood in his veins. He was just a kid—no more than twenty-five, younger than Tom Stanley—dressed in a rumpled white shirt with the tie pulled askew. He kept tugging at his mustache and scratching at his nose, covering his face one way or another. He was sitting between Ian Carpenter of the Union—sorry, "Association"—and somebody who I thought for a minute was Melvin Belli, but turned out to be just a hopeful imitator. He couldn't have looked more like a lawyer if he had the word stenciled on his forehead.

We were back in the small conference room at the Oakland airport and it was getting on toward two in the afternoon. All I'd had that day was a donut and a ham sandwich so my stomach wasn't in the greatest shape, but they finally had the DC-10 tape ready to play and I wanted to do it while Janz was there to listen.

It's not strictly going by the book to play the cockpit voice tape at the investigation site. The actual tape was already on its way to Washington. There the Board maintains sophisticated machines that clean up, enhance, and analyze the usually awful recordings we get off CVR's. It takes a couple weeks putting the tapes through that mill. So I sometimes have a copy made before sending it off. That's what we'd be listening to.

The room had been cleared of reporters. I started out by watching Janz as it was played, but soon I was engrossed.

Somebody said: "United three-five, this is Oakland. I have you at twenty-three thousand, descending to fifteen. There is traffic below you, bearing . . ." and so forth. I saw Janz jump at the sound of his own voice. At least, though I'd never heard him speak, I assumed it was him. The quality of the voice was pretty good.

There were several exchanges, all routine, and some of the usual cockpit chatter, though by and large the two in the DC-10 didn't have a lot to say to each other. We heard a stewardess come in at one point, and heard the door shut behind her.

This sort of thing went on for ten or fifteen minutes. It was useful to get the names associated with the voices. We had the Chief pilots for Pan Am and United in the room to help us with that, and by the time things started to get interesting I had them sorted out.

In the DC-10 had been Captain Vern Rockwell, First Officer Harold Davis, and Flight Engineer Thomas Abayta. I wondered what nationality he was. Every once in a while we'd hear the voice of Captain Gilbert Crain, the pilot of the Pan Am 747, coming over the radio, responding to calls from Janz. There were also many other planes in the area, and we heard the parts of their communications that reached the DC-10 cockpit through their radio.

United 35 was descending, coming through cloud layers from the north and east, and Janz was guiding it through a series of turns that would have it heading almost due west when he handed it over to the Oakland tower for landing. Davis said something about the clouds, and Rockwell griped about the weather in Oakland. It seemed he didn't care much for the city. Abayta said something about a date he had that night, and it sounded like the other two laughed. Then things started to happen.

Janz said, "United three-five, I make you too far south. There is another aircraft in your path. Advise you increase speed and turn left."

Rockwell said, "Roger, Oakland, but—" and that was it, because Janz was on the air again immediately.

"Pan Am eight-eight-oh, advise you initiate left turn and decrease speed at once. What is your altitude, eight-eight-oh?"

I glanced at Janz again. He wouldn't have had to ask that unless his computer was down. It would be displaying altitude right next to 880's blip. Janz had no reaction. I wasn't even sure he was hearing anymore.

Somebody—I'm pretty sure it was Davis, the co-pilot—said, "What the hell?"

"I don't know," Rockwell said. "I better do it. Call him back."

"Oakland, this is United three-five, turning—"

But he was cut off again by Janz, who said, "United three-five, can you see anything out your right window?"

There was a pause. I could imagine Davis looking out the window. He'd have to get his face real close to it, because with the plane already in a left turn his side would be tilted sharply.

"Negative, Oakland," Davis said. "We are in a cloud layer at this time. Do you advise—"

"Jesus! Right over—"

That was Rockwell again, and that's all he had time to say.

We could hear the screech of metal, far away and indistinct, and instantly alarms started to go off. That's all we heard for maybe five seconds. Then Rockwell came back on.

"Uh . . . Oakland, this is . . . uh-oh, get that, get it!"

The engineer, Abayta, was shouting something in the background. We might retrieve his words in the lab; we'd listen to it over and over and eventually work up a fairly complete script. For now, we all listened to Vern Rockwell's last words, delivered in a calm, almost bored voice.

"Oakland, this is United three-five . . . uh, we have collided with something and the . . . uh, the aircraft is not responding . . . uh, to control. No rudder function. Ah . . . no response from the elevators. We have lost most of our left wing and the aircraft is on fire, repeat, the aircraft is on fire."

"Out of the clouds now," Davis put in. "Come on, come on, pull it up, get up, get up, get up."

Rockwell again: "The aircraft is in a tight roll to the left."

Abayta: "Fifteen hundred feet."

Rockwell: "Applying . . . right aileron . . . the stick is shaking."

Davis: "Get the nose up . . . we're going down, Vern."

Rockwell: "Looks like it."

Abayta: "Hydraulic pressure is gone, back-up hydraulics . . ."

Rockwell: "I'm trying to . . . I'm going to try . . . that didn't do it, okay, uh, let's try . . . shit."

I've never yet heard a pilot crying about it on the way down. Some of them are more excited than Rockwell was, but there's never anything that sounds like panic. These are men who have learned there is always something else you can do, something that, if you forget to do it, you're going to feel pretty silly. So they try and they try and they keep trying until the ground is about an inch from the windshield, and then what I think they tend to feel is foolish. They finally realize they don't have time to do anything about anything. They've missed it. They've fucked up. They feel disgusted that they didn't solve the problem in time, and they say *Aw, shit!*

Sure, he's afraid. At least the ones I've talked to who made it through say they felt something that was an awful lot like fear. But his job is to keep the thing in the air, and he's still doing his job when he hits.

You can define heroism any way you want, but that's it for me. It's sticking in there no matter what. Whether it's a pilot fighting his plane down through that last mile, or switchboard operators and doctors and nurses staying at their posts while the bombs blitz London, or even the dance band on the *Titanic* playing while the ship goes down...

It's fulfilling your responsibilities.

The room was silent for a while. Nobody could think of anything to say. Rockwell hadn't said anything deathless, anything quotable as being a heroic thing to say, but no one wanted to spoil the moment.

That's *my* job.

"Let's hear the other tape," I said, and everyone began murmuring at once. I glanced to my left, where a stenographer from United was sitting with a notepad in her lap. She was pale and her eyes were shiny. I gave her a smile that I meant to tell her *it's okay, I understand,* but from the way she looked at me she probably thought I was leering at her. My face is like that, sad to report. I'm told I usually look a little mean, or a little excited.

"They're still working on the other," Eli said. He looked meaningfully over at Janz, flanked by his protectors. I sighed, and went to him.

I dragged a chair around and straddled it, facing him. I was introduced to his attorney, but I'm afraid the name has gone clear out of my head.

You can't run an investigation without lawyers. They'd soon be as thick as maggots in a week-old carcass.

"I had both 35 and 880 where I wanted them," Janz said, dully. He kept looking at his hands, clasped in his lap. You couldn't help thinking, looking at him, that the guy would fall over any minute. His eyelids kept drooping, then they'd jerk open and he'd study his hands some more. He had two ways of talking: too fast, and too slow. We'd get a burst of something, then he'd sit there looking vague and mumbling things we couldn't understand.

"And where was that, Don?" I said, encouragingly.

"Huh?"

"In what order? They were both going toward an approach to Oakland, right? Which one were you going to hand over first?"

"Uh . . ." His eyes got spacey.

I should have known better. The lawyer cleared his throat again. We'd already listened to a lecture about how this whole interview was against his advice, and at several points he'd broken in, accusing me of manhandling his client. Manhandling! He was a lousy jerk in a three-piece suit, and dammit, I knew better than to push this kid. My big fear was that he'd start to cry.

"Okay, counselor," I said, holding up my hands. "No more questions, okay? I'll just sit back and listen." It was probably the best course, anyway. Questions just seemed to befuddle Janz.

"You were saying, Don?"

It took him a few minutes to recall where we'd been.

"Oh, right. Which one was ahead. I . . . I . . . can't remember."

"It's not important. Go ahead."

"Huh? Oh, okay."

He showed no inclination to do so, then started to talk rapidly again.

"I think there were fifteen commercial flights on my board. I don't know how many private planes. Some military . . . it was a fast night, but we were doing okay, I was on top of it. I brought them in, and I could see they were going to get close, but I'd have plenty of time to straighten them out.

"Not a collision course. No way. Even if they'd never heard from me again, they should have missed each other by . . . oh, four, five miles.

"So I gave 35 a . . . it was a right turn. Just a hair. I was feeling pretty good about it, since I'd just made a bigger hole *behind* 35 for somebody else . . . ah, it was PSA something-or-other from . . . ah, Bakersfield. Eleven-oh-one, that was it."

He smiled faintly, remembering how neatly he'd done it. Then his face fell apart.

"That's when the computer dropped out.

"I got real busy. I think I sort of put 35 and 880 in the back of my mind; I'd just dealt with them, and I knew they were okay. I had another situa—There were a couple other aircraft . . . uh, a couple others that needed looking after just then." Janz looked at Carpenter. "How long did the computer stay down?"

"Nine minutes," Carpenter said, quietly.

"Nine minutes." Janz shrugged. "Time sort of gets mixed up. I had 'em all labeled . . ." He looked up at me, puzzled. "You know what it's like when the computer goes down? You know how we—"

"I know," I said. "You go back to manual marking."

"Right. Manual." He laughed, with no humor. "They didn't tell me it was gonna be that hard. I mean, I just about had it back under control . . . and the next thing I know the computer was back on. There were even a couple of flights labeled, but not much altitude information available yet. It's like that, sometimes, when we're getting back on line. Some things get lost, and others—"

"I know," I said. I was visualizing him trying to switch from one system to another, with inadequate data.

"Well, the computer was still slow. It wasn't real-time yet."

"It hardly ever is," Carpenter said, with a scowl directed at me.

The lawyer looked confused, and I thought he was about to make an objection. He was obviously out of his depth, and didn't know if he ought to let his client talk on about things he couldn't advise him about. Carpenter noticed it, and shook his head.

"Don't worry," he said. "Don's just saying the computer was running behind. We make it about fifteen seconds, which is about average on a busy night." The lawyer still looked confused, which exasperated Carpenter. "It means the picture Don was seeing on his screen was fifteen seconds old. And it's all he had to go by. Sometimes the computer falls behind as much as a minute and a half. There's no way anybody can blame Don because the computer is an antique."

I could tell from Carpenter's look that *he* had a pretty good idea who to blame, but he wouldn't say anything just now. The lawyer seemed satisfied.

Janz didn't seem to have noticed the exchange. He was still back there in the ARTCC, coping with a new situation.

"Right off, I could see three-five and eight-eighty were a problem. They weren't close enough yet to set off the alarm, but they were getting that way. Or at least, considering the computer lagtime, I didn't *think* they were in trouble yet. But they weren't where they ought to be.

"They were on the wrong side of each other. Damn it, I couldn't figure out *how* the fuckers had passed each other like that. It didn't seem like they'd had enough time, no matter *how* bad my course figures were. But 35 should have been north of 880, and it was the other way around. And they were drifting back toward each other."

He put his head in his hands again, and shook it slowly.

"There wasn't a hell of a lot of time to make the decision. I figured they had about three minutes. But the fucking *crash* alarm wasn't going off, and I couldn't figure that, either. I turned them away from each other damn quick, and figured I'd sort it out later, in the incident report.

"That's when they switched places."

I looked up, and over at Carpenter. He nodded grimly at me.

"You're saying, Don, that the computer had mislabeled the two planes?"

He was nodding.

"Just for a couple of sweeps. I don't know . . . transponder trouble, simultaneous signals . . . what the hell. Whatever happened, for a minute there the computer was telling me the Pan Am was the United and the United was the Pan Am." He looked up at me for the first time, and in his eyes was a terrible emptiness.

"And . . . see, what I had to do . . . from what the computer was saying . . ." He choked, but struggled on. "See, I tried to turn them away from each other. But since they were exactly reversed on my screen, what I ended up telling them to do was to steer straight toward each other."

There was a short silence in the room. A couple of my people looked skeptical—hell, maybe I was, myself, in a way. But it was hard to believe, looking at him, that he was lying. He went on, still calm.

"And then, see, when the computer got them straightened out, there was just time for the alarm to go off, and I looked down and you couldn't tell the blips apart anymore. They were just one blip.

"And the blip dropped right off my board."

6

"As Never Was"

Testimony of Louise Baltimore

Sherman took me in hand when I finally got home. He didn't ask any questions, and he didn't say anything. A very quiet machine, is Sherman. I suppose it's a result of his near-total identification with me, his near-perfect reading of my moods and his near-perfect knowledge of what is best to do about them. One might even be moved to call it empathy, if one wasn't such a cynical bitch.

And of course he read that, too.

"I talk to you when you need talk, Louise," he said. "And for you, cynicism is probably a necessary armor."

Maybe I need to talk now, I thought. This, after an hour soaking in a hot tub as Sherman scrubbed and scrubbed at the blood that had vanished long ago but still needed cleansing. Out, damned spot.

"Maybe you *do* need to talk," he said.

"Ah *ha*! You *do* read minds, you devious android."

"I read bodies. The print is much clearer. But I know your thought processes, and your education. You just thought of *Macbeth*."

"Lady Macbeth," I said. "Tell me why."

"You know, but it would be easier to hear me tell it."

"So I won't let you. Keep washing while I talk; maybe you can get the guilt out."

"You're indulging yourself. But if you wish to wallow in it a little longer, who am I to object? Merely a devious android."

"Wallowing in it? Bite your tongue."

"I was speaking of the bathwater."

I knew what he was speaking about, but I still needed to talk.

"It was Ralph's stunner. He's dead, of course, so he can't be blamed. But then who should be? Lilly was second in command; no point in trying to find *her* for a drumhead trial and execution. That leaves me. I was in command; I should have brought the stunner back with me. Two stunners left behind in one day!"

Sherman continued to scrub. I looked at his blank face, for once wishing there was an expression I could read.

"Honorable behavior," he said, finally, "demands *seppuku*. Do you want me to go get the knife?"

"Don't ridicule me."

"There's not much else I can do. If you insist that someone die for the mistake you all made in a chaotic situation, you are the logical choice."

"That's what I told the others."

"And what did they say?"

I didn't answer him. I was still confused about it. What they said was, fine, Louise, but we'll have to be killed, too. They maintained—every one of them—that responsibility for overlooking the stunner was spread out among all of us. They further pointed out that Ralph and Lilly were already dead, and it would be terribly wasteful to kill everyone else, too.

I didn't know about that, but I did know that if any of them ever needed my hide for a doormat, I'd cheerfully skin myself. There *are* rewards in being a leader, dammit.

"Haven't you been scrubbing there a little too long?" I said.

"I'm not distracting you, am I?"

"I don't need that. It's not the right time."

As usual, I was wrong.

And that is how William Archibald "Bill" Smith entered my life.

Not there in the bathtub, of course; later, back at the Gate, in the first anxious hours as we all waited as best we could while the temporal technicians took the pulse of the timeline, checking for damage.

Martin Coventry explained it to me and Lawrence and a few of my top operatives and Lawrence's deputy gnomes. He gathered us all around a time tank he had set up near Lawrence's console and outlined the situation.

I had to admit I liked Coventry. He was a walkie, and a worker, but not a snatcher. His field was temporal theory, which made him one of about a dozen people on the planet who could claim to understand a little of what time travel was all about.

What first made me like him was his skinsuit. I'm not sure how old he was, but it must have been the early twenties. It was rumored that he had just about every mutated disease it was possible to have and still retain a brain, but then one hears those rumors about a lot of people. I thought it likely he was closer to gnomehood than I was, even though I was older. And yet he chose to wear a skinsuit that made him look like a man in his early sixties.

That's rare. Even I have fallen prey to the cultural imperative of our day that says if you're going to lie about how you look, then *really* lie. The face I wear could grace magazine covers—had done so, in fact. And my body was a twentieth-century adolescent's dream.

Then here comes Martin Coventry mugging at the world behind a face that only a mother could love, pretending he's older than anyone has actually been for thousands of years.

But he couldn't have made a more brilliant choice. The drones probably back away from him in horror, but he doesn't have to deal with them any more than I do. The people he works with are all involved in time travel. We *know* what age looks like, and deep down where we aren't even aware of it there is something that still respects the wisdom of the Elder. Coventry plays on that for all it's worth. With that face and that bearing, he was able to stand before us and lecture us as if we were a bunch of schoolkids. I can't think of another person I'd have taken that from.

"Let us consider the case of the first twonky," he said. "The stunner lost in 1955, over Arizona.

"In 1955, accident investigation was the responsibility of the Federal Aviation Administration. In addition to FAA personnel, members of the sheriffs' departments of Coconino and Navajo counties in Arizona, and of Kane and San Juan counties in Utah visited the site in an official capacity. Constables, police, and volunteer firemen from Red Lake, Cow Springs, Tonolea, Desert View and several other tiny Arizona communities arrived within six to twelve hours, in addition to units from Flagstaff. United States Park Service rangers from the nearby Grand Canyon National Park were there and thought they were the first, but actually the site had been already seen by members of the Hopi and Navajo nations. These were ethnic groups living in subjugation in the wasteland.

"Over the next several days people from the Federal Bureau of Investigation—a sort of national police force who maintained extensive fingerprint files—the Lockheed Aircraft Company, Trans World Airlines, and the Allison Corporation, manufacturers of the powerplants, visited the site. Several trucking firms were engaged to haul away the major or interesting portions of the wreckage, but a great deal of assorted trash was left behind as not worth carrying out. Seven local mortuaries were hired to cart away the organic debris generated by the crash, with eventual disposal and burial in fifteen of the United States and two foreign countries.

"In all, a total of five hundred and twelve people came and went at the crash site in the seven days following the crash. Another twenty-two, mostly morbid curiosity-seekers, came in the subsequent seven days, and the numbers tail off drastically from that point.

"We have done a scan over the ensuing three centuries. We have observed thousands of Navajos and Hopis, hundreds of hikers, and tens of thousands of coyotes in that time, and the Big Computer is following up on each potential contact. However, as you must realize, a completely thorough search of each person's life from the time he contacted the wreckage would take longer than the real-time events themselves; we must be content with a scan.

"In addition, if you go to the site of the crash even today and dig down about fifty feet it is possible to find pieces of airframe and engine. We have done that; it will take another day to completely sift the ground for a radius of three miles from the impact site, but the outlook for finding the stunner is not good. I will keep you posted on the results.

"The most promising avenue, naturally, is with the FAA investigators. We are looking into their subsequent lives minutely. There is still a chance that someone who went to the crash site picked up the stunner and carried it away—indeed, if we don't find it in our digging, we must assume that someone did so. The problem, of course, is that the wreckage has been lying there for fifty thousand years, and the stunner could have been taken during any of the twenty-six billion minutes that have elapsed since that time."

I wondered why I'd ever liked him. The bastard was showing off. Facts at his fingertips, here's what we're doing, the investigation was in good hands... I'd never have tolerated that kind of report from one of my people for even *one* of those twenty-six billion minutes. But since I wasn't in charge here I merely swallowed my anger and wondered when he'd get to the important part.

"The important factor," he said, confirming my judgement of what had gone before, "is the timestream itself. All the measurements we have taken so far show the timestream has absorbed this twonky with no disturbance."

I sat back and breathed a little easier. To sum up what he'd said so far, in a less windy way:

Two guns had been left behind. One of them, so far as we could tell, would probably never be found. If it wasn't, then its mere presence in the past would not be enough to upset the delicate balance of events. We were home free.

Even if someone did find it, it did not necessarily mean disaster. It could have been rendered inoperative in the crash, in which case it was just an odd hunk of plastic and other junk. It might raise a few eyebrows, but nothing more. We could live with raised eyebrows.

We speak of the rigid framework of events, but the fact is there is some leeway. Apparently things *tend* to happen the way they *should* happen, according to whatever plan was dictated by whoever's in charge of this stinking universe. Changes, if they are minor, correct themselves in ways no one understands but which tend to make a hash of anybody's theory of free will.

Picture an Indian passing through the site of the 1955 crash, many years later. He stumbles over Pinky's lost weapon—broken, useless, but something that shouldn't have been there. He picks it up, scratches his head, and tosses it away.

If the universe were absolutely rigid then we'd be sunk. The time he wasted picking up the gun and throwing it away would change his life minutely, but the change would reverberate through time, growing larger with each passing year.

You could imagine any chain of events you wanted to.

The Indian gets back to his teepee five seconds later than he would have. The phone is ringing but he just misses a call he would have gotten if he hadn't stopped for the gun. (Do teepees have phones? Did Indians still live in them in 1955? Never mind.) If he'd gotten the call he'd have jumped on his horse and ridden into town and been struck by a car—driven by a guy who was on his way to murder someone but now had to deal with a dead Indian—so the guy who would have died didn't die, with the result that in a few years he'd discover a cure for a type of cancer—which would afflict a President of the United States in 1996—so the President would be cured instead of dying when he should have died—and a war would happen that shouldn't have happened.

If it worked that way we wouldn't be able to make time snatches.

But the way it really works leaves us a loophole. There are two salient facts to keep in mind:

One: Things can be taken from the past as long as reasonable substitutes are left in their place.

Two: Events tend toward their predestined pattern.

Suffering from an energy shortage? Why not use the Gate to go back to 5000 B.C. and swipe a trillion barrels of crude oil out from under Saudi Arabia before there is any such thing as an uppity oil sheik?

Fine. No sweat. Just as long as you *replace* it with a trillion barrels of crude that cannot be distinguished from the oil that was stolen.

We can only take things that will not be missed, or that can logically vanish. (Who knows how many paper clips are in a box? Who is upset if one carton of cigarettes is missing out of a shipment of 10,000? A rational person assumes petty pilferage if he misses it at all; I have pilfered many a carton in my day.)

But it's a very strict rule. It means we can only take things from narrowly defined times and places, and if we take anything major we have to leave behind good copies of what we took.

So if somebody is about to die and no one will *ever* see him alive again, why not kidnap him while he's still alive and leave in his place a wimp that is indistinguishable from the dead body he was about to become?

Rule two makes that possible. The copy is not going to be exact, not down to the genetic level, not down to the sub-atomic level. It's going to weigh a few ounces more or less than the original. There will always be subtle differences, but the universe adjusts to them, short of a critical threshold.

And so we snatch.

But beyond these small, acceptable changes, things get very risky indeed.

The generic description for the trouble we were afraid of is "The Grandfather Paradox." Simply stated, I go back in time, do something foolish, and as a result my grandfather dies at the age of eight. That means he never met my grandmother, and my father was never born, and I was never born. The paradox is that if I was never born, how did I go back and kill my grandfather?

Nobody knows for sure. Theories about the Gate abound, some of them contradictory, but it is generally accepted that the universe readjusts along the simplest lines. It shifts around in some multidimensional fashion, and when it's through, no time machine ever existed. My grandfather lived, and my father was born because I never went back to fool with causality.

What that would mean to *me*, I don't know. Probably I'd have been a drone, laughing it up, having a great time, and finally learning to skydive. My entire life has been lived around the Gate. I have difficulty imagining myself without it.

On the other hand ...

(And there's always another hand in Time Travel ...)

My people did not invent the Gate. It's been sitting right

where it is for thousands of years as civilizations grew up and fell around it.

We believe it was invented by humans, but we can't look into that time, obviously, since the Gate was in operation then.

And something happened to those people.

I wish I knew what. Possibly they got so scared of what they were fooling with they just turned it off and left it there, afraid or unable to destroy it, and wandered off into the desert. We do know that the end of the First Gate Civilization coincided with a big war and a dark age. The survivors didn't write history books. It's the biggest gap between my time and the twentieth century.

People from my time have gone back to that era of the first Gate shutdown. So many of them that it is useless to scan it; the period is riddled with the blank spots of temporal censorship.

And none of them ever came back.

Perhaps this is tied up with causality and the Grandfather Paradox, but the connection is beyond me.

The point is, if the Gate had never existed I would be living in a very different world. Possibly a better one, but it's more likely it would be worse. How could it be worse? Easy. The Last Age could have been three or four thousand years ago instead of right now. The human race could already be extinct instead of just racing toward oblivion. It's sort of miraculous that we've lasted as long as we have.

That's one theory. It's the best one. The worst . . .

It could very well be that if a grandfather paradox really gets going and history from the point of the twonky forward starts to come unglued . . .

. . . we all softly and suddenly vanish away.

Not just you and me, but the Sun, Jupiter, Alpha Centauri, and the Andromeda Galaxy.

And so forth.

This is known as the Cosmic Disgust Theory. Or: *If you're going to play games like that, I'll take my marbles and go home. Signed, God.*

Coventry went on with quite a bit more eyewash about the Herculean effort his department was carrying out, peering into the intimate moments in the lives of around six thousand people who had been dead for millennia. It seemed to me like a good time to get some sleep. I probably would have, too—let's face it, in just ten hours Coventry and his team *had* done a remarkable job, and so far seemed to have ruled out the 1955 accident as a source of temporal disturbance. I was feeling much relieved.

Then he got to the second twonky.

"Here," he said, "the situation seems hopeless."

Did you ever have the short hairs on the back of your neck stand up? Mine did. I heard a roaring in my ears, a sound of thunder like an earthquake building up steam, or the winds of change blowing through the ruins of time. I could hear God clearing his throat: *Okay, folks, I warned you . . .*

"Ralph's stunner came down with the DC-10 in a pasture north of Interstate 580, not far from Livermore, California. There it was picked up by a recovery worker and taken with the rest of the wreckage to a hangar at Oakland International Airport, where it sat for about forty-eight hours. At the end of that time, it seems to have come into the possession of a Mister William Archibald "Bill" Smith, an employee of the National Transportation Safety Board. Of all the people who might have found the weapon, he is probably the worst possibility. He has technical training and an inquisitive mind.

"What he learned from his examination of the weapon is impossible for us to determine. All we know is that he entered the hangar where the weapon was being stored at eleven P.M. on the night of December 13. We can observe him inside the hangar for only a short time; then a temporal blank intervenes, a period of censorship lasting two hours. When he emerges from the hangar, we can describe his actions only in terms of probabilities."

Somebody groaned—it might even have been me. There was excited talk, worried looks thrown back and forth, haunted eyes, the old smell of fear. You could hardly blame us. When we have to speak in terms of probabilities concerning events in the immutable past it means the shit has already hit the fan and the only reason we don't smell it is it hasn't hit *us* yet.

I won't go on quoting Martin. It's not really fair to him; he was as scared as the rest of us, and with him, fear shows up as pedantry. He got even more insufferably, prissily dry and didactic as he told us the story leading up to the casting of Bill Smith as the Most Important Man in the Universe, using the time tank as a visual aid.

My first thought when I finally saw Bill Smith there in the time scanner was *maybe I should go back and kill him.*

Not the best way to begin a relationship. But if killing him would prevent him from upsetting the framework of fated events, I would have done it without batting an eye.

Naturally, that was the worst thing I possibly could have done. According to Martin's scanning, Smith had years to live. He was supposed to die in 1996, by drowning, and to kill him in Oakland could not fail to affect the timestream.

I sat and listened to the buzz of conversation after Coventry's exit, but I didn't join in. I was having an idea, and I didn't want to force it.

Finally, still not sure what I was doing, I left the others and went to a terminal.

"Listen up . . ." I started, then decided I was in no mood for those sorts of games just now.

"BC, on-line, please," I said.

"On-line," it replied. "Am I addressing Louise Baltimore?"

"Yes, and don't sound so damned shocked. I'd like a straight answer."

"Very well. What is the question?"

"What do you know about Jack London Square?"

"Jack London Square is/was an area near the waterfront of Oakland, California. It was named for a famous writer. It came into being as an urban redevelopment project in the mid-twentieth century, and was something of a tourist attraction for those few people who visited Oakland for reasons of tourism. Do you want more?"

"No, I think that's enough."

I found Martin Coventry on the balcony outside the Gate building, looking over the derelict field. Or, as we snatchers sometimes call it, the Bermuda Triangle. In another age the place might have qualified as a museum. In our day, it was simply an historical junkyard. I joined Coventry and stood with him looking at the debris of five hundred years of Gate operations.

How would you go about snatching a one-seat fighter plane? What about a plane that gets into trouble over the ocean and vanishes without a trace? Or a Spanish galleon going down in a hurricane? Or a space capsule that falls into the sun, killing all aboard?

The best way to handle those types of disasters is to take the entire vehicle through the Gate. If it's a jet fighter, we field it in the retarder rings. The plane slows to a stop, we take the pilot off—usually quite confused—and then, depending on where he was going to crash, either catapult his wimp-piloted plane back a thousandth of a second later than we took it, or just dump it in the derelict field. Any vehicle which will never be found ends up out there on the field. Why send it back? It takes a lot of energy to send an ocean liner back through the Gate. There's a very good reason why nobody's ever found the wreck of the *Titanic:* it's sitting out there rusting away.

Right next to the pride of Cunard is a starship from the twenty-eighth century.

The derelict field is roughly triangular, five miles on a side, and is chock-a-block with every land, sea, air, and space vehicle imaginable. Right in front of me were four propeller-driven aircraft that, if memory serves, actually *did* come from the Bermuda Triangle.

They were in pretty bad shape. We'd taken them about fifty years ago and, like everything else on the field, the chemicals in the air had not done them any good. A rain shower in the Glorious Future I call home is not something to take lightly.

"I was born to be an historian," Coventry said, unexpectedly. I looked at him. I couldn't have been more befuddled if he'd told me what he wanted Santa Claus to bring him for Christmas.

"Were you?" I said, helpfully.

"I was. What more honorable profession in the Last Age than that of historian?"

And what more futile, I thought, but kept it to myself. Historians, as I understood, existed to pass down knowledge and lore to future generations. Without descendants, the compilation of history struck me as a fairly dry business. But he was way ahead of me.

"I know I was born in the wrong age for it," he conceded, looking at me for the first time. "Still, this breaks my heart. What a memorial this could have made. What a testament to the human will to keep going. Look at that."

He was pointing to what remained of a Viking longboat I'd helped snatch no more than six months before. The thick fluid we are pleased to call air had eaten gaping holes in it already; out here, you might as well build something out of cheese as to build it of wood.

"Can you imagine setting out to row across the Atlantic Ocean in that . . . that . . ."

"Yeah, yeah, I know what you mean," I said. "But what you don't know is it was a real ship of fools. You didn't have to deal with a berserk Captain. Lars, Cleaver-of-Heads, he was called. He told me that Thor had called him to sail to Greenland. He hadn't messed with navigation, even though he knew more about it than you'd think, because it was a divine sailing. I picked up him and his crew becalmed in the horse latitudes, rowing to beat the band. They were about two days from starvation. Before long they would have been eating their shipmates who'd already crossed over to Valhalla. Let me tell you, the *stink* on that—"

"You don't have much romance in your soul, Louise."

I thought it over.

"I can't afford it," I said, finally. "There's still too much work to do."

"That's my point. You've got a lot in common with Lars, whether you understand that or not."

"I hope I don't smell like him."

Some of my best comebacks just go right over people's heads; he went on like he hadn't heard me.

"Your will to keep going is the strongest I have ever encountered. There are no new frontiers to push back. In fact, the best you can do is push back the date of the final blackout by a day or a week—but you push!"

He was making me uncomfortable. There's no doubt he'd

read me right in one way: I don't have much truck with romantic notions of human destiny, or Gods, or Good Guys winning out in the end. I have seen destiny in action, and I can tell you, it stinks.

"What's the consensus back there?" he said. "How are they taking my analysis of the situation?"

"Nobody's very happy about it. You said it's hopeless; I guess they all agree with you. You're pretty much the voice of authority when it comes to the Gate and the timestream."

"So no one has anything to suggest? No course of action?"

"How could they? They're all looking to you to show them a way out. You said there wasn't any way out. If they had anybody to leave anything to, they'd all be writing their wills, I guess."

He looked at me, and smiled.

"Right. So what's your plan?"

7

Guardians of Time

There are nine people on the Council. I don't know why, though the BC might tell me if I asked, since it nominates and elects Council members. I've always fancied it's so in case we ever screw up so totally that the universe does come apart at the seams and all eras coexist, we can field a team in the Never-neverland World Series.

Technically it's called the Programmers' Council. That's a polite fiction. They don't do any programming. Computers long ago grew too complex and too accurate to allow a mere human to fuck around with their instructions.

Yet there are qualities no one has ever succeeded in placing into the memory banks.

Don't ask me what they are.

Imagination might be one of them, empathy another. Or I could just be giving the human race credit for more than it deserves. Maybe the BC supports and maintains the Council to keep itself in check, to prevent it from actually becoming God. There *is* that hazard. Possibly the BC needs an element of foolhardiness and prejudice and meanness and ornery self-interest to give it perspective. Or maybe, like the rest of us, it just needs a giggle now and then.

For whatever reason, the Council is the nearest thing we have to a government. To get on it you need to be incredibly ancient— say thirty-six or thirty-seven; well beyond the median mortality age.

That they are gnomes goes without saying. Most are little more than a brain and a central nervous system. Sometimes only the cerebrum is left, and in more than one case I've suspected even that is gone.

There are requirements other than sheer age, but I've never been able to figure them out. Intelligence is a good one, and so is eccentricity. If you're a thirty-eight-year-old super-genius and a real pain in the ass, your chances of ending up on the Council are excellent.

They are an odd lot. Most of them are not nearly as concerned with outward appearance as most gnomes. Several have elected to house their brains in full prosthetic bodies, but more often than not they don't look any more realistic than Sherman. Ali Teheran is like Larry: a torso fastened to a pedestal. Marybeth Brest is a talking head, a puss on a post, like from a cheap horror film. Nancy Yokohama is a brain in a tank, and The Nameless One is just a speaker sitting on a desk. Only the BC knows who, where, or what he is.

Who knows how important they are? I doubt if even they could answer that. But the fact is, I'd never heard of a case where the BC overruled one of the Council's decisions. And the Gate Project, the last feeble hope of the human race, had originated in the Council Chamber, not in the BC's supercooled synapses.

Understand then that I was a trifle twitchy to appear in their august presences. I'd known it was coming: the time capsule had said so. What I hadn't known was that I'd request the audience—I had expected to be summoned. It didn't make me any happier to be there.

I wished Martin Coventry had come with me, but he had refused. Looking at them, I thought I knew why. He hated them, hated with an unreasoning passion I knew only too well. Whereas I was destined to rot away until I was installed with the other gnomes in Operations, this is where Martin Coventry would come. He'd been a prime candidate for the Council since he was nine. I don't blame him for not wishing to see his future.

A Hollywood set designer would have loved the Council Chamber. It was futuristic as shit. You couldn't find the walls unless you blundered into them; it was like standing in a vast, featureless plain, all white, with nine oddballs sitting behind—or on—a curved, black table.

Well, if it made them happy, it was no skin off my suit.

I assumed Peter Phoenix was the leader since he sat in the middle. He looked more human than the rest of them put together, if a trifle like an Old Testament God. He started the festivities.

"I understand there has been a twonky, and that you have a plan for correcting it."

"Two twonkies," I said, wondering if that was the correct plural.

"And that you might have been responsible for one of them?" Phoenix lifted one massive eyebrow. I could almost hear the pulleys creaking.

"It may be. I stand ready to accept your judgement on that matter, and your penalty."

"Report, then."

I filled them in on the disastrous day that had seen the deaths of Pinky, Ralph, and probably Lilly. I told the tale of the hijacker as straight as I knew how, relating every circumstance I thought might have a bearing on the case. It had been about forty-eight hours, straight-time, since Pinky died. I had spent the last twenty-four of those, after my conversation with Coventry, peering into a time-scan tank, getting to know Mr. Bill Smith better than probably even his ex-wife had ever known him. He's the man I wanted to talk to the Council about, but I thought it best to lead up to it gradually.

So I summarized Coventry's lecture of the previous day, telling them the tale of the first twonky, the one I had no responsibility for—other than the transferred responsibility of being in command of someone who makes a mistake. I told them we had found no trace of it, and that the probability was nearly one hundred percent that whoever found it in the last five hundred centuries had done nothing with it, that it had not altered his, her, or its life.

"Some good news for a change," Nancy Yokohama opined.

You want some more, O disgusting one? I just released a school of piranha in that fishtank your gray matter swims in . . .

I cut that thought short, I'm afraid. There are limits even to *my* irreverence.

"Yes, it is, isn't it?" I beamed. "Now for the classical rejoinder. The *bad* news is that we have located the other weapon. It's going to be a bitch to get it back. Can I have the tank, please?"

A time-scan tank rose from the floor beside me. In rapid succession we watched the results of thirty hours of scanning by almost a thousand operatives.

The first scene was the site of the DC-10 crash. The tank was almost black, punctuated by tiny, exquisitely lovely flames. The viewpoint zoomed in until most of the tank was filled by one worker looking dazed and dragging a plastic sack behind him. He stooped, picked up something, and started to put it in his bag. The picture froze and we zoomed in closer, to see the object in his hand. It was Ralph's stunner, much the worse for wear. Deep inside it a red light glowed.

"This is the first human contact with the twonky. It's nothing serious, as you can see. The man has no idea what he's handling. His actions are not altered enough to produce change in the timestream.

"The twonky is taken to this building, which has been set aside to collect the non-organic debris generated by the crash."

I let them study the interior of the building as displayed in the tank. I surreptitiously wiped my palms on my hips. "Non-organic debris generated . . ."

This was all getting to me. I'd been around Martin Coventry too much, and, to make it worse, much of the time-windows we could look into in our study of Bill Smith had been consumed by endless meetings. And suddenly I was babbling fluent techspeak, that universal human gobbledegook patois designed by "experts" to overawe the unwashed. It probably got started about the time of the flint hand-axe and has been getting denser and more impenetrable ever since.

I couldn't help it. For twenty-four hours I'd been observing masters of the tongue outdoing themselves at the subsequent meetings and hearings and press conferences generated by the crash.

Still, I'd have to watch it. Before I knew it I'd be on speaking terms with bureaucrats and from there it's only one short step downward to the nadir of language, which, in the twentieth century, was known as The Law.

"We can't trace it in here," I went on. "We're hampered by the fact that no less than four distinct blank spots exist between the time the Gate was turned off at the end of the snatch, and the critical time, forty-eight hours later, when the paradox situation becomes inherent. Naturally, we can't know for what purpose the Gate was used those four times. But we do know none of them are the result of operations conducted by us prior to this time."

Ali Teheran spoke up. "Ergo, they will be caused by excursions into the past yet to be taken."

For brilliant observations like this I hold the Council in awe? Oh, well. I nodded, and went on.

"Skipping over that for now . . . when we again pick up the twonky it is only in terms of probabilities."

That statement produced much the same reaction it had earlier when Martin Coventry made it; I even heard someone groan, though this time I was sure it wasn't me. I believe it was The Nameless One.

"Right now everything seems to hinge on the actions of this man. William 'Bill' Smith, forty-something years old, chief on-site investigator for the National Transportation Safety Board."

In the tank, the image was of an unkempt, slightly rheumy, tall, brown-haired guy I'd come to know all too well in the last hours. I let him linger there while the Council studied the man who had suddenly become the pivot of history as we knew it. I couldn't help taking another look myself. He was not the guy I'd have ordered up from central casting to be the Man for All Seasons.

Oddly, he looked a little like Robert Redford, my Hollywood heartthrob. If Redford had been a heavy drinker weighed down by fifteen years of quiet despair and burdened with an unfortunate way of holding his mouth and a pair of slightly misfocused eyes straddling a nose that leaned to the left . . . if Redford had been a rummy and a loser, he'd have been Bill Smith. It was as if two people had built a model using identical parts, but one had followed the instructions and the other had just bashed it together and left glue oozing from the cracks.

I resumed.

"Smith's actions following the last of the blank spots are crucial. We have established that he entered the hangar containing the wrecked airplanes forty-eight hours after the crash itself. When he emerges, he has come unstuck from the timestream." I let that sequence unfold in the tank. I was weary of talking.

We saw him come out, but he was no longer the sharp, perfect little model of a man he had been when he went in. He was fuzzy around the edges. He was like a badly focused film, a vidscreen tuned incorrectly, or, more to the point, a photographic quintuple-exposure.

"We have identified five distinct main lines of action from this departure point—or cusp, if you will. In two of them he emerges from the hangar with the weapon—at least we think he does. He's very hard to see. In one of those two, the weapon is not sufficient as a disruptive force in his life. He eventually reenters his predestined lifeline. In the other, finding the weapon changes his life forever, with consequences for us I need not detail.

"In three other scenarios he does *not* have the weapon when he comes out. In two of those, he once more reintegrates into the path of history. But again, in the fifth and last, he departs radically."

"Even though he does not have the stunner," Peter Phoenix said.

"That's right. We don't know why."

"Something happened to him in there," Yokohama said.

"Yes. Naturally, we tried to find out what it was, but since the event happened during a period of temporal censorship we're unlikely to ever know." I was assuming they didn't need that phenomenon explained to them, but perhaps a few more words about it are in order, since I was now bracing to hit them with my plan, and it hinged on the laws of censorship.

There is absolute temporal censorship, and there is the censorship of proximity. The presence of the Gate is the best example of the first; when it is in operation, when it has actually appeared at a particular time, we can neither see nor go anywhere in that time ever again.

The Proximity Effect is a bit different. My recent trip back to 1983 New York is a good example. The Gate appeared, I zapped Mary Sondergard back through it, and it vanished. It didn't reenter 1983 until the next day. But for almost twenty-four hours I had been living in the past. *I* became a sort of twonky. If I tried to look into those twenty-four hours in New York, I'd see nothing but static; I was a disruptive factor in the timestream. An inanimate twonky did the same thing, but much less so.

You can't meet yourself. As far as we know, that's an absolutely inflexible rule of time-traveling. It extends even to seeing yourself, and further, to someone else seeing you and giving you a report. Thus, Martin Coventry could not look into that motel room where I spent the night and see anything but static, nor could anyone from my time. That area was sealed to us.

In fact, my presence in that room had created a zone of censorship that took in most of the Eastern Seaboard. We could still scan in California during that night, but we'd have no luck seeing what had been happening in Baltimore.

For much the same reason, we could no longer follow Smith very accurately after he got to California to begin his investigation— and that's what my argument to the Council would be based around. In addition to the windows of absolute censorship that told us when the Gate would be used—might be used—there was a great deal of proximity effect to be seen.

This probably meant that one of us had been involved in the events in the hangar. It meant, to Coventry and me, anyway, that somebody from our time was going to be moving around in 1983, with the result that temporal censorship was preventing us from learning anything that could be useful in planning what we would do—had done.

If you don't understand that, take fifty aspirin and call me in the morning.

"I take it you are in favor of a mission to repair this situation," Phoenix said, anticipating me.

"Yes, I am. For two reasons. If we do nothing, the cumulative effects of this thing are going to work their way up the timeline. I believe I was told the rate of approach of this . . . one of the engineers called it a 'timequake' . . . is on the order of two hundred years per hour. If you can make any sense out of a figure like that. I—''

''We are familiar with the concept,'' Teheran chided me. ''When the timequake arrives here where the disturbance originated, the readjustment in reality will take place all up and down the timeline.''

''And we'll all be edited out of it,'' I finished for him. ''Us, and all the effects of our work. A hundred thousand rescued humans will reappear on falling airplanes, in sinking ships and exploding factories and on battlefields and in the bottom of mineshafts. The Gate Project will be over. I don't suppose it will matter to us since we won't be around to witness it. We'll be never-born.''

''There are other theories,'' The Nameless One said.

''I'm aware of that. Yet in five hundred years of snatch operations no one has suggested we rely on any of them. A few hours ago I let a girl die because it has been so strongly impressed on me that we must treat this theory as if it were proven fact. Are you telling me we're changing theories now?'' Do it, you impossible obscenity; tell me that, and I'll find you, and find a way to make you hurt.

''No,'' it said. ''Get on with it. You mentioned a second reason for undertaking this project.''

''Which, in my opinion,'' Teheran added, ''might well produce the very temporal catastrophe we are trying to avoid.''

''I have to defer to your judgement on that,'' I said. ''I suspect it may be true, myself. However. The second reason has to do with the time capsule message I opened and read two days ago.''

That got a stir out of them. Who says we highly evolved future types aren't superstitious? That message was in my handwriting. That meant I was going to write it when I was a little older, and presumably a little wiser.

But just as cynical. The message had said: ''I don't know if it is [vital], but tell them anyway.''

There had been no need for her/me to add "don't let anybody see this message." A con like that wouldn't work if anybody but me had seen it.

So I said, "The message said this mission is vital to the success of the Gate Project." And I sat back, not pushing.

Sure enough, in twenty minutes I had the authorization I needed.

8

"Me, Myself, and I"

There were four days to consider: the tenth through the thirteenth of December. During those four days the Gate had made/would make six different appearances.

The first was my entrance on the 10th, in the New York motel.

The second was actually many trips, carefully spaced, from the afternoon through the evening and early night of the 11th, during the flights of the two aircraft. Both these periods were now closed to us. It hardly mattered: both periods were before the loss of the stunner.

The planes crashed at 9:11 P.M., Pacific Standard Time. The first temporal blank after that was from eight to nine A.M. on the following morning, the 12th. We decided to call that Window A, since it was the first period we knew we had not yet sent the Gate to—which meant we would do so some day.

The second window—which we called, with fine lack of imagination, B—was later that same day, from two to four in the afternoon.

Window C was a long one. It started at nine in the evening on the 12th, and went all the way to ten in the morning the next day.

And Window D was the paradox window. It coincided with Smith's visit to the hangar on the night of the 13th.

Each of these windows had advantages and disadvantages.

A was far enough downtime from the paradox that Smith would be unlikely to be alert to anything. Our research showed that at the time of Window A the wreckage of both planes was, in large part, already in the hangar. If we used that window, it would be in an attempt to find the stunner in the unsorted wreckage and bring it back. If we could do that, all our troubles were over.

B seemed the least promising. What was happening at that time, most probably, was the first playing of the cockpit tape from the 747. I figured I'd go back to that one if and when my first option failed, as it still involved the least interference possible.

As for Window C . . .

I was the only one who had read the time capsule message, and even that early in the preparations I had developed a dread for C. I couldn't tell you why. I just know that I felt very bad when I thought of going back and spending a night in Oakland. *Tell him about the kid. She's only a wimp.*

No thank you.

Coventry argued for D. Take the bull by the horns, was his feeling. I wondered if he'd started seeing himself as Lars, Cleaver-of-Heads—a man of action if there ever was one—instead of an historian. And I wondered if he'd feel the same way if *he* was the one going back to confront the site of a paradox.

Again, no thank you.

I voted for A, and by voting very hard and as often as I could, eventually got my way. I further decided the expedition should be as small as possible: that is, one person. Coventry had to admit the wisdom of this. When messing with the timestream, you push as gently as possible.

And when you want to be sure a job is done right, there is only one possible person you can send.

At the rate of two hundred years per hour, we had just over eight days to work on the problem. It was not a lot of time. On the other hand, it was enough that I felt I should use every advantage available to me. So instead of hopping through the Gate to the morning of December 12th and simply sifting through the rubble, I decided to take the time to get an education.

It was ten hours well spent.

What I did was undergo extensive data dumping into the three temporary cybernetic memories implanted in my brain. The BC took everything it had in storage concerning the twentieth century up to the early eighties and unloaded it into my cerebral microprocessors.

I shouldn't make fun of the mental capacities of twentieth-century natives. They did the best they could with what they had. In five hundred centuries the human brain had evolved a little—I could learn a language the conventional way in about two days—but the qualitative change was not much. A good comparison might be the times clocked for running the mile. At one time four minutes seemed unreachable. Later, it was routine, and people were shooting for three and a half. But nobody was planning to do it in two seconds flat.

Still, traveling a mile in *one* second is no problem if you have the help of a jet engine.

In the same way, learning to speak Swahili in one minute or soaking up the contents of a library in an hour is no special trick if you have the appropriate data storage, sorting, and access facilities built into your head.

It's a great tool. You learn to speak a language idiomatically, like a native, and you get a great deal of cultural context in which to speak it.

Those three tiny crystalline memories soaked up encyclopedias, news, movies, television shows, fads, fantasies, and fallacies with equal facility. When I was done I had the lore of a century at my fingertips. I could feel right at home in the 1980s.

Like any tool, the cyber-booster had its drawbacks. It was better at language and facts than it was at pattern recognition. I still would not be able to look at a dress and *know,* as a native would, whether it came from 1968 or 1978. I could move through the twentieth century with reasonable assurance. If I stayed there very long I'd surely pull some anachronistic boner.

But what could happen in one hour?

It was a terrible day. It had been raining all night; the only good thing about the day was that the rain had finally stopped. But with it had gone the cloud cover and, worse, all that precipitation had washed most of the flavor out of the air. The sky was this great, thundering, alien *blue,* and about a billion miles away. The sun was so bright I couldn't look at it without risking damage to my retinas. It was bad enough that the thing was showering me with unhealthy radiation; how could these people live with such an oppressive weight hanging over them? And the air was so bland and clear I could see Marin County.

Words are funny things. I realize I've just described what certainly was, to a 20th, a beautiful morning. Cool, crisp, clean air; lots of bright, healthy sunshine; so clear you can see forever.

So there I stood, gasping for breath, feeling naked beneath the awful sky.

The shortness of breath was ninety percent anxiety. Still, I felt a lot better after a few snorts from the Vicks inhaler I'd brought with me. If anybody else took a sniff from it they'd be most disagreeably surprised. The chemicals in it would kill roaches and discolor stainless steel.

The Gate had dumped me near the east side of the giant steel hangar which was being used to receive the remains of the two aircraft. At least, that had been the theory. When I walked around to the front doors I found them open. Inside were two PSA 727's and a lot of mechanics.

I didn't like that at all. It meant disruption in the timeline. Glancing around, orienting myself, I saw the proper hangar about a quarter mile away.

That far in the other direction would have dropped me into the Bay. And of course, there was always the *other* direction. I could have shown up a quarter of a mile *above* the field . . .

It was a long quarter mile. I felt like a bug on a plate. There was just this endless concrete, still damp from the night's rain, and the infinite, awful sky. You'd think that after five hundred centuries we'd have developed a pill for agoraphobia.

One of the first things I saw when I got inside was two women dressed just like me. That was reassuring; it put me on familiar ground. I'd spent a lot of time blending in with other uniformed women. I studied them to see what they were doing, and it turned out to be wonderfully prosaic. The recovery workers had been working through the night, most of them without time to stop and grab a bite to eat. So United had sent some women over to serve coffee and donuts. Nothing could have been more in line with my experience. Snatching a commercial jetliner is ninety-nine percent serving coffee and one percent snatching.

I found the table where the coffeepot had been set up, exchanged a few pleasantries with the woman behind it. She was perfectly willing to accept me as what I seemed to be. I took a tray, arranged a dozen styrofoam cups on it, filled them, grabbed a handful of those paper packets of sugar and non-dairy creamer, and set off to serve.

Or at least to look like I was serving. I quickly saw that one woman could easily have handled the job United had given to three. That was no surprise—since the days of mud huts it's been a rule that it always takes at least three to get something done: one to do it, one to supervise, and one to offer helpful suggestions. I've seen it in mammoth hunts in 40,000 B.C. and I've seen it in interstellar spaceships. I'd have been in trouble but for another universal trait of humanity. If you look busy and seem to know what you're doing, nobody is likely to bother you.

So I kept moving and looked very efficient. In the first twenty minutes I handed out one cup of coffee and almost disposed of a donut, but the guy thought better of it in the end. No doubt after the things he'd seen that morning he was wondering if he'd ever eat again.

When I got a chance I would steal a look at my wristwatch. It was a Seiko digital this time, and no more genuine than the greenbacks in my purse. It contained an indicator that was supposed to home in on the energy leakage we'd seen coming from the damaged stunner.

Lanes had been left between the heaps of wreckage, some of them big enough to drive a truck through; literally—a stream of trucks was arriving from Livermore all the time I was there, and fifty or sixty men were constantly employed unloading them. Two or three men directed the distribution of the junk, which fell into several broad categories: airframe, powerplant, electronics, hydraulics, and so forth. There was an area for interior furnishings, most of which were the burned shells of seats.

There was a lot of gaily-colored paper and foil, most of it charred around the edges. I had to consult my cybernet memories before I knew what it was: the remains of Christmas presents. I saw new clothes, some still in plastic wrappers, and other things I was pretty sure were gifts. There was one heap of things that could only have been children's toys. It was all badly burned.

There was another area, the largest by far, where they had dumped a category of wreckage best defined as "?".

It looked like it covered about an acre, and my Seiko said the stunner was in there.

The stuff was contained in big Hefty trash bags. Some of the bags had fallen on their sides and spilled their contents, and I'd have been hard pressed to determine what most of it was myself. It was even possible there were some bits of passengers in there. Obviously, the crews had walked over the site picking up everything that didn't look as if it belonged in a cow pasture, and if they couldn't tell what it was it had been dumped here for someone to go over later.

I counted a hundred bags and I wasn't a quarter of the way through.

I tried to think of some plausible reason for me to go wading into the middle of that, breaking open bags and dumping the contents on the concrete floor and rooting around in them. I couldn't think of a good reason. I still can't. If I'd had ten people alone and five or six hours to search, I probably would have found it. What I had was thirty minutes, me myself and I, and a hundred and fifty people to provide an interested audience. ("What're ya looking for, babe?" Souvenirs? Fingers with diamond rings on them? The most important object in the universe?)

"I could use some of that coffee."

Coffee? Oh, right, I was here to pass out coffee, wasn't I? I turned, with a carefully calculated smile on my face, and there he was.

Bill Smith. The star of the show.

Time is my stock in trade. I shouldn't be surprised, by now, at the tricks it can play. But that moment was very much like another one, not much earlier, when a hijacker's bullet had hit me in the shoulder. Time slowed down, and a moment became an eternity.

I remember fear. I was an actress, playing a part on a stage before the most important audience I would ever face, and I couldn't remember my lines. I was an imposter: everyone could instantly see it, there was no escape from exposure. I was a pitiful freak hiding in a lying skinsuit, a monster from an unimaginable future. And the whole world hinged on this one man, and on what I did to or with him, and I was now expected to speak to him, offer him a cup of coffee, just as if he were an ordinary mortal.

At the same time, that's just what he was. I knew Bill Smith: divorce, incipient ulcer, drinking problem, and all. I'd read his biography from the childhood in Ohio right through Naval flight school and carrier landings and commercial aviation and the job with Boeing and the gradual rise through the Safety Board and the early retirement and the boating accident that would kill him.

And that's what hurt. I knew how this man was going to die. If I succeeded in my project, if I could turn the course of events back to what the timestream could tolerate, back to predestination, he would continue his slow decline. He would eat away at himself until his death would be a mercy.

For the first time, a goat had acquired a name and a history. And a lopsided, tired grin.

I turned, having looked at him for no more than a second, and started to walk away.

"Hey, how about that coffee?"

I walked faster. In no time I was almost running.

I've made other mistakes in my career with the Gate. I did other things badly. After I got the top job, everyone's mistakes were my mistakes, in a sense. I will always bear a load for the mistake Pinky made, for instance. It meant I hadn't trained her well enough.

But a special guilt attaches to that day, to that first trip back to correct the paradox, because I don't know why I did what I did.

I ran out of the hangar and ran the quarter-mile to the place where the Gate had dropped me. I cowered there beneath that hateful sky until the Gate appeared again on schedule and I stepped through.

Predestination is the ugliest word in any human language.

That first meeting was the one and only chance I'd ever have to cut the paradox knot cleanly, right at the source, and I bungled it. Do I mention predestination to excuse my failure, or did inexorable fate really grab me like a marionette and frogmarch me through the stations of some cosmic ritual?

Sometimes I wish I'd never been born.

Then again, you have to be born to wish such a thing. And if I flubbed again as badly as I did the first time, that's exactly the situation we'd all be facing. Never-born, never-lived, never having tasted either success or failure. Bad as it is, my life is my own, and I accept it without reservation.

I returned with my sense of determination intact. We'd never expected this first trip to show much result; it was simply the direct approach, and the only one that could stop the paradox completely. Now we'd try more subtle avenues. Now we'd start the war of containment. Our goal would be to confine the paradox to limits the universe could withstand—we'd seal it off, encapsulate it, turn events gently back toward what they should have been, and, though the timeline might vibrate like a plucked guitar string eight billion years long, pray that its fundamental elasticity would eventually prevail.

"It's like stuffing neutrons back into a critical mass of uranium," Martin Coventry said.

"Fine," I said. "You've got a machine that will do that, don't you? Let's start stuffing."

"I think he was speaking in twentieth-century terms," Sherman said.

That's right. Sherman.

I glared at him. Apparently I didn't have enough odd things in my life. Now my robot had started to act funny.

He had been there when I came back through the Gate, smiling and looking a bit guilty. Both of those things are hard to do without a face, so he had grown one for the occasion. His presence there was bad enough. So far as I knew, he'd never been out of the apartment since I uncrated him. But the face was utterly impossible.

Now the three of us were closeted in a room just off the operations level, discussing the shambles of the first trip. Lawrence was also present, via two-way remote, and I suspect somebody from the Council might have been listening in through the BC.

Three of us! That shows how much Sherman had shaken me. Before, I'd no more have counted Sherman in our number than I would a chair or a table.

"I think Louise is right," Lawrence said. I looked at his image in the vidscreen. "We shouldn't make too much of this. The thing to do is move on to the next phase."

"I'm afraid too much damage has already been done," said Martin. He really looked scared. His man-of-action phase had apparently faded; he was once again the cautious historian—worse, a *practical* historian, with the terrifying capability to write his own history.

"What damage?" I wanted to know. "Okay, I didn't get what I went back for. We didn't estimate my chances were very good even before I went."

"I agree," said Sherman. I waited for Martin or Lawrence to protest the idiocy of letting an animated dildo have a voice in these proceedings, but neither of them batted an eye. They turned to listen to Sherman, so I did, too.

"To sum up what happened," he went on, "Smith saw her, she looked at him, and she ran. Is that accurate, Louise? Don't bare your teeth like that; it's not attractive."

"Wait until I get you home with a screwdriver and a soldering iron."

"That's as may be. Right now we're talking about your recent failure. Is my account of your failure an accurate one?"

"I'll peel that smarmy face right off your head, you—"

"This is not germane to the question of your—"

"Stop using that word!"

"—failure. Sit down, Louise. Breathe regularly; the faintness will pass."

I did, and it did.

Sherman leaned closer to me and spoke in a voice I'm pretty sure the others couldn't hear.

"I have taken certain actions I thought appropriate," he said. "The new face is one of them. The induced catharsis was another.

If you're calm enough to continue and if you'll concede my right to be here in this conference, we can proceed, and discuss your grievances when we're alone."

I swallowed hard, and nodded. I didn't trust myself to talk.

"So he saw you, and you ran. Does that sum it up?"

I nodded again.

"Then I don't think the damage is great. There was no question of him penetrating your disguise."

"That's right," Lawrence said. "Look at it from his viewpoint. He saw a woman in a United Airlines uniform, and she ran from him."

"An odd thing to do," Martin said.

"Sure, but she can explain it to him the next time she meets him. We can think of some kind of story to—"

"Wait a minute. What's this about me meeting him again?"

"That was my idea," Sherman said.

I looked from one to the other, taking my time about it.

"You didn't suggest it while I was here," I said. "So the three of you were talking while I was gone."

"That's right," Lawrence said. "Sherman arrived just as we were getting the new information."

"What new information?"

"Lawrence expressed it badly," Sherman said. "I arrived, and after a great deal of trouble making myself heard, managed to communicate to the operations team that I knew what they were about to discover. Shortly afterward, they discovered it."

"We're still not sure about the time sequence," Lawrence said, defensively.

"I'm sure," Sherman said.

"Will someone tell it to me straight?" I asked. "Start to finish, just the way things happen in real time?"

The three of them looked at each other, and I swear, Martin and Lawrence were the ones who looked uncertain while Sherman was stolid as a stone.

"He'd better tell it," Lawrence conceded.

"Very well," Sherman said. "Thirty seconds before you went through the Gate, I was at the Post Office, where the Big Computer had summoned me. I read the message that was waiting for me just as you stepped through. Pursuant to instruction in the message, I came here."

I hadn't known there was a message waiting for Sherman. I hadn't known that *any* robot had ever gotten a time capsule.

There was a good reason for that. This was an unusual message. It specified on the outside that no human was to be notified of the identity of the recipient, nor of the date of its opening. The BC, as I said, follows these instructions literally. Technically, the Programming Council has *instructed* the BC to follow the directions on time capsules, but I wonder what the BC would have done if the Council had said otherwise.

Well, "would have done" is nothing but a rarefied form of the verb "to do." And a very pointless one.

The message told Sherman—among other things, and we'll get to that—to go to Gate operations and tell Lawrence that I was going to have a face-to-face meeting with Bill Smith, and that I would fail in my mission. That word again.

He did that, or tried to. It was hard to get their attention, for two reasons: the operations team was still probing in and around the era with their time-scan tanks and things were clearing up a little, and . . . well, he was a robot. Most people were astonished that he was there. It was as if my refrigerator had come into Operations, tap-dancing and singing *Suwannee,* wearing a sandwich board proclaiming the end of the world.

But he managed to tell them. Simultaneously, or a few seconds later, depending on who you believe, one of the operatives spotted Bill Smith in a helicopter returning from the 747 crash site and someone else found the same helicopter parked on the apron outside the hangar I was visiting. Inference: Smith and I could meet inside that hangar.

That's when they started listening to Sherman. It was a matter of a few seconds to confirm that he had indeed received a time capsule, at which point his stock went up tremendously. I'd recently experienced the same effect. Me and my people tend to listen to somebody who's just received a message from the future.

And of course that's when he started to clam up.

*   *   *

"The message was quite specific," he said. "There are certain things I can tell you, and other things that I must keep secret."

"Come on," I said. "Don't bullshit a bullsh—" That's as far as I got, and wished I'd buttoned my lip about five syllables earlier. I remembered my suspicion that the Council might be listening in, and the recent time-capsule-inspired performance I'd given them to get this operation authorized.

"There are a few more things I can say," Sherman went on. "The first is that my message confirmed yours, Louise. It said this operation is vital to the success of the Gate Project." He glanced at me, and I wished I'd had more experience at reading his eyes, but you can't read what isn't there. His new eyes were fake, of course, but looked very natural. His mouth was just a sketch. It could convey expression in the same way a cartoon can. He hadn't bothered with a nose.

"The second thing concerns the next phase, since we all agree the excursion back to window A was of no use."

So the subject was back to windows. What we had was B, C, and D. I thought D was too dangerous, B too unlikely to produce results, and C . . .

Tell him about the kid. She's just a wimp.

Nobody knew it but me, but I wasn't going back to Window C. I took a deep breath, got ready to do a cowardly thing, which was to put all my weight behind a trip back to B. I was pretty sure Martin would vote with me, and I thought I could swing Lawrence. The one thing I was sure of was that nobody would go for D. D was the site of the paradox, and surely too dangerous to visit.

"The third thing I can tell you now," Sherman went on, "is that the next visit must be to 2300 hours, Pacific time, on the night of the 13th of December. This is the window you have referred to as D. And Louise should lead the operation."

9

The Shadow Girl

Testimony of Bill Smith

There was one of those stand-up places not too far from our conference room. We went in there because we didn't think we'd have time for much more than that. I've seen those places in airports from LAX to Orly, and I've always wondered why people would want to stand up to eat their stale hot dogs. I guess the answer was obvious: they were in a hurry, like us.

I got something they claimed was roast beef, then I spent a lot of time tearing open and squeezing those little packets of mustard and ketchup and some unidentifiable white sauce to kill the gluey taste of the meat. Tom got a chili dog he had to eat with a plastic fork.

"Had you heard that story before?" I asked him.

"Some of it. I had some idea that's what he'd say."

"What'd you think of it?"

Tom took some time with his answer. I was interested, because ground control and operations was his specialty, and he knows a lot about electronics in general—an area I'll admit isn't my strongest. He was an M.I.T. graduate in computer science, whereas I was a member of the last generation who still knew what a slide rule looked like. You have to know something about computers in my line of work, and I did, but I'd never grown to love them.

"It could happen," he said, at last.

"Do you think it did?"

"I believed him, if that's what you're asking. We may even get corroboration out of the computer. It'll take some work."

I chewed that over.

"Okay. Assuming it's true. Who do you think we hang for it?"

"What, are you asking for a guess?"

"Why not?"

"Hell, I don't know if we can hang anybody at all. It's early, you understand. There may be something we can turn up that'll—"

"Off the record, Tom."

He nodded. "Right. We still might not find anybody to blame."

"Listen, Tom. If a tornado springs out of a clear blue sky and wrecks a plane, I'll concede it wasn't anybody's fault. If a meteor falls on a plane, we probably couldn't have done anything about it. If—"

"Spare me the speech," he said. "I've heard it. What if it turns out that the people to blame are us? You and me and the Board."

"It's *been* me. It'll be me again." I didn't go on, because he knew what I was talking about. Sometimes we can't find out exactly what went wrong and you never know if it's just because you did't look hard enough. Then again, sometimes you find the cause, put it in the report, tell the folks who are supposed to fix it, and they don't fix it. You keep after them to do something about it, but you'll never know if you pushed them hard enough. Did you really go to the wall over it, and was it worth risking your job for . . . and so forth. So far there'd never been a clear-cut case where a plane had crashed because I'd overlooked something, let something go that I should have done. But there were any number of crashes that left me wondering if I'd pushed just a *little* bit harder . . .

"Eli said he's seen this before," Tom said.

"Did he report it?" I mean, Eli was a friend, but there are limits.

"He says he did. He's only seen it once, but he's heard of two or three more times it's happened. It's just been such a small problem that nobody's gotten around to doing anything. You know, the problem of the old computers in general outweighs this glitch in particular. There's a file on it back in Washington.''

"You've seen it?"

"Yeah. I've even fiddled with a solution, but I don't know if it'd work. Short of getting new hardware.''

"What does that mean?"

"It's a one-in-a-million thing. It can happen when two planes are in the same section of the sky and the same distance from the radar dish. The ground station queries the on-board transponders, and they respond, and the signals get to the ground at the same time. It's got to be *real* close; thousandths of a second. And then, sometimes, the computer can't handle it. They mistake the signals and put the wrong numbers up on the screen. It's garbage in, garbage out.''

I knew what he was talking about, but I wasn't sure he was right. Computers, contrary to what you may have been told, are not smart. They're just fast. They can be programmed to act smart, but then it's the programmer who's actually smart and not the computer. If you give a computer long enough to chew on a problem it will usually solve it. And since a long time to a computer is about a millionth of a second, they give the illusion of being smart.

"Okay," I said. "So the information the computer got was garbage, or at least misleading. An ATC computer shouldn't accept information that's *obvious* garbage.''

"But how obvious was it? And don't forget it was just shut down. Maybe it didn't have anything to work from. Maybe it was starting from scratch, and it seemed perfectly reasonable that two planes had changed positions.''

"It should have been obvious.''

"Well," he said, with a sigh, "it *would* have been obvious to the new computers, which wouldn't have gone down in the first place.''

I looked at him for a while, and for a while he kept chewing on his hot dog, which seemed tougher than any hot dog had a right to be.

"You're saying the new computers could have handled this?"

"Damn right they could have. They do it every day. The ones

we've got in place. Hell, there were computers around seven or eight years ago that wouldn't have got into the bind this one did.''

''We should have pushed harder.''

''How much harder can you push?''

He was talking about a meeting six months before. Because of a computer overload in the Boston area there had been a situation that had been brought to our attention. In this case the planes didn't hit, they just sort of played chicken with each other until one pilot pulled up in time. So once again we brought up the subject of computer replacement.

Most of the FAA computers were bought and installed in 1968. Somebody had what must have seemed like a good idea at the time, which was to buy the hardware instead of lease it. So the U.S. Government soon owned many millions of dollars worth of computers, which they operated and maintained themselves.

Years went by.

If you know anything about the computer field, you know that a computer built ten years ago might as well come from the stone age. It doesn't matter that the thing has been well-maintained, that it works wonderfully at what it was designed to do: it's worth nothing at all. If you can sell it for scrap metal you're lucky, because who wants to buy a big mainframe computer that can't do half the stuff that can be done better nowadays by a machine a hundredth the size?

The FAA computers were now white elephants. They worked— though they were approaching the limits of their design load and as a result suffering a lot of downtime. We were in the process of replacing them, but it's expensive and budgets are tight. It would take a while.

And what the hell? In that business, about the time you take the dust-covers off and plug them in, somebody's got something twice as good on the market at half the price. We find ourselves always looking down the road at what'll be available next year and wondering if it might not make more sense to wait just a little longer.

I'd been opposed to the slow schedule. I wanted to get them all replaced within a year, and the hell with next year's models. But it wasn't something worth losing my job over.

If you look hard enough, you'll find the person responsible.

When we got back they were ready to play the copy of the tape from the 747 CVR.

We all gathered around again—more people this time; I don't know how it happens but an investigation accumulates people like a dog picks up fleas—and the tape was started. There was a bad hiss that came and went, but we were able to hear most of it.

There were four people in this cockpit. They were having a good time, chattering back and forth, telling jokes.

Gil Crain, the pilot, was the easiest voice for me to place. I'd known him, and besides, he had a strong Southern accent. A legitimate accent, by the way. Half the commercial airline pilots in the sky affect a West Virginia drawl over the radio, pretending they're Chuck Yeager, who started the whole thing back in the '50s. The rest of them use a bored sing-song patois I've started to call Viet-Nam Jet Jockey. Sometimes you'd think you were listening to a lot of interstate truckers on their CB's. But Gil Crain was born and raised on Dixie soil. He'd soon be buried in it.

He spent a lot of his time talking about his kids. That wasn't easy to listen to, considering what was about to happen to him. I recall the cockpit tape from the San Diego crash. They were discussing life insurance, little knowing how badly they'd need it in a few minutes.

The guy with the giggle was Lloyd Whitmore, the engineer. John Sianis, the co-pilot, had a faint foreign accent—something middle-eastern, I thought—and a crisp, precise way of talking.

The last guy up there was Wayne DeLisle. He was listed as an observer, but it would be more accurate to call him a deadhead. He was a Pan Am pilot hitching a ride in the cockpit jumpseat. He'd been due to take a flight out of San Francisco the next day, bound for Hong Kong. He hadn't been too close to the mike and his voice wasn't very distinctive, but he talked so much I soon had no trouble picking him out from the rest.

The trouble started in pretty much the same way. Captain Crain tried to protest Janz's order, since it didn't make any sense to him, but I knew he wouldn't have hesitated long. He had to assume the ground controller looking at his radar display knew a lot more about the situation than he, Crain, flying through a cloud layer with nothing but fog outside his windshield.

The cockpit got quiet and businesslike instantly.

Crain said, "I wonder what he's got in mind?" He started to say something else, and stopped. It got noisy as the planes hit. Apparently the cockpit crew never even got a glimpse of the other plane, or at least they never mentioned seeing it.

Somebody shouted something, then they got down to the business of flying the disabled plane.

We listened to the activity as three of them went to work. It was by the book. Crain was testing to see what he had left, reporting everything he did, and gradually began to sound optimistic. The aircraft was still going down but he was wrestling the nose up and thought he still had enough control to get it level. I agreed with him, from what I knew, but I also knew something he didn't, which was that he didn't have any rudder left at all and that there was a mountain down there waiting for him that he couldn't turn away from. Then I heard DeLisle.

"Back it up a minute," I said. "What did he say?"

"Sounded like 'see the passengers,'" somebody suggested. The tape started again, and we heard Gil talking about rudder function. I was leaning forward to catch the next line, which would be DeLisle's, when a voice spoke close to my ear.

"Would you like some coffee, Mr. Smith?"

I had missed it again. I turned, furious, ready to shout something about getting this bitch out of here . . . and found myself looking into the face of my movie star/stewardess from the hangar. She had a beautiful smile, and it was as guileless and innocent as a saint's. I thought it a little odd for somebody who'd run like a thief the last time I saw her, no more than a few hours ago.

"What are you doing over—"

"He said 'I'm going to see to the passengers,'" Jerry said at my other side. "Why would he . . . Bill? Are you listening?"

Part of me had been, but the rest had been wrapped up in the woman. I was torn two ways. I looked at Jerry, then back to the woman and she was already walking away with her tray of coffee.

"Why do you think he'd say that?" Jerry repeated. "Things must have been pretty grim in there."

"You'd think he'd be afraid to unstrap," somebody else contributed.

My attention was back on the problem.

"There's not much point in asking why he'd leave," I said. "He didn't have any duties in the cockpit, so we can't fault him for it. He was dead weight, but maybe he thought he could help out the flight attendants in the cabin."

"I'm just surprised he thought of it so soon," Craig said.

"I'm not," said Carole. "Think about it. He's a pilot in a cockpit and he's useless. Everything in his training is telling him to do something, but that's the Captain's job. So he's been trained to save the passengers, so he gets out of the cockpit where he can't do anything to help and goes back into the cabin where maybe he can."

I nodded at her. It made sense. Tom thought so, too.

"That would do it," he said. "But from an Operations standpoint, he's not part of the crew and his impulse should have been to do what the crew told him to do, not take off on his own initiative. He should have waited for orders from Crain."

"Crain was pretty busy to be bothered with suggestions."

It was batted around some more, until I called it off.

"Turn it back on."

This one went on a little longer than the other had. It was worse, in a way. You could tell that Gil really thought he had it. He reported his altimeter readings and they were looking better. His angle of attack was improving. He had his co-pilot calling around, asking about places they might ditch, wondering if they could reach the shallows of the Bay or the Sacramento River or something, they were talking about fields and country roads...and suddenly his ground avoidance alarm started to shout at him. And there was the mountain.

It would have been hard to miss even with a rudder. He tried everything he had, all his control surfaces, spoilers, ailerons, flaps, elevators, trying to wrestle the big beast into a turn. The talk in the cockpit became even more rapid, but still ordered, as Crain and his crew worked on it.

He decided to get the nose up, flaps down, pull back on the engines, and try to stall into the ground, pancake it on that hillside and hope it wouldn't slide too far. By then he was out of good options and seemed to be thinking in terms of minimizing the violence.

Then we heard a most surprising sound. Someone was screaming in the cockpit. I was pretty sure it was a man, and he sounded hysterical.

The words were tumbling out almost too fast to be understood. I found myself on the edge of my seat, my eyes squeezed shut, in an effort to hear what the voice was saying. I had by then identified it as DeLisle. He'd come back.

But why? And what was he saying?

That's when the tape stopped abruptly and something heavy bumped into my side. I jerked in surprise and opened my eyes and looked down at my lap. There was a styrofoam coffee cup there, on its side. Warm brown liquid was soaking into my pants.

"I'm so *sorry,* oh my goodness, here, let me help you with that. I'm such a klutz, no wonder they didn't want me for a stewardess."

She went on like that for a while, crouching at my side and dabbing my lap with a tiny handkerchief.

For a while there I was at a loss. I had been jerked away from total concentration on those dead guys in the cockpit, and then all this fell, literally, into my lap. She was inches away from me, looking up at my face with a strange expression, and she was stroking my thighs with a wet handkerchief. All I could do was stare at her.

"It's okay," I said, finally. "Accidents will happen."

"But always to *me,*" she said, plaintively.

It had been quite an accident, really.

She had tripped over the power cord on the floor, which is why the tape machine went off. Her tray of coffee cups went one way and she, holding a cup in her hand, had gone the other. She'd ended up on the floor beside me, and the tray had ended up all over the tape machine.

I went over to assess the damage.

"I'll have to get another machine," the operator said. "Goddam stupid bitch. This is a five-thousand-dollar set-up here, and coffee's not going to—"

"How about the tape?" I'd had a chilling thought. Once, I played the original CVR tape before sending it on to the Washington lab. I was damn lucky this was only a copy. Nobody at the Board would be too amused if a tape came through a crash and then got ruined by spilled coffee.

"It ought to be okay. I'll put it on a reel and dry it by hand." He glanced at his watch. "Give me half an hour."

I nodded at him and turned to go find the girl, but she was gone.

10

"The Man Who Came Early"

Testimony of Louise Baltimore

I got a taste of what the Council must have felt. I had told those nine pitiful geniuses that my mission was vital to the success of the Gate project, and they had fallen over like ninepins. Now Sherman was doing the same thing to me. I suspected his authority was as spurious as mine had been, but didn't dare say it, and . . . he could have been right. I felt the same superstitious dread of disobeying a message from the future.

At that, I had healthy self-interest—one might call it fear—pushing me to argue against the proposal. Lawrence and Martin didn't even have that. It was fine with them if, assuming anyone had to go back at all, I lead a commando raid into that fateful hangar on that fateful night. They could sit safely uptime and have the great pleasure of second-guessing me when I came back with another failure.

I had a very unscientific, very primitive premonition. I was going to fail again. I think Sherman knew it.

It went off very quickly. There were details to iron out.

Lawrence was horrified to learn how far he had deposited me from my goal. He set his teams to work on the problem, and shortly was able to assure me that he could get me to within ten inches of my intended destination. I didn't believe it, but why tell him that?

The practical details, on my end, were a lot less complicated. It *would* be a commando raid. I picked a team of my three best operatives to go back with me: Mandy Djakarta, Tony Louisville, and Minoru Hanoi. There would be no masquerade this time. We'd go back as thieves in the night. Our objective would be to get into that hangar, find the stunner, and get out without being seen.

I put Tony in charge of equipment selection and planning.

I guess Tony had been subjected to the same data-dump I had. At least he'd seen the same films. The uniforms he picked for us to wear wouldn't have been out of place in a World War Two movie. We were dressed all in black, with gloves and soft black shoes, and he even had soot for us to smear on our faces—except for Mandy, who didn't need any.

We had equipment belts, but all we wore on them was detection gear that we hoped would help us locate the stunner. No weapons on this trip. Stunning someone would only magnify our problems.

Martin Coventry hovered over us like a nervous stage mother as we stood in line waiting for Gate congruency. He was full of last-minute bits of advice.

"You'll be there from eleven to midnight," he was saying. "We show Smith arriving at 11:30 and leaving an hour later. So for half an hour you'll be there in the hangar with him, and—"

"We'll walk on tippy-toe," Minoru finished for him. "We've been through this, Martin. You want to come along and hold our hands?"

"It never hurts to go over these things."

"We have, Martin," I assured him. "It's a big hangar. There's a million places for us to hide, and it won't be lit very well."

"I'm more worried about your end," Tony said. "If we're going to get out of there while he's snooping around, you'd better ease that Gate in real slow and real quiet."

"I don't like it," Mandy said. "Why don't we put the Gate outside the hangar and break in?"

Martin looked pained. "Because there were guards around it that night."

"I don't like *that*," Tony said, darkly.

"It can't be helped. You just trust us. Lawrence and I will have all the suppressors operating. The Gate will show where we planned, and it will come in without any noise."

Be that as it may, the Gate didn't *arrive* all that quietly.

I could hear echoes reverberating in the empty hangar as we stepped out. I wasn't worried, because we knew we were alone in there and the noise wasn't loud enough to carry outside the building. But I remember thinking Lawrence had better do a better job on the pick-up.

"Right on the button," Mandy whispered, pointing to the concrete floor.

She was right. My brief excursion through the building a few hours ago—or about thirty-nine hours ago, depending on how you looked at it—had been useful in selecting an entry and exit point for the Gate. We'd selected the northwest corner, behind what was left of the 747 tail section and other large pieces of Boeing fuselage. It was shadowy enough that we had to get out our pencil-beams for a few quick looks around or we might have stumbled over something.

When I had my bearings I gestured silently to the team to spread out and start looking around. Myself, I got out my detector and headed toward where the stunner had been the last time I was in the hangar.

All the trash bags had been moved. It made sense. They'd had almost two days to sort the junk, and they'd made a lot of progress. So I started searching, creeping silently as any cat through the nightmarish mounds of wreckage.

Fifteen minutes later I was still creeping, and the indicator dial hadn't jiggled half a millimeter.

I gave a low whistle, and pretty soon my comrades material-ized out of the darkness and we put our heads together.

"I'm getting nothing at all," I said.

"Me either," said Tony.

"Nothing."

Minoru just shrugged and shook his head.

"Ideas?"

"These things home on the power source. Maybe it ran out of juice."

"Or somebody's taken it out of the hanger."

"Not likely." I realized I was chewing on a thumbnail. "He'll be here in fifteen minutes. We'll take ten of those, leave ourselves a safety margin. Turn on your lights, look everywhere you can, don't worry so much about noise. If we don't find it, we'll hide under the tail section and wait for the Gate."

"This is going to be dry, isn't it?" Mandy said.

"Don't be such a pessimist."

"All time travelers are pessimists."

That was Minoru's contribution to the conversation. Me, I don't know if I was born a pessimist or had pessimism thrust upon me. What I do know is that I've had ample reason to embrace the philosophy. A case in point:

I'd been turning over small items for three or four minutes when I heard Tony make the low warbling call we'd agreed on in the ready-room. We stole the call from some Cherokees in a film from the 1930s, and what it was supposed to mean was "I've found it!"

He sure had. We converged on him. My heart was pounding. We were actually going to get out of this. Then I saw Tony waving at Mandy, telling her to stop. She did, skidding silently, crouching twenty meters away. I did the same, and watched as Tony motioned her closer. Minoru appeared silently at my elbow, and we creeped the last thirty meters.

The light was very bad. It took a while to be sure what we were seeing. The first thing I identified was the stunner, lying all by itself about ten feet from a line of folding tables that were heaped with debris. There was a long object lying in shadow just in front of the tables, a few feet from the stunner. Gradually, my eyes confirmed my first gut reaction. It was a human body.

"Who is it?" Mandy whispered.

"Who do you think?" I said, bitterly.

We moved in closer. I turned my light beam on low. It was Bill Smith.

"Is he breathing?"

"I can't tell for sure."

"Yeah, he's breathing. He's just stunned."

"Then he can probably hear us."

Mandy and Tony started to back away.

"Shit!" I shouted. I went on in a lower voice. "If he can hear us, then the cat's already hit the fan."

"There's no need to make it worse," Mandy suggested. I supposed she was right. We all backed away and crouched down.

"Are his eyes open or closed?" I asked.

"Open," Tony said. "I'm sure he saw me."

"What do you think happened here?"

We all surveyed the still-life of disaster, and pretty soon the scenario became apparent.

He was on his back. His legs were out, one of them slightly bent and folded under the other; that bottom leg was probably going to sleep, and would hurt like hell when he could move again. The stunner was a few feet from his outstretched left hand. Inches from his right hand was a Swiss Army knife with the long blade opened.

Minoru put it all together for us.

"He came in here before we arrived. He found the stunner. On the time-scans, we saw a red light coming from it. Power leakage. That's probably what he saw, too. He got out that knife and started poking around inside it, and shorted something out."

"It's been damaged enough that the stun beam wouldn't be focused anymore."

"Damn lucky it was set on 'stun.' We could be looking at a dead man."

"I don't want to hear about 'could be,' " I said. "He could have gotten here when he was supposed to, at 11:30. What the hell is he doing here now? Why was he here before we got here?"

"We'll have to sort that out when we get back."

"What do we do now? Should we take the stunner?"

I chewed that one over. I knew the damage had been done,

but we'd come back to get it and there it was, so I scooped it up. I opened it and confirmed that it was all out of power, which is why it hadn't showed up on our detectors.

"We take it." I looked at my watch. "Shit. We've been here fifteen minutes just talking it over. The Gate's due in twenty minutes. Let's get the hell out of here."

"He's sure sweating a lot."

I played my light over him. Tony was right. Pretty soon Mr. Smith would be lying in a puddle. I tried to figure what all this would sound like to him. He couldn't have gotten more than a few glimpses of us, but it would have been enough to scare the hell out of him. He'd heard a few phrases. I didn't know exactly what we'd said that he might have overheard.

Any way you looked at it, though, we must have looked menacing as hell.

And what could I do about it? Nothing. I motioned the team back toward the northwest corner of the hangar.

I even followed them, for about twenty meters.

Then I found myself stopped. I don't remember stopping. It was as if there was something in the air so thick I couldn't move through it. I wanted to go on, and I couldn't. I turned, and hurried back to him.

He hadn't moved. I knelt beside him and leaned over until I was sure he could see me. I remembered the blackface I was wearing; surely he couldn't recognize me from our brief encounter almost two days ago.

"Smith," I said. "You don't know me. I can't tell you who I am. You're going to be all right. You're just stunned. You messed with something you . . ." Stop, Louise, I told myself. You're saying too much. But how much was enough, and why was I even talking to him?

I was sweating as much as he was, by then.

"I wanted . . . Smith, you're endangering a project bigger than you can imagine. *Forget* about this."

Christ. How could he forget? Would I have forgotten? Would you?

"There's going to be a paradox if you don't leave this alone."

I suddenly went cold all over. I *knew* what he was thinking.

"Oh, no. We didn't. You think we made those planes crash, but we didn't, I swear to you, they were going . . ."

Shit. I'd said too much already. I thought I saw one corner of his mouth twitch, but it might have been my imagination. There was just the slow rise and fall of his chest, and the rivers of sweat.

Everything I touched seemed to turn to shit. Believe it or not, up until recently I'd been a crackerjack operative.

I turned from him and hurried back to my team.

In due course, the Gate appeared and the four of us stepped through it.

There were recriminations. I spent an unprofitable time yelling at Lawrence and Martin about the wondrous power of their prognostications. I recall saying things like I could have done better with a crystal ball and tea leaves. I could feel properly self-righteous about it; I hadn't screwed up this time. We'd been told Smith wouldn't show until 11:30. I didn't mention my brief monologue with Smith, and neither did any of my team. Not that they knew what I'd said to him, but they could hardly have failed to notice I went back and said *something*.

It didn't do any good, unless an unworthy feeling of redemption could be regarded as a good. I knew as well as they did that the readings they had taken before we left had been invalidated by the chaotic state of the timestream. We all should have realized that we could no longer count on the time tanks to tell us anything reliable.

And once again, there had been changes during my brief absence.

Apparently, as soon as my team had stepped through the Gate, many things had suddenly become clearer in the time tanks. Some of the censorship had eased, and the operators could see things that had previously been clouded. One of the first things they saw was that Smith had entered the hangar at 10:30. They even were able to see him find the stunner, pick it up, and, like a fool, start poking around in it. The whole thing had gone off pretty much as Minoru had described it. And, of course, by the time they saw it it was too late to call us back.

Martin was having a fit trying to understand why the temporal censorship was lifting. I certainly didn't have anything to contribute; I've never been a theoretician. If I had an opinion in the matter it was simply that God was having his innings, playing his little jokes on us. Free will, indeed!

The other big change was Sherman. His mouth was now a much more realistic creation. He had added a nose to his facial accomplishments. He was still quite unlikely to pass for human, even on the darkest night, but he had at least become an interesting humanoid.

I kept looking at his mouth. I finally convinced myself there really was no resemblance at all. Only a badly frightened, obsessed, defensive, and emotionally exhausted zombie could have found a lopsided grin on that plastic face.

I was the only one who even wanted to consider Window B. I still hadn't revealed to anyone that I had ruled out Window C, so that made it harder to argue my position. Everyone kept looking to Sherman for guidance. He kept quiet.

Then we heard I was being summoned to the Council again, so the decision was postponed. Martin and Lawrence admitted they welcomed the delay, since they wanted to run tests on their temporal equipment. The goal was to create a statistical universe that had some things in common with the "real" universe, whatever that meant at this point. They knew they couldn't look into the past any more and be sure what they were seeing was reality or probability, but they hoped to at least be able to express things in percentages. I thought that might be nice, especially if they were going to send *me* back again. So far we'd had a quarter-mile miss in one spatial dimension, and a one-hour miss in the time dimension. Martin once told me that twelve dimensions were involved in operating the Gate. I didn't want to miss in any of the remaining ten.

The Council meeting was more of the same. I offered my resignation twice, and I think the second time they almost took it. I told them once again that this mission was vital to the success of the Gate Project, but I suspect that was starting to wear a little thin.

I couldn't follow a lot of it. Much of it was technical, way over my head. The rest seemed tied up in the internal politics of the Council. There were at least three factions—actually, not too bad a split for a group as large as that—and one of them kept swaying back and forth. In the end, I was authorized for another trip.

Martin had conquered his distaste for the Council chamber and was with me during this second meeting. He told the members that nothing could be done for at least ten hours. I said a silent prayer of thanks to whatever gods there be. I hadn't had a rest in almost two days.

And I needed to talk to Sherman.

11

Behold the Man

Sherman said, "Call me Jesus."

I threw my cigarette at him, simply because I didn't have anything heavier close at hand. The butt never reached him. There's a little laser mounted in one corner of my room, equipped with a little radar and a little brain; it tracked the butt and zapped it to plasma before it had gone two feet. I know, I know, what will modern science think of next, but it beats hell out of ashtrays.

"I'll call you an ambulance in a minute."

"There are some things I honestly can't tell you, Louise," he said.

"What can you tell me, then?"

He seemed to think it over for a while.

"Did your message really say you couldn't tell anybody what was in it?" I prompted.

"Yes. With certain exceptions."

"Like what?"

"Like you. I am allowed to tell you certain things. At certain times."

"To manipulate me."

"Yes."

I stared at him bleakly, and he stared back. To give him credit, he didn't look smug about it.

"So many levels..." I said.

"Yes."

"I mean, you telling me, *admitting* to me, that you can tell

me certain things at certain times, for purposes of manipulation
. . . that's manipulation right there."

"Yes."

"It makes me feel so . . . responsible! I know you're using
me, and I have to assume it's for a good reason, so I ought to do
what you want me to do . . . but how do I know what that *is*?"

"You simply must behave naturally. Do what you would
normally have done."

"But what you just told me alters the equation. Now that I
know that you're guiding me—however subtly—the awareness of
it will make me do things differently than . . ." I sputtered to a
stop. He was still regarding me innocently.

"So I have to assume that these layers of confusion are just
part of your plan, whatever it may be . . ." That wasn't going
anywhere, either.

"Fuck you," I said.

"Wonderful," he said, and clapped his hands together. "You're
back on track."

I had to smile at that.

"I'm going to melt you down and use the scrap to make a tin
can, then kick the can."

"Great, great, get it all out."

"Your mother was a vending machine and your father was a
roto-rooter."

"My, didn't that twentieth-century tape work well? Every
little detail of daily life, at your fingertips."

I gave him a few more half-hearted insults in modern idiom,
but they were just as useless. You can't argue with Sherman. Even
trying to is frustrating, and that's the last thing I needed. So I tried
to clear it all out of my mind and start from scratch.

"Okay. You're Jesus. Will you tell me what you mean by
that?"

"Yes. Jesus Christ was a prevalent myth-figure in the twentieth century, the Son of the Supreme Being, worshipped by a sect
whose chief fetishes were a cross, a chalice or grail, and—"

"Crap, I know all that. Their big line was 'He died for our
sins.'" I looked hopeful. "Is that what you had in mind?"

"Not precisely. I had in mind his role as savior of humankind."

I looked at him. Remember, at this stage his face was a simple cartoon, so ineptly drawn that Walt Disney must have been spinning in his cryo-suspension fluid. Parts of his body were straight out of *The Wizard of Oz*. I won't say he clanked when he walked, but one look at him and you just *knew* he was the lineal descendant of a video arcade. This was the entity holding himself up to me as humanity's savior.

"Call me dubious," I said.

"Nevertheless, it's true. The message in my time capsule was quite lengthy. It delineated the events of the past few days in great detail, and went on to describe the events of the next . . . six days. Having read it, I immediately saw what I must do, and when, to effect the salvation of the human race. Musing on this, I was struck by the parallels with the biblical story of Jesus. Perhaps this is *hubris* on my part, and I don't intend to seriously stress it, but if you cast the Big Computer as God, it's not unreasonable to see me—the only robot ever to receive a time-capsule message—as its only begotten son."

"And *you* were supposed to psychoanalyze *me*," I said. "Have you listened to yourself? You're no more unique than a Model-T. A savior with a serial number."

" 'Big Computer, all things are possible unto thee; take away this cup from me: nevertheless, not what I will, but what thou wilt.' "

That time I wished I had an ashtray; nevertheless, I didn't throw my cigarette at him; it was only half-smoked, and it's a sin to waste good tobacco.

"I didn't ask for the time capsule, Louise," he said, "any more than you asked for yours. You play the cards as they are dealt. I must do likewise."

I smoked in silence for a while, trying my best to read something in that travesty he was using for a face. And I swear, after a while he began to seem almost human. I began to feel sorry for him. If even *half* of what he was saying was true, he'd been given a much heavier load than I had.

"Can you prove any of this?" I asked.

"Easily. Though I don't guarantee to prove it all. You'll remain too dubious for that. I can tell you what was in your time capsule."

And he did, word for word. I let him go right through it, even the part about the kid, and the business about not fucking him unless I wanted to.

"Will I . . ."

"That's one of the things I can't tell you."

"But you know."

"Yes. I know."

I studied him some more. It would be pointless to mention the mazes of probabilities, lies, and deceptions my mind navigated while I watched him, because in the end I arrived right back where I started.

"The Big Computer could have told you what was in my time capsule."

"You think it would do that? With strict instructions from the Council not to?"

"I know it *could* do it, so it's possible it *did* do it."

"Wonderful," Sherman said, and he really seemed pleased. "Your suspicious mind will serve you well in the coming days, just as it has in the past."

"Meaning it won't do me any good, but it'll keep me on my toes."

"Exactly." He leaned forward, and regarded me with a reasonable approximation of an earnest expression. "Louise, I don't ask you to like the situation. I don't like it myself."

"You? Or the Big Computer?"

"Sometimes it's pointless to speak of a distinction. But I do have feelings. I don't have to like what I have to do, and at the same time, I *know* it is my only course. There are bad times ahead. We are headed for a disaster that is inevitable, impossible to avoid. And yet, at the same time, there is a way out. We can't reach it until the whole sorry spectacle has been performed, but in the end, I will deliver humanity to the promised land."

"Humanity. That's a nice broad term. I've been working all my life to save humanity." I stubbed out my cigarette. "But what about me?'' I wasn't sure I really wanted to hear that, but I had to ask it.

"For you, Louise, there are some bad times ahead. I can't be more specific. Ultimately, there is a happy ending.''

"For me?'' I was incredulous. The *last* thing I anticipated was a happy ending.

"Happier than you have ever expected. Is that enough?''

For a long-time, rock-ribbed, true-blue pessimist, I guess it was. At least I found myself feeling unaccountably better, though I never for a moment thought that my own ending would be any better than bittersweet. But the nice thing about being a pessimist is that bittersweet is an improvement.

"Okay,'' I said. "But you got your biblical allusions wrong. You said you were going to lead us to the promised land. Jesus didn't do that.''

Sherman looked surprised as an infallible Pope holding a losing ticket at the racetrack. It pleased the perverse side of me; I mean, maybe his history of the future hadn't contained that line of dialogue.

"Call me Moses,'' he said.

So it was Window B. That decision got made the way so many are made in our rather informal organization: by consensus.

There was a nation in the twentieth century that styled itself the People's Republic of China. It was a dictatorship of the proletariat—a phrase which struck me as the worst of both worlds— and decisions were made through processes like criticism/self-criticism, dialectic analysis, and similar buzzwords. In theory, the answer that emerged expressed the will of the masses. In fact, the Politically Correct answer always turned out to be the Chairman's answer, whatever that happened to be at the moment.

Early in my career with the Gate Project I noticed that, informal or not, things got done in a certain manner. I made a study of it. Putting that together with my data-dumped knowledge of the PRC in the twentieth century, I learned a few things about how to arrive at a consensus: you kick ass until everybody decides to do things the way you want to do them.

Some asses were kicked. I never had to tell anyone that I had absolutely ruled out a trip back to Window C. It just happened that, when all the dust had settled, the obvious course was to go back to Window B.

I'll admit that it helped when Sherman made no objection to B. And I could see that might be a problem down the road if this trip didn't work out and we were left with only one alternative, but as we say in the Time Travel Business, tomorrow can take care of itself.

Monday, December 12, Oakland International Airport.

I had been to this day before, from eight to nine in the morning, but for me it had been almost two days ago. I had to bear in mind that for Bill Smith it had been only five hours. He was likely to recognize me if he had any memory for faces. I was assuming he would, as my face and body are quite memorable.

The Gate dropped me at a little-used location inside the terminal building. I had argued about that some, wondering if they had really recalibrated the Gate as finely as they claimed. But in the end I let Lawrence have his way, since he was the expert. At some point you have to rely on expert opinion. I didn't figure this was an important enough point to force for a "consensus."

He turned out to be right. I was within six inches of the spot he had been aiming for. And the Gate had arrived quietly, as Lawrence had guaranteed. I looked around quickly to be sure I hadn't been observed, and headed down the hallway toward the room the National Transportation Safety Board had been given for their private meetings.

It took me through the main part of the terminal, which was jammed. It would get worse in the coming days. We were in the middle of a festival known as Christmas, which seemed to take up the whole month of December. There was a big tree decorated with lights, and various other decorations hung around the buildings. Christmas was a time for spending money, traveling, and getting drunk. It had originally been a celebration of the birth of Jesus Christ, but by the 1980s that had been largely forgotten, replaced by a new totem in a red suit and a false beard.

Everyone around me looked quite grim, in keeping with the

season. The grimmest of all were gathered around a booth that sold flight insurance. There could be few people in the terminal who were not thinking about the recent mid-air collision. Many had decided to buy an insurance policy—which actually insured nothing, and was in fact a bet made with a large company concerning your survival. To win the bet, you had to die. Maybe that would make more sense to me if I expected to have descendants.

It wasn't hard getting to the meeting. I had to go through several doors marked AUTHORIZED PERSONNEL ONLY, and at one point I had to deal with a guard posted to keep out the press and other busybodies. But I was liberally armed with identification, I was wearing the right clothes, and I knew all the right names to drop. We had researched the investigation thoroughly, and knew who pulled enough weight to break the rules. So I simply flashed an I.D. badge and about eighteen perfect teeth at the guard and told him Mister Smith was waiting to see me, and I was in.

Not too long after that, I was out.

My pretty little dress was soaked with coffee, but I was feeling pretty good about myself. Laurel and Hardy couldn't have handled it better. It had been one of the all-time great pratfalls. The tray had gone just where I'd aimed it. Nobody would be listening to that tape for a while.

The good feeling didn't last long, though.

This had been the *craziest* damn trip of them all. Both times before, I'd been hoping to come up with the twonky and get the whole paradox resolved. This time all I'd tried to do was a diversion, and probably a fairly useless one. There were things on that tape we didn't want Mr. Smith to brood about. We had figured the later in the day he heard them, the less alert he'd be, and the less likely to attach any importance to them.

It sounded damn thin, even to me. There was even a chance that my outrageous behavior would draw his attention *to* DeLisle's words, rather than away.

Once more, my only consolation was that it was all we had. The only thing left was Window C.

And there was something I didn't like about that, too.

I'd felt those strings very strongly there in that room: the strings held by the temporal puppet master, Mister Pre-Destination, Professor Fate, Karma, the Black Magic Woman, or whatever the hell you wanted to call him/her/it. Whoever or whatever it was, I felt like I was being jerked around.

There had been that one moment . . .

Squatting there on the floor beside him while he looked down at me in his befuddled way . . .

What the hell am I doing here? I had wondered. And why do his eyes look like that?

I was being set up. There was no way around it. There was no way to look at this trip except as a preparation for a trip to Window C. *Don't fuck him unless you want to. And tell him about the kid. She's just a wimp.*

The puppet master was pulling very hard. And his name was Sherman.

It no longer surprised me to see that Sherman had changed. I came through the Gate and he was waiting for me. His face wasn't cartoon-like any more, though it was still far from human. I'd half-expected he'd look like Bill Smith—I'd caught the ghost of him in Sherman's earlier incarnation—but he didn't. He was just an android, but now he looked like one to be taken seriously.

Everybody was treating him as such. They kept out of his way as he led me to a room where we could talk in private.

"How did it go?" he asked.

"Why don't *you* tell *me*?"

"Very well. You succeeded in distracting him the first time DeLisle's words came up on the tape. He saw you up close, and he recognized you. Your face is now firmly fixed in his mind. He is still going to think what DeLisle had to say when he returned to the cockpit was *odd,* but then that was never very important. It will be easy for him to dismiss it, because everyone else will be helping him out. Tom Stanley will hold out the longest, but eventually he will decide, with the rest, that DeLisle simply went crazy."

"I'm not going to do it, Sherman."

He went on as if I hadn't spoken.

"The new Board Member, Mister Petcher—or Gordy, as he

prefers to be called—will not make it to California on the night of the twelfth. Much as Bill Smith hates it, he will have to hold a press conference that evening. It will be the usual fruitless exercise: Smith has nothing he can tell them, and they will harry him with speculations. He will spend the evening saying 'No comment.' "

"I won't do it, Sherman."

"At this press conference Smith will get his first glimpse of Mister Arnold Mayer, the mystic physicist, the well-known crackpot. Mayer's questions will seem idiotic to Smith, but his name and face will stick in his mind. It wouldn't hurt if he had another name and another face that impressed him even more that night. We're doing better, Louise, but we're far from out of the woods."

"I won't do it."

He looked at me for a long time, in silence. At last he steepled his fingers in a very human-like gesture, put them to his chin, and rocked back and forth. He sighed, if you can believe that.

"Tell him about the kid, Louise," he said. "She's only a wimp."

I stood up, intending to go over and dismantle him, but I guess standing up was a mistake. I passed out.

12

The Productions of Time

Testimony of Bill Smith

It came out like this:

"...dead! They're all dead, every one of them! They're *burnt*, Gil, they're dead and burned up and torn to pieces, all dead—"

Then the plane hit the mountain and Wayne DeLisle had nothing more to say.

It was getting on in the evening when we finally had the tape cleaned up and processed enough to hear those words clearly. When the operator shut off his machine we all just sat there for a while.

I couldn't begin to describe the sheer horror in the man's voice. It came through, though, even with the poor technical quality.

To say we were shocked would be an understatement. None of us had ever heard anything quite like that from a CVR. Fear, tension...sure. They're not robots, the people who fly these planes. They try to conceal their emotions in a moment like that—I guess it's a reflex—but it comes through.

No. It just didn't make sense. I've come to expect heroic

behavior, or at least stoicism, when monitoring a CVR tape, but panic would not throw me too much. Pilots are just like the rest of us. They suffer mental problems, drinking problems, marital problems. They go crazy, but hardly ever as the result of an emergency in the air.

They don't have *time*. Not even *passengers* go crazy that quickly. Contrary to what you've seen in the *Airport* movies, in the first few moments after an impact a few people will scream a little and maybe jump up in reaction, but that generally calms down pretty quickly. After that, the dominant reaction is to just sit there in their seats, stunned, for a fairly long time. They don't know what to do. The common response to that, in a plane, is to do nothing. They become pliant, eager to do what the flight attendants tell them. It's only if the emergency stretches out and they get time to form their own hare-brained ideas that you have to watch out for them.

Wayne DeLisle just shouldn't have gone that nutty that quickly.

In thirty-three seconds he'd gone from a competent pilot, a take-charge guy who was willing to get out of his secure seat and go moving around in a plane that was bucking and turning like a rock rolling down a hill just so he could try to help the passengers, to a gibbering . . . well, *coward,* crying about how they were all dead. Dead and burned.

We spent some time discussing it.

Jerry: "Maybe they *were* all dead. There's indications that the fuselage might have been breached. We found some bodies and debris a good ways from the main site." The verdict on that was in pretty soon; even Jerry didn't stick to it long. If there was cabin depressurization it would have blown out the cockpit door and maybe DeLisle with it. Some people would have been sucked out, but the rest would have been all right. They were only at five thousand feet, so decompression was no problem, nor lack of oxygen.

Craig: "He said they were burned, too. Maybe there was a fire in the cabin before it went in."

Eli: "In the first-class lounge? I don't buy it. Everything I saw looks like the fire was restricted to the engines ... maybe the wings, but no further. At least until it hit, when everything went up. I don't see a wing fire spreading that far forward that quickly.''

Craig: "Maybe it was downstairs. Maybe he got back to tourist.''

Tom: "In a 747? Listen, we're assuming the plane wasn't holed, or we'd have heard it on the tape. It makes a hell of a noise.''

Jerry: "We might not hear it if the hole was toward the back.''

Tom: "Yeah, but how's he going to get there? Into the first-class lounge, down the stairs, back to tourist, and then all the way back to the cockpit in thirty-three seconds? Not in that plane. It would be a miracle if he got down the stairs without breaking his fucking neck.''

I agreed. It would have been easier to walk on a roller coaster.

"So," I said, "we can postulate he didn't get much farther than the stairway. It doesn't seem reasonable that he'd see anything there but a bunch of scared people.''

Carole interrupted us after we'd gone on like that for quite a while.

"You guys are going to have to learn to accept the obvious,'' she said.

"What's that?'' Jerry wanted to know.

"That he simply went crazy.''

"I thought you psychologists didn't like that word.''

She shrugged. "I'm not prejudiced against it when it's the simplest one that fits. But I used it to rub your faces in it. I know you don't want to believe that a pilot could flip out like that, and I'll admit it's rare. But you've all pretty well proved that when he went back into the lounge all he could have seen were frightened people, not burnt corpses.''

Tom protested. "But he *said* he saw—''

"He didn't say he *saw* anything. Don't treat it as a reliable eyewitness account of anything. Treat it as the last realization of a man pushed beyond his limits. He said they were all dead and urned. He was a man trained to fly a plane but he couldn't do it ecause it wasn't his plane. He knew more than the passengers; he ad more reason to panic, because he knew they were all doomed. Ie could look at the reality Gil Crain and the others could keep lenying because they had things they could do. He just gave in nd said what he knew would happen—that they were all going to lie. And he was right.''

None of us liked it, but it ended the discussion, at least for hen. Carole was the human-factors expert. Thinking it over, I had o agree that the main reason I was reluctant to accept her explanation was the one she'd mentioned: I didn't want to believe a pilot could come unglued that fast. But he must have.

We held our nightly meeting—the first of many—not long after the first run-through of the 747 tape.

It was all we could do to squeeze everyone into the smaller of the two airport rooms. There must have been over a hundred people there who had a right to be present. I'm afraid I dozed through a lot of it, but I can doze with my eyes open, so nobody noticed. I hope.

The nightly meetings are a fixture of any investigation. Everybody that's been working on the crash gets together and compares notes. Decisions are made about what avenues to pursue.

We agreed that the computer at Fremont—which is where the Oakland Air Region Traffic Control Center is actually located— would have to be gone over by an expert team. Tom already had some people in mind. Otherwise, it was mostly a matter of confirming things already done and telling everybody to keep doing them. Many of the physical aspects of an investigation take quite a while.

After that the meeting could have gone on for ten more hours. Any meeting will, if you let it. But in the early stages I've found it's just a lot of wind. Later on some longer meetings would be in order, but when I saw by my watch that this one had been going on for two hours I chopped it off short and told everybody not actually working in the hangar to go home and get some sleep.

Some of them didn't like that, but they couldn't do anything about it. It was my investigation. Maybe on paper it was C. Gordon Petcher's, but in fact it was mine. And speaking of good old Gordy . . .

Briley came up to me as everybody was shuffling out, looking like he had bad news. I let him off easy.

"I already know," I told him. "Gordy didn't make the evening flight. He'll show up in the morning. I heard he held a press conference in Washington."

"That's what I was told."

"It must have been a cute one. I haven't talked with him, so I wonder what he told them?"

"That the situation was well in hand, I gather. Just like you're going to have to do in about twenty minutes."

I groaned, but I was already resigned to it. The press had been promised a conference. All it would really be, to my way of thinking, was what they call a "photo opportunity." They'd have footage of me to put on the late news. There was certainly damn little I could tell them.

I hate inefficiency. You'd have to look a long, long ways before you found a better example of it than the press conference.

The duplication of effort is enough to make you break down and cry. Is it really necessary for the evening Eyewash News in Kankakee, Illinois, to send a cameraman to cover an airline disaster in California?

And it's not just television, though every major station in the seven surrounding states had a camera there. All the newspapers were there, too. Reporters from India and Japan and England and, for all I know, Bali, the Maldive Islands, and Kampuchea. There were the magazine reporters and the columnists. There must have been a hundred just from the aviation journals. There were scientists from every university in the state. There were the nonfiction authors who specialize in quickie news books, and concept people whose job it is to swarm around Patty Hearst or Gary Gilmore or anybody and anything that captures the country's attention for a few days and assign pimp writers and pimp producers to write cash-in books and make cash-in television movies. They are the packagers of disaster. In a couple months we'd be seeing the results of their efforts: "The Last Seconds of Flight 35" and "Collision!" and "Mount Diablo" and "Crash of the Jumbos."

I wondered who they'd get to play Bill Smith.

I'd have been tickled pink if all they wanted to do was stand in front of wreckage in the middle of the night in mud up to their knees, hold mikes up to their faces, and look solemn. But they wanted to talk to *me*, and all I'd ever wanted to know was *why*? There was *no story* from me. They knew that as well as I did, but they had to have a circus, anyway.

So I stood up there in front of a forest of microphones and squinted into the lights and cursed C. Gordon Petcher, who should have had this job. If he wasn't good for this, what *was* he good for?

I started out with the standard statement that there'd be no comment about facts still under investigation. Then I gave them the things we knew, which they all knew already. It was just a dry recital of where the planes came from, where they were bound, the time of impact, the location of the sites. I told them how many passengers and crew had been on each plane (we'd finally gotten those figures: 637 total), that there were ten missing and probably dead on the ground, and seven injuries on the ground, all hit by the DC-10. Names of the dead were being withheld pending notification... Well, you fill it in. You've heard it on the evening news. Causes of the crash were still under investigation.

Questions, anyone?

Well, my God, don't everyone shout at once.

"Mr. Smith, was everyone on the basketball team killed?"

That was the first I'd heard of a basketball team. It turned out some collegiate team was on the 747. I told the reporter that if they were on the plane, they were certainly dead, as there had been no, repeat no, survivors. How many times would I have to say that?

"What about Senator Gray?"

"Was he on one of the planes?"

"That's our information."

"I can't confirm or deny that. If he was on it, he's dead."

"I'm talking about State Senator Eleanor Gray."

"Okay. It's not my department. The list will be released when identities are confirmed. Next question."

They asked me about ground control and about pilot error. No comment. They wanted to know about radar transponders. No comment. Are you talking to a man by the name of Donald Janz? No comment. Was there a computer failure? We don't know. No comment. I couldn't say. That's under investigation. We're looking into it. Not to my knowledge. The investigation is continuing.

What they did was turn me into one of those squirming public officials you see on the news or on "60 Minutes" who won't commit themselves on whether or not this is the month of December. I get as burned about them as you do, and I don't appreciate being made to look like that. But, you know, sometimes when Mike Wallace asks somebody a question and he says, "That's still in litigation" or words to that effect, he's not covering up anything. He *can't* talk. It wouldn't be proper. Any public pronouncements I made at that conference could damage innocent parties.

We waltzed around like that for almost an hour.

There was only one thing about the conference that was worth remembering. It came toward the end, when most of the serious organizations had given up and only the crackpots remained. The TV cameras, of course, had started leaving after they had five minutes of film.

This one fellow stood up and I could tell right off he thought he was Ralph Nader.

"Mister Smith, I represent the Air-Line Passengers Organization."

I couldn't resist it.

"A.L.P.O.? You're the man from ALPO?"

It got a good laugh. In fact, I think I was responsible for that group changing its name.

He asked his question, red-faced, and I brushed it off. Surely there had to be a few more people here I could insult without fearing reprisals. I looked around, hoping to pick out the man from the *National Enquirer*.

What I got instead was a dignified, white-haired gentleman, a little portly, a bit old-fashioned in his dress. His hair was unruly, but it was the only thing about him that wasn't neat. He stood out in that audience.

"Mister Smith, I am Arnold Mayer. My question has nothing to do with overloaded computers or negligent air-traffic controllers."

"That would be a relief."

"I doubt it. I'd like to know what unusual facts you have developed so far in your investigation."

"I'm afraid I can't comment on..." I stopped, thinking about all those watches. Not that I was about to tell him about them.

"That's about as broad a question as I've ever heard, Mr. Mayer."

The old fellow gave me a wry smile, ducking his head quickly. I'd already decided this was going to be the last question of the night, and I wondered if I could finish with something that didn't make me out as such a bastard.

"If you could be a little more specific," I prompted.

Again he shrugged.

"If I knew how to describe the facts they wouldn't be unusual. Have you found any unusual item associated with the crash? Were there any unexplained observations? Is there any indication that this crash was caused by something less obvious than a computer overload?"

"Without in any way endorsing that computer overload hypothesis, I can say that, no, there has been nothing unexplained thus far." That's right. Lie, you wonderful public servant, you. "Of course, every crash is unique, and—"

"—yet they share common factors. There are things you expect to find, and things you don't. I've heard, for instance, that the cockpit voice recording—or CVR as you people refer to it—contains something a little out of the ordinary."

So something had leaked. I can't say I was surprised. Things always do. I *was* a little taken aback that the leak had come to this old guy and not the people from CBS or *Time* magazine.

"I can't comment on that until the CVR has been processed and analyzed. Since you seem to know so much about our workings, you know that will take about two weeks. Then the relevant portions will be released and you can listen yourself."

He jumped in again, quick, before I had time to call an end.

"All right, but is there anything else odd? Something that may not in itself appear significant. Any discrepancies in the sequence of the crash. Any inexplicable item found in the wreckage. Most particularly, anything having to do with time."

Once again I thought of the watches, but I was distracted by someone in the back of the big room having a coughing fit. It was a woman, and she had her back to me. Somebody was holding her arm and leaning toward her as she doubled over, clearly concerned that she was going to choke to death. She was waving him away.

"I still don't know what you're driving at," I told Mayer.

"I can't be more plain without sounding like a fool," he said, wryly. "I'm simply looking for the inexplicable. I usually find it."

"You won't here," I said. "In a few days or weeks I'll be able to tell you exactly what happened last night. No doubt about it. There's . . ."

The woman in back had straightened up at last, and it was her. The one who wouldn't give me any coffee in the hangar and then gave me entirely too much of it a few hours ago. She was on her way out of the room.

"There's nothing inexplicable in my line of work, Mister Mayer. And that's the end of the press conference, ladies and gentlemen."

I stepped off the platform and hurried toward the back of the room.

She wasn't in the hallway outside. I went down it a little ways, to where it made a right angle, and looked around that. There were some reporters straggling away, but she wasn't among them. At the end of that corridor was the door to the public part of the terminal. No point in looking for her out there.

"What are you in such a hurry for?"

I glanced back at Tom. He looked about as tired as I felt. We stood there at the side of the hallway while the last of the reporters went by us, including Mayer, who gave me what might have been a wink.

"I saw her again. I thought she came this way."

"Who? Oh, your mystery woman. You think a cup of coffee in the lap is a sufficient introduction?"

"Hell, I don't know. I just wanted to talk to her."

"Sure." He shook his head in disbelief. "I don't know how you hold up. I'm half dead, and you're looking for a party."

"It's not like that. It's just . . ." I realized I didn't know just why I wanted to talk to her. But I did want to. I thought about calling up United and seeing if I could trace her down, decided to put it off until tomorrow.

"Is that all for today, boss-man?" Tom asked.

I glanced at my watch. "Damn right. The night crew's got their orders?"

"They do. Want to go get something to eat?"

"No, thanks. I'll just head back to that motel room I heard a rumor about seven or eight days ago. See if I can make it to the bed."

"Two to one you don't sleep alone."

13

"As Time Goes By"

There's not much more depressing than to be alone in a crowd listening to Christmas carols.

I shuffled through the terminal, feeling about ninety years old. It was about 9:30. Just about time for three or four drinks in the motel bar and then to bed.

I didn't put much stock in Tom's odds. Even if he'd been right, I wasn't sure I'd know what to do with my good fortune in my present state. The one thing about Tom that irritates me is his belief that I live some kind of wild bachelor life.

Hell, in Kensington, Maryland?

I'm not saying it hadn't occurred to me to take an apartment in town. Washington is and always has been blessed with an abundance of lovely, young government workers. Plenty of them will go to bed with you for a couple drinks and a turn around the dance floor. Then they'll get up in the morning, peck you on the cheek, and you never see them again. Quick and easy and fun, and no strings attached. I know what I'm talking about; I tried it a few times not long after the divorce.

The thing is, it was good, athletic fun at night, but it always left me feeling shitty. I wanted to know the girl, I wanted—to use a devalued word—a relationship. I didn't insist on marriage. I wasn't *that* far behind the times. But I thought we should get to know each other.

My wife would have had a good laugh over that.

I patronized a certain massage parlor on Q Street. I didn't do it more than once every two or three weeks; my sexual urges didn't seem to be what they once were. What I liked was the no-nonsense atmosphere. It was quick and efficient, and though I felt bad when I left, it wasn't so bad as the one-night stands had been.

That was the wild and free bachelor life that happily married Tom Stanley seemed to delight in thinking about. And that's what had happened to the carefree jet-jockey too young for Korea and out of the service by the time of Nam but who had so goddam much of the Right Stuff he could have written the goddam book. Somehow, he didn't quite remember how, he'd ended up at a desk. For a good time he got drunk and went to bed with whores.

In that frame of mind I hardly noticed where I was going. Keeping my eyes on my feet, I stepped on a down escalator, and a pair of low-cut brown shoes stepped on with me. I looked up the nylons to the skirt, then quickly to her face.

"We do keep running into each other, don't we?" she said, with a smile.

I was still staring at her when there was a jolt. I had one hand on the rubber rail; with the other I grabbed her arm. For one wild moment I thought *earthquake*! Then I looked around and realized the escalator had stopped.

"Maybe we'd better get acquainted," she said. "We might be stuck here for hours."

I laughed. "You've got the advantage on me," I said. "You know my name, but I've never had time to ask you yours."

"It's Louise Ba—" She covered her mouth and coughed. There was a cigarette going in her other hand. "Louise Ball." She looked at me with a tentative smile, like she wanted to know if that was okay with me, her being Louise Ball. Well, I don't meet a lot of Louises anymore, but it was better than Luci or Lori or any of the cutesy names moms were giving their girls these days.

I smiled back at her, and her full-blown smile emerged. You could have used it to light candles. I became aware I was still holding her elbow, so I let it go.

"No relation to the famous redhead?" I asked.

She looked blank for a moment and I thought I might have dated myself with a reference to ancient history, then she had it. It was only later that I thought it odd she'd miss a reference to "I

Love Lucy." With a name like hers, wise guys like me must have brought it up a hundred times.

"No relation. I hope I didn't embarrass you. I'm always doing things like that."

I thought we were still talking about Lucille Ball, then realized she was referring to the coffee she'd spilled on me. It seemed like a trifle compared with the privilege of sharing an escalator step with her.

"No problem."

The people below us were moving, so we started down the unnaturally high steps.

I considered and rejected several things to say to her. I was attracted to her as I hadn't been attracted to a woman in a long time. I wanted to talk to her. I wanted to dance the night away with her, sweep her off her feet, laugh with her, cry with her, say bright, witty, gay things to her. Okay, I wouldn't have minded going to bed with her, either. To do any of those things, I should start by enchanting her, fascinating her with my wit, deliver some of those fine lines movie stars toss off with such ease in screwball comedies.

"You live around here?" I asked. Brilliant conversation opener number 192. I've got a million of 'em.

"Uh-huh. In Menlo Park."

"I don't know the area. I've only been here a couple of times, and hardly ever left the airport." *Will you show me the city?* But I couldn't quite bring myself to ask her that. We had come to rest in a quiet little eddy beside the rushing river of humanity. We almost had to shout to hear each other.

"It's across San Francisco Bay. On the peninsula. I ride the underground to work."

"You mean BART?"

Again there was that pause; she looked blank, like computer tapes were whirling around in her head, then, *bingo*.

"Yes, of course, the Bay Area Rapid Transit."

An embarrassing silence began to settle over us. I had the gloomy feeling she'd be away in a moment unless Cary Grant stepped to my rescue with a good line.

"So you probably don't know the East Bay very well."

"Why do you ask?"

"I was wondering if you knew a good restaurant. All I know are the ones around the airport."

"I've been told there are some nice ones in Jack London Square."

And she just stood there, smiling at me. I hesitated again—frankly, I'm always awkward with people I've just met, unless it's in the line of business. But she clearly wasn't in a hurry to get anywhere, so what the hell?

"Would you like to have dinner with me, then?"

"I thought you'd never ask."

Her smile was better than amphetamines, and worse than heroin. I mean, here I'd been feeling like I'd been stepped on by an elephant, and then we were together, and just like that it was like I was twenty years old and just woke up from a good night's sleep.

On the other hand, I felt it might be habit-forming, and it sure as hell did disorient me. We were already walking through the public parking lot in the drizzle—with me babbling away like a speed freak—before I recalled I had a car of my own, over at the Hertz lot. I told her about it, and she looked up at the sky. It was starting to rain harder.

"Why don't we take mine, anyway?" she said. "I can drop you off here later."

It sounded like a good idea, until I saw her car.

It was one hell of a car. I looked at it, then at her. She was smiling innocently at me, so I looked back at the car.

I'm not even sure what it *was*, but it was Italian, looked like it had been built about twenty or thirty years from now, was about eighteen inches high and thirty feet long, and seemed to be doing sixty just sitting there. I figured it had to cost eighty or ninety grand.

Okay. This is her boyfriend's car. Or she has a lucrative side income. Maybe a rich uncle just died, or her parents had money. There was no way she could have paid for it on an airline ticket agent's salary.

Frankly, I was getting a little dubious about her. Small things were adding up the wrong way. For instance, with this sitting in the garage she rode the "underground" to work?

And let's be brutally frank. With a face and a body like that, she was eager to go out with a guy like me?

I began to fear she might be a disaster groupie. They exist, though they tend to be male. But when they're female, they can be very weird. Suddenly I remembered that morning in the hangar, when she'd run away from me. She'd been looking very hard at those plastic bags full of debris. Was she getting some kind of kick out of it?

Back in the airport she had seemed like an impossible dream. So when I finally understood that she was trying to help me, that she actually *wanted* to go to dinner with me and was doing her best to get me to ask, I hadn't questioned my good fortune. But what did she really want from me? I doubted it was my dashing good looks and suave conversation.

I shoehorned myself into the passenger seat and she backed out, the foreign fireball under the hood rumbling like a big cat. The car purred along to the parking lot gate and we got in line. She looked over at me.

"Was it very bad today?" she asked.

Right. Here we go. I get to trot out my gruesome stories for the lady.

"It was terrible."

"Then let's forget about it. Let's ban all talk about crashes. Let's don't even talk about airplanes."

So there was another theory out the window. I just couldn't figure where she was coming from. As we neared the toll gate I studied her again in the blue glare of the parking lot lights. Something else had been bothering me.

It was her clothes. There was nothing wrong with them. She looked good in them. But they were old-fashioned. She was in her civilian clothes now, and I hadn't seen anything quite like them for ten years. I don't claim to be a fashion expert, but even I could see they didn't go together. The skirt didn't match the blouse. The hemline was too high on her skirt. Her blouse was thin enough for me to tell she *was* wearing a bra.

I was still puzzling over it when she paid the parking charge by dumping a fistful of coins into the attendant's hand and letting him pick out what he needed. I remembered doing much the same thing at the Calcutta airport.

Then she eased the lean, hungry machine out onto the access road, and we took off without waiting for clearance from the tower. It was like being in one of those car commercials where they try to prove their machine is more suited for aviation than for mere highways. We made the freeway in one piece, and then she really opened it up. She cut in and out of holes I never even saw, like the other cars were stationary obstacles.

After the first surge of fear I stopped reaching for the brake that wasn't there, sat back, and admired the performance.

Damn it, that lady could *drive*.

She took me to Jack London Square. I'd heard about it but never seen it. It looked touristy, but then I'm not a gourmet.

She parked, and I pried my fingers loose from the sides of the seat and managed to sort of roll out, amazed to be able to breathe, thankful for my life. She looked at me like she couldn't figure out what was wrong. I felt very old all of a sudden. I decided she probably hadn't been going all that fast, it was just me turning into a fossil. I'm sure I drove just as fast in my own hot-rod days, and as for some of the stunts we pulled in our Navy jets . . .

We went into a place called *Antoine's*, which was crowded. Naturally, we didn't have a reservation. The *maitre d'* told me it would be about forty-five minutes. I reached for my wallet, thinking I might grease his palm a little, when a magic thing happened. He got a look at Louise.

I guess he couldn't bear the thought of having her cool her heels in the lobby. I didn't see her do anything; hypnosis, maybe. Whatever it was, there was suddenly an available table by the window overlooking the water.

There were a lot of little boats out there, bobbing at anchor and drenched with rain. It was beautiful. I ordered a double scotch on the rocks, and she said she'd have the same. That pleased me. I never did understand why people want drinks that taste like candy and have paper umbrellas in them.

The menu was in French. Guess what? She spoke it like a

native. So I let her order, hoping she wouldn't saddle me with snails or eels or something.

Our drinks arrived at a close approximation of the speed of light. I could see in our waiter's eyes that Louise had made another conquest.

Somebody started playing a piano. Louise paused, and I saw that look again. She was consulting the memory banks, but she couldn't have had to look hard for that one.

" 'As Time Goes By,' " she said.

"Here's looking at *you*, kid," I said, and raised my glass.

She drained hers neat. I must have stared.

"I needed that," she said.

I motioned for the waiter, and sure enough, he'd been looking at Louise and some of her magic rubbed off on me, because he was there very quickly with another of the same.

"It certainly looked like it." I needed one, too, but I sipped at mine. She sat sort of sideways in the chair, one arm draped along the back, her legs stretched out to the side of the table. She seemed totally relaxed, and more beautiful than ever. She cocked her head slightly.

"What's the matter?" she asked.

"Nothing. Nothing at all. Don't get mad, but I've got to say it. You're very beautiful, and I'm doing my best not to stare too much."

She dimpled at that, and accepted it with a wry nod.

"I can hardly believe my good fortune."

The smile faded a little. "I'm not sure how I should take that."

"What I mean is, I know anybody could see what I see in you, but I'm having a hard time understanding what you see in me."

She sat up a little straighter, and her smile faded some more. Actually, by then it was almost a frown.

"At the risk of letting you think I was feeling sorry for you, you looked lonely and depressed. You looked like you needed a friend. Well, so do I, and I don't have any. I wanted to get my mind off the things I saw today and I thought it probably wouldn't do you any harm, either. But if you—"

"Wait, I'm sorry I said—"

"No, let me finish. I'm not doing you any favors. And I'm not out to get anything from you. I'm not a reporter. I'm not a disaster freak. Don't talk about me like I'm your 'good fortune.' I'm me, and when I accepted your invitation it was because I was impressed at how you handled all those fools at the press conference and how you seem to be working so hard at unraveling the mistakes made by the people I work for and I thought I might like to get to know you."

She looked me up and down, clinically.

"Of course, I could have been wrong."

I hadn't until that moment thought she might have been a reporter. I still didn't think so. But I wasn't spending a lot of time worrying about it one way or the other, as all I could see just then was something beautiful in danger of being wrecked by my suspicions.

"I wish I hadn't said that," I said.

"Well, you did." She sighed, and looked away from me. "Maybe I did come down on you a bit hard."

"I was asking for it."

"It's been a hard day." She looked at her second drink. She tossed it down. I did the same, hoping her opinion of her own capacity for liquor was close to the truth. It wouldn't be much fun if she got sloppy drunk.

"How old are you?" she asked.

"You're certainly direct."

"It saves time."

"I'm forty-four."

"Good God," she said. "Were you worried that I was too young for you? Is that what you couldn't figure out?"

"Part of it."

"I'm thirty-three. Does that make you feel better?"

"Yeah. I figured you for twenty-six." That wasn't quite true. When I first saw her I thought she was a lot younger, and later I thought she might be a little older. Twenty-six was splitting the difference.

"I wish I could just wipe out the last couple minutes and start all over with you," I told her.

"I'm willing." She lit another cigarette from the butt of the one she had been smoking. It was the only thing about her I didn't like, but you can't have everything.

"You were right about me," I said. It wasn't as hard to say as I'd thought it would be. "I am lonely, and I've been depressed. Or I was. I felt a lot better as soon as you bumped into me."

"Even with coffee in your lap?"

"I meant later, on the escalator—"

She reached over the table and touched my hand.

"I know what you meant. I hate airports in strange towns. You feel so anonymous. All those people."

"Especially this time of the year."

"I know. They're all frowning. It's better out at the gates. People are happier out there, meeting the people they came to pick up. But I hate to work the main terminal. Everybody's in a hurry, and there are always computer problems. Reservations getting lost . . . you know."

I felt a chill there. What if she *was* a reporter?

"When they pulled me off the ticket desk and sent me out to the hangar I was almost relieved, can you imagine that? I mean, after they promised me there wouldn't be any dead bodies out there."

I didn't say anything. If she wanted horror stories, this was the time to ask me about them.

"But we weren't going to talk about work," she said. "Except I would like to know how a man who's only forty-four years old came to have such a sad face."

"I put it together here and there over the years. But you don't want to hear about that."

So that's exactly what we talked about: my life and hard times. I tried to stop myself but it was no good. I didn't get weepy about it, thank all the gods, and beyond a certain point and a certain number of drinks I can't recall exactly what I *did* say except I'm sure it wasn't about the details of my work. At least we stuck to that part of the agreement. Mostly I told her about what the job was doing to me. About what had happened to my marriage, about waking up with a fear of falling, and the dream where I'm moving through this long dark tunnel full of flashing lights.

The drinks didn't hurt anything. By the time dinner came we'd each had quite a few, and I was feeling as relaxed and unguarded as I ever get. There's a wonderful feeling of release in talking about things you've held inside too long.

But when the food arrived I calmed down enough to realize what we'd been having could hardly be called a conversation. Her part in it had been to provide the ears and a sympathetic comment or two.

"So how do you like your job?" I asked, and she laughed. I met her eyes for a moment, and saw no reproach there. "Listen, I'm sorry I've been carrying on like this."

"Hush and eat your dinner. I don't mind listening. I told you, I thought you looked like you needed a friend."

"You said you did, too. I haven't been a very good one so far."

"You needed to talk worse than I did. I'm flattered that you chose me to talk to. I must have an honest face, or something."

"Or something."

I'd almost forgotten what it was like, feeling good about myself, and I was grateful. So I asked her about herself and she told me a few things while we ate.

Her father had a lot of money. She had a degree in art from some college back east. She hadn't grown up thinking she'd ever have to support herself. She married the right guy, who turned out to be not so right after all. She left him and had been trying to make it on her own. There'd been a miscarriage.

I gathered the art career was a failure. She'd been shocked to discover how hard it was to make a living, but she did not want to return to her father. He kept sending her gifts that she didn't have the will power to refuse, like the car outside.

She told the whole story very glibly, and finished up before the dessert came. Every time I asked for a detail she had it ready. It was fascinating, really, because about halfway through the story I realized I didn't believe a word of it.

You know what? I didn't give a shit. By then I had a pleasant glow that was a long way from being drunk but felt very nice indeed. She'd matched me drink for drink and, as far as I could see, was completely sober.

"Can you fly?" I asked her.

She looked startled, then suspicious.

"What do you mean?"

"I don't know. I just thought you could."

"I've flown small planes."

"I thought so."

She'd hardly touched her dessert. Come to think of it, she'd hardly touched anything, though the food was excellent. And she'd smoked all the time. She'd gone through one pack and put a dent in another.

I started to think about riding back to the airport with her in that rolling bomb. And I wondered why she'd lied to me. Don't ask me how I knew she had been lying; I *knew*.

"Can you take me home?" I said.

"I don't know if anyone can do that, Bill. I'll try."

She did all right. Maybe she'd realized my terror on the way to the restaurant, because she slowed down considerably.

Then I was dropped off in front of the hotel, like a coed at the dorm. I felt a little funny about it, but I figured I shouldn't come on too heavy. I expected to see her in the morning, anyway.

I found my room in a warm glow that lasted until I had the door shut behind me. Then I was once again in a strange hotel room, far from home, alone. I wished I had a drink, knew it was the worst possible thing for me, and wished for it again. I dialed room service and then, in a rare display of will power, hung up before they answered. I opened the drapes and looked out at the lights. I sat by the window.

I'm sure I would have gone to sleep there in that chair, but about twenty minutes later there was a knock on my door. I almost didn't answer; it had to be Tom or somebody from the investigation with a problem I wasn't up to solving.

But I did go to the door and when I opened it Louise was

standing there with a paper sack and two glasses, trying to look cheerful and not doing a very good job of it.

"I thought you might like a nightcap," she said, and started to cry.

14

"Poor Little Warrior!"

Testimony of Louise Baltimore

"Sherman, set the dial on the Wayback Machine for the evening of December twelfth, nineteen eighty-something-or-other."

"You got it, Mr. Peabody," Sherman piped up.

Sherman. The bastard.

Our story thus far...

If you'll recall, when we left our heroine she was heroically passed out at the mere mention of an historically insignificant miscarriage. That the miscarriage occurred a couple years after the baby was born was not worthy of special remark; it happened all the time, these days. In fact, now it was happening *every* time. I'd had my baby for two years. I suppose that could be seen as good fortune.

What's Fortune? A magazine. What does it cost? Ten cents. But I've only got a nickel. That's your good fortune.

If I get any heavier I'll drop through the floor. Historical allusions, ten cents per kilobyte, courtesy of your local data-dumper. Nineteen-eighties our specialty.

My head was crammed with so much data about the era that I could hardly clear my throat without coming up with an advertising jingle, movie synopsis, television show, or hoary joke.

"Sherman, what I am is a jokey whore."

"Don't fuck him unless you want to, Louise."

"I don't want to!"

The Gate opened up, and I . . . stepped through.

I sat through most of his news conference. It was fully as boring as I'd expected it to be, though of course we'd not been able to observe it since I was sitting there exerting temporal censorship.

There was only one bad moment. At the end of the press conference Mayer started asking the damndest questions. Looking for unusual data, he said. I don't know what it is, but I'll know it when I see it. And by the way, Mister Smith, have you found anything unusual having to do with time?

I nearly swallowed my cigarette.

What did that bastard know?

I spotted Smith across the crowded airport lobby. I didn't have much trouble reaching him as he stepped on the escalator, though a couple people who hadn't gotten out of my way didn't like my methods. I didn't care. They were all my ancestors, but I'd had it with ancestors. I'd spent my life trying to make a future for them, and look where it had got me.

We had worked hard on this moment, Sherman and I.

(This was after, *long* after, he threw water on my face or pinched my earlobe or slapped me or whatever he did to bring me around. My memories of that period are rather vague and I'd just as soon not discuss them, thank you. My memories of the hours following that, when Sherman and I had discussed the kid, are clear as can be, and I'd just as soon not discuss them either. I'm supposed to tell everything, but there are limits.)

"Meet cute," Sherman had said.

"What is that supposed to mean?"

"It's a term popular in various eras of twentieth-century Hollywood, describing devices whose purpose is to effect the first plot element of the favorite story of the time, which began 'boy meets girl.' "

" 'Boy loses girl, boy gets girl,' right?"

"Right. We needn't concern ourselves too much with the second part. He'll lose you without our help, in the natural order of things, and of course he can't get you in the end."

"Whatever happened to happy endings?" I asked. "Don't answer. They died out about the time I was born. So give me an example of meeting cute."

"Veronica Lake as a disillusioned woman on her way out of Hollywood, who spends her last dollar on ham and eggs for Joel McRae, who turns out to be a famous director dressed as a bum to gather material for a movie he plans to make. *Sullivan's Travels*, Preston Sturges, 1942."

"You've been watching a lot of movies," I said.

"About as many as you. Of course, my data-dumping capacity is larger, and I have better access to it."

"You were thinking along these lines when you told me to dump the coffee in his lap."

"Yes. Now he knows you. We must give him an opportunity to know you better."

"So what's your idea?"

Sherman told me, and here I was, getting onto an escalator in Oakland.

I reached into my purse just about the time Smith saw me. I smiled at him, and pressed a button in the purse, and the escalator ground to a stop.

"We do keep running into each other, don't we?" I said.

I hadn't counted on him being so shy. I had to drag a dinner invitation out of him. I was beginning to wonder if the fancy skinsuit I was wearing was really all it was cracked up to be.

Thinking it over, I suppose I'd been expecting him to know his lines as well as I did. I just assumed he was feeling the puppet master's strings pulling him as strongly as they were pulling me. But why should he? If anything, I was his puppet master, and he had no way of knowing that. I was the one who'd seen the script—or at least the proposal—for the way the evening should proceed.

Since he didn't suggest driving I assumed he didn't have a car. So I steered him toward the parking lot, where we'd prepared a contingency plan. That's when I almost got into trouble.

As I said, data-dumping can fill me with facts, but it's not much help at pattern recognition. There were a million vehicles in the lot and I didn't know much about any of them. Oh, I knew the brand names; other than that, I had to go by instinct in selecting "my" automobile.

Logically, I thought I should choose a small one to go with my presumed socio-economic status. But sometimes logic doesn't help. How was I to know that big cars don't always cost more, nor small ones less.

The one I picked was low and uncomfortable-looking. As soon as I indicated it I knew I was wrong. Smith looked at me strangely. Well, it was too late to change my mind. I reached in my purse and all the door locks sprang open before he could get close enough to see it happening. Then we got in and I scanned the controls. They seemed simple and straightforward, though I thought radar might have been helpful. I inserted a key in the ignition. It felt out the proper combination, started the car for me, and I got it in motion.

It was even easier than I'd thought. The vehicle was much faster than anything else on the road. I used the reserve speed to hurry through the smaller autos, keeping the tachometer as close as possible to the red line. I followed the signs to Jack London Square.

I shouldn't have admitted I spoke French. By the time I realized it was out of character to do so, I'd already been speaking it to the waiter.

The food was pretty bad. I'm sure everyone else enjoyed it, but to me, it was tasteless, like chewing cardboard. We require quite different chemicals in our diets than 20ths, including a lot of things that would surely kill Bill Smith, or at least make him very sick. I'd come prepared. I had some capsules that contained all the poisons a self-respecting creature from the ninety-ninth century could ever need. I kept palming them all night and dropping them into my drinks. They had the added advantage of neutralizing the ethanol. I pecked at my food; it was the double scotches that sustained me.

He told me a lot of things I already knew; after all, Bill Smith had become the most extensively researched person in the twentieth century. We had scanned him from his birth (by Caesarean section) to his death.

I'd entered the twentieth century with a good deal of contempt for Mister Smith. Looking at his life from the outside, you just had to wonder why a guy who had so much going for him had done so little with it. He struck me as a whiner, soon to be a wino. He had a responsible position and he was in the process of throwing it away. He'd been a failure at marriage.

He was living in the era that, from my perspective, was about as close to heaven on Earth as the human race had ever come, and in a nation that had more wealth—however you want to measure it—than any other nation ever achieved. From here on up it was going to be downhill all the way, until the human race reached its nadir: those good old days of the far future I called home.

It was only natural I'd find myself thinking *what the hell did he have to complain about?*

Yet the twentieth century was bursting with complainers. They worried about meaningful relationships. They complained about the high cost of living. They had a whole battery of words to describe the things that afflicted them: words like *angst, ennui, malaise.* They took pills to cure something called depression. They went to classes to learn how to feel good about themselves. They aborted about one out of four of their children. They really felt they had problems.

And at the same time they were busy as beavers destroying the world. They built—eventually—over three hundred gigatons of nuclear weapons and then pretended they'd never use them. They set in motion the processes that would eventually kill all animal species but themselves and a few insects and a million quick-mutating microbes, and that would leave their descendants—such as myself—catastrophically evolving toward oblivion. They were doing things right then that would change me so much that I could no longer breathe their air or eat their food for any length of time.

I guess it's no wonder they invented existential despair.

Still, it's one thing to see a man's life in overview, and another to hear him tell it. I'd been prepared for the tale, had expected to do my best to smile all the way through it.

But when he started to talk, I found things shifting around. *The poor guy,* I'd think, and then catch myself thinking it.

He didn't whine. He didn't even really complain. I found myself wishing he would; it would be so much easier to feel a healthy contempt for him. But what he told me was the simple truth. He was lonely. He didn't know what to do about it. He used to be able to lose himself in his job, but that didn't work anymore. He knew it was silly, he couldn't figure out why nothing seemed to mean anything. Working as his own physician, he had prescribed ethanol as a possible cure. It seemed to work some of the time, but the results weren't all in yet. He knew, without knowing how he knew, that he'd reached for something, missed it, and was on his way down. It wouldn't get any better.

So I vacillated between feeling sorry for him and wanting to jerk him up by the collar and slap him around until he came to his senses. I guess if I'd been born in the twentieth century, I'd have been a social worker. I couldn't seem to deal with a goat as a *person* without getting all fouled up inside. I couldn't stay out of his shoes.

Damn, it's so much easier to knock the fuckers out and kick their asses through the Gate. Then all the crying is done far from my sight.

The man could hold his liquor. He probably thought the same thing about me.

He held it so well that, by the time the food came, he realized he'd been pouring out his life story in an uninterrupted monologue, and he had the grace to feel guilty about it. So he asked me about myself.

Not that I hadn't come prepared. Sherman and I had worked up a life story. I just didn't want to tell it. I was sick of lying. But I told it, and I thought I did a pretty good job. He nodded in the right places, asked sympathetic but not probing questions.

I was going right along, feeling pleased with myself, when I realized he didn't believe a word I was saying.

There was a funny look in his eyes. Maybe it was just liquor. I told myself it was, but I didn't believe it.

No, he just thought there was something I didn't want to talk about, and he was perfectly right.

I dropped him off at his hotel, drove a few blocks away, parked, and then just sat there and shook.

When I stopped shaking, I looked at my watch. It was a little after midnight. I knew what I had to do. Sherman and I had worked out the approach and I thought it would work. I just couldn't seem to get moving.

It's not that I was afraid to go to bed with him. Sherman and I had talked that out, and I felt a lot better about the sex question. Why be afraid of having a baby when you only have a couple days to live? And it wasn't that I was too uppity to go to bed with a man for the sake of the Gate Project. There was a long list of unsavory things I'd do to save the project, and fucking somebody I didn't like was a long ways from the bottom.

It's not even that I didn't like him. It was a job to do and I don't turn away from my job any more than any good soldier should . . . but all that aside, I *did* like him. And the time capsule had been easy about that part, anyway. I didn't have to unless I wanted to.

She's only a wimp.

There was a liquor store not far from where I was parked. I got out of my car, walked down the sidewalk, went in, and bought a bottle of scotch.

On my way back somebody stepped out of a dark doorway and started to follow me. I turned around. He was a dark man, possibly a negro, though to my eyes races are as hard to distinguish as fashions. He pushed a gun toward me.

"Let's have the purse, cunt," he said.

"Are you a mugger or a rapist?" I asked him. Then I took his gun, threw him on the ground, and stood on his neck. He tried to throw me off, so I kicked his face and stood on his neck again. He gurgled. I let up the pressure.

"I think you broke my wrist," he said.

"No, it was either the radius or the ulna. You'd better have a doctor set it." I looked at his bare arm. "You're a junkie, aren't you?"

He didn't say anything.

Well, you don't get a lot of choice in your ancestors, but he was one, so I couldn't kill him. There was the possibility I'd already done a lot of damage to the timestream...but I didn't care.

It was a feeling of relief. I was going to do what I wanted to do, if I could just discover what that was.

I took the bullets out of his gun and gave it back to him. Then I reached in my purse and handed him a wad of American currency—twenty thousand dollars, minus the $15.86 I'd spent for the scotch.

"Have a good time," I said.

Free will was an odd feeling. If that's what it was.

I let my hands do the driving. They brought me back to Bill's hotel, and they parked the car.

My feet seemed to have similar ideas, though they didn't do as neat a job. In the hall outside Bill's room I stumbled over a room-service tray that had two empty highball glasses on it. I picked them up, and my feet took me to his door and parked me there. I was about to scratch on the door, remembered that was a different time and place, so I hit it with my fist instead.

Knock, knock.

Who's there?

Your good fortune.

What's fortune?

Just stick out your palm, Mister Smith. Louise tells all.

15

"Compounded Interest"

Testimony of Bill Smith

I hadn't smoked a cigarette in nine years. But when she got up off the bed and went to the bathroom, I grabbed the pack she'd left on the nightstand and lit one up. They were Virginia Slims. I started coughing on the second puff, and by the fourth I was feeling light-headed, so I stubbed it out.

What a night.

I glanced at the clock. It was one in the morning. She was going to turn into a pumpkin at ten. It was one of many things she'd said, and it made about as much sense as any of the other things.

I listened to the water running behind the closed door. It sounded like she was taking a shower.

All I knew for sure was she'd had a daughter, and the kid had died. The rest of it didn't add up.

"Can I tell you something?" she had said, after she managed to stop crying. We were sitting on the edge of the bed and I had my arms around her. She was as beautiful an armful as I had ever had, but sex was very far from my mind.

"Sure. Anything."

"It's a long story," she warned me.

"I figured."

She laughed. It was a shaky laugh and it threatened to become something else, but she controlled herself.

"Where I come from, everybody dies," she said.

And I swear, it got crazier from there.

Testimony of Louise Baltimore

"We don't name our babies until their second birthday," I told him.

"Why is that?"

"Isn't it obvious?" I wondered again how much of this he was believing. About one percent, I decided. Still, if I was going to tell *this* story I couldn't put it into safe, 1980s terms.

"We don't name them because the chances are less than one percent they'll live to their second birthday. After that you can take a chance. Maybe they'll make it."

"What was it this child had?"

"Nothing. At least, that's how it looked. I was twelve, you understand, I'd had my first period and it looked like I was fertile. Genalysis hadn't turned up any major problems."

I looked at him. Sometimes the truth just won't do.

"I have a fertility problem," I said. "The doctors told me I wouldn't be able to have children. And then I got pregnant anyway."

"At twelve?" he said.

"Forget twelve. I'm drunk, okay? I had . . . what's the word? Amniocentesis. Everybody thought that if I *did* get pregnant, the kid would be . . . mongoloid."

"They call it Down's syndrome these days."

"Right. Right. Forgot the local jargon. So then the baby was born, and she was perfect. The sweetest, prettiest thing ever. The most perfect baby born in a hundred years."

I was swigging right from the bottle. No pills, no nothing. It turned out ethanol ain't such a bad prescription for despair, after all.

"She was my life. She was everything I ever wanted. Oh, they tried to take her away, they tried to put her in a hospital where they could keep a close eye on her all the time.

"And smart? The kid was a genius. She was walking at six months, talking at nine. She was the earth, moon, and stars."

"What did you say her name was?" he asked.

I looked at him again. Okay, so he didn't even believe one percent.

And why should he? And why should I?

I started to cry again.

Testimony of Bill Smith

The lady was a lot more disturbed than I'd figured. I did my best to piece it together, almost like I'd handle an airplane crash.

The baby had some sort of congenital disease. I'm not an expert on those kinds of problems, but a couple of things occurred to me. Such as: the mother had syphilis, or she was a heroin addict while she was carrying the child. What else could have given her such guilt? Why else would she be telling her story in such crazy metaphors?

The child died before her second birthday. Or maybe not. There was a possibility she was a vegetable kept alive by machines.

Come to that, the welfare department might have taken the kid. Maybe she was living with her foster parents. There was just no way I could tell.

So it was well established Louise was crazy. The more she talked, the more certain it was. I've got a reaction to crazy people. I'd prefer to have nothing to do with them. She might get violent. There was no telling what she might imagine, what she might decide to blame me for.

Yet I didn't feel it this time.

It's true I was emotionally exhausted when she was through. It's true the back of my neck was getting sore from all the sympathetic nods I'd been giving her. But it didn't matter. I still liked her. I still wanted to be with her.

Testimony of Louise Baltimore

"I haven't got much time left," I said, when I'd finished telling him a story he had no background to comprehend. "I think I'll go freshen up." I glanced at my watch. "After all, at ten in the morning I turn into a pumpkin."

I studied my face in the bathroom mirror. Same old Louise. Same old idiot.

"See," I told myself. "You were making a lot of fuss about nothing. You told him the thing you least wanted to talk about, and he didn't believe a word. You might call that an anticlimax."

I started coughing before I got through the speech. I found my Vicks inhaler and took a deep whiff, hoping the stench—to Bill's nose—wouldn't foul up the whole room. Then I took off my clothes and got in the shower.

Sherman had cooked up a whole sub-plot to begin at this point. It was cuter than hell, chock full of lines borrowed from the likes of Katharine Hepburn and Jean Arthur, that ended up with me falling into his arms and—I presume—waves crashing on the beach as we faded tastefully away. Trouble was, it only works like that in movies. We'd met cute; that was about all the cuteness I could stand. It was time to leave the thirties and forties and get right into the explicit eighties.

So I got out of the shower and opened the door.

Testimony of Bill Smith

She seemed to enjoy it. At least, if she didn't, she made all the right noises. God knows *I* enjoyed it. I felt she was at least as hungry for sex as I was, and I'd never been so hungry.

When it was over she reached for her cigarettes, and that annoyed me just a little. Maybe I needed something to complain about. Maybe all of a sudden my life was too good.

"Do you always smoke right after you make love?"

She looked down at her crotch, and the punch line passed

between us without her needing to deliver it. We both laughed. She lit up, and took a long drag, let the smoke out very slowly. She seemed utterly content.

"I smoke after everything, Bill. I smoke before everything. If I could figure out a way to smoke while I was sleeping, I'd do it. It's only my inhuman self-restraint that leads me to smoke them one at a time in your presence."

"I suppose you know what the Surgeon General has determined."

"I can read the side of the box."

"Then why do you smoke?"

"Because I like the taste. It reminds me of home. And because getting lung cancer would be like a half-inch snowfall at the north pole."

"What do you mean?"

"I mean I'm already dying of a horrible disease."

I looked at her, but her eyes weren't giving anything away. It could be the literal truth, or another of her weird delusions, or she could just be pulling my leg.

I'd been proud of myself when I'd decided, back at the restaurant, that she was lying to me. Now, I couldn't read her at all.

"We're all dying, Bill," she said. "Life is invariably fatal."

"I'd say you had quite a while to live yet, though."

"You'd be wrong."

"Why did you run yesterday morning? When I asked you for a cup of coffee?"

She stubbed out her smoke, lit another.

"I didn't expect to see you there. I was looking for something else."

"Do you really work for United?"

She grinned at me.

"What do you think?"

"I think you're crazy."

"I know that. The truth just isn't good enough for some people."

I thought it over.

"Yeah. I do think you work for United. I think you just have fun making people feel foolish. You like to keep them off-balance."

"If you insist."

"I think you were shocked by something else. Like bloody toys, and torn-up Christmas presents."

She sighed, and looked at me with sad eyes.

"You've discovered my dark secret. I've got a soft heart." She looked away from my face, down quite a bit lower, and stubbed out a cigarette half-smoked. From her, it was a startling gesture.

"You ready to do it again?" she asked.

Testimony of Louise Baltimore

The mission was still there, though I'd practically forgotten it. I had to keep reminding myself: what you're here for is to change him, to keep him from going back to that hangar in the middle of the night and meeting an earlier version of Louise Baltimore.

The fact that if he *didn't* go there a part of my life I'd already lived would be cancelled out, would never have happened, didn't bother me much. If the universe cancelled me out at least I'd fade away a contented woman. That's a *lot* better than I ever expected to get.

When I looked at my watch it was seven in the morning, and we were still sitting there in bed, naked, laughing and talking as the sun came up outside. I don't know who suggested sleeping, but eventually we seemed headed in that direction. I didn't think I'd have much trouble keeping him away from the investigation tomorrow. For one thing, this C. Gordon Petcher item was certain to arrive some time that morning, taking a lot of pressure off Bill. He could plead illness, spend the day in bed.

At least I kept telling myself that.

The whole Window C business had turned out very strange. I had broken security up one side and down the other. I had told him the *literal truth* about many things. And I had not been believed.

Strangely, I saw that as a good sign. He thought I was a kook, and yet he didn't seem to mind too much. Could it be so hard for the lovely kook with all the crazy stories to enchant this man long enough to keep him out of that hangar tonight?

Even if she was destined to turn into a pumpkin at ten A.M., Pacific Standard Time?

Testimony of Bill Smith

We laughed in each other's arms, roaring drunk, and made love again, more slowly. We laughed some more, and made love some more. I impressed even myself. I hope she appreciated it.

I have no idea when I got to sleep. It didn't seem to matter. But it did. Oh, it did.

I came out of bed like a guided missile . . .

. . . and bumped my nose on the wall. I stood staring stupidly at it as my hungover thoughts arranged themselves into a dim state of awareness.

The alarm didn't ring. What's this wall doing here? Who am I where am I what am I why am I . . .

Oh.

"Good morning," she said. She was sitting on the bed, nude, propped on some pillows with her feet out in front of her. She took a drag on her cigarette. She was so heartbreakingly beautiful I thought I might cry.

"Please," I croaked. "Don't smoke so loud."

"Pretty feeble. You did a lot better last night." But she stubbed it out.

"I was feeling a lot funnier last night."

"I was just sitting here wondering," she said. "While you woke up on your feet, I mean. It took a while for your eyes to focus."

"They aren't focused yet."

"Yes they are." She stretched, and I guess she was right. It was impossible not to focus on someone as spectacular as that.

"What I was wondering is, what woke you up? I didn't hear

anything and I didn't do anything. But brother, you sure as hell woke up."

"What time is it?"

"Eight-thirty."

I sat on the edge of the bed and told her about my alarm clock. What I had to assume was I had just pulled a variation of the old story about the man at the lighthouse. Twenty years he sits out there, and the foghorn goes off in his ear every thirty seconds. One night it misses a blast and he jumps out of bed screaming, *"What was that?"*

She listened solemnly, reached for another smoke, looked at me, and decided against it. She held out her arms.

"Bill. Listen to me. You've been asleep for one hour. Your Mister Petcher can handle your duties this morning. Come back to bed. I'll rub your back."

I sat back down, and she did rub it. She used a lot more than her hands, too, and I didn't complain. Then I did the hardest thing I ever did. I stood up.

"Got to get to work," I said.

She sat there like something out of the middle of *Penthouse*, even to the vaseline on the lens—though that might have been simply the condition of my eyeballs. She just kept looking up at me.

"This job is killing you, Bill."

"Yeah. I know."

"Stay with me today. I'll show you San Francisco."

"I thought you had to go at ten."

Her face fell. I didn't know what I'd said. She hadn't exactly said where she had to go at ten. Maybe to visit her baby in the hospital.

The shower curtain rings rattled as she yanked the curtain open and stepped in with me. She shuddered when the cold water hit her and for a moment we clung together like children. I turned the tap over toward warm, and hugged her. She leaned back in my arms. I saw that her nipples hadn't crinkled up from the cold like my wife's used to in a cold shower. Funny the things you notice at a time like that.

"I don't like to see you killing yourself. Take the day off."

"Louise, don't bitch at me. I have a job, and I have to do it."

"Don't work late, then. I'll be here at ten this evening."

"That I can do. I'll be here, too."

Testimony of Louise Baltimore

He left, and I had no idea what he was going to do that night. Either way, it didn't look good.

He could go to the hangar, meet me, and screw up the timeline. Or he could not go to a place I'd already been, to a place that, in *my* version of reality, he had already been. I didn't know what that would do to me.

Either way, sitting there on the bed in my damp skinsuit, I figured I could be smoking my last cigarette. I made it last, savored every carcinogenic puff.

Then the Gate arrived in the bathroom and I stepped through. For all I knew, there might be nothing on the other side. The thought didn't bother me much. For a night, anyway, I had lived.

16
A Night to Remember

Testimony of Bill Smith

There were two cops at the desk as I went through the lobby. They were talking to the manager. I didn't think anything about it until I got outside and saw two more cops, two police cars, and a tow truck pulling Louise's Italian sports car out of its parking slot.

I started over there. I was going to ask what the hell was going on, but something made me stop. Instead, I found a spectator and asked him what was going on.

"The cop said it was stolen," the man said.

"Stolen?"

"That's what he said. Must have been a kid. Who the hell else would be dumb enough to steal a thing like that? I bet there's no more than six or seven of them in the whole country."

I got out of the elevator and ran down the hall toward my room. I was getting out my key when a strange noise started. I looked around, up and down the hall, but I couldn't locate its source.

We weren't that far from the airport, so I dismissed the noise. I had my key, so I started to put it in the lock.

At least, I tried to.

The door bulged away from me, like it was made of rubber.

I almost fell over; putting out a hand, I caught myself against the wall, which had also distorted. Then, slowly, it eased back into position.

I stood there, sweating. I backed away from the door, studied it and the wall. No paint was cracked. I ran my hand over the door, and around the frame. Nothing was warped, there were no splinters.

Jesus. I'd had bad hangovers before, but nothing like that. I rubbed my hands over my face, and unlocked the door.

For just a second it looked very odd in there. At the far end of the room were sliding glass doors that led to a coffin-sized balcony. The doors were shut, but the drapes were blowing as if in a high wind. I couldn't feel the slightest breeze. And everything in the room seemed to be coated with ice.

Maybe ice isn't the right word. Frost, or powdered sugar.

I blinked, and it was all gone. The curtains were barely stirring, and there was nothing wrong with the walls or the unmade bed.

She was gone.

I did everything I could think of. It didn't bring her back.

The balcony door was locked from the inside. I opened it and stepped out, looked around, couldn't see how she could have gotten out from the fourth floor. There was no rope of knotted bedsheets or anything.

I hadn't been gone that long. I suppose she could have come down one elevator while I was going up the other, or she might have used the stairs, but there was something that made me doubt that. Her clothes were still there. All of them, from the brown shoes to the cotton bra.

Her purse was gone, though. Could she have had some clothes in there?

The only other evidence she had ever been there were the stained sheets and the heaping ashtrays.

I stayed in the room for almost half an hour, trying to put it together.

A stolen car. A night to remember. A strange story about a

place where everybody died. A dead or stillborn or heroin-addicted infant.

Oh, yes, and two more clues. In the bathroom trash can I found a Vicks inhaler and an empty package of Clorets breath freshener. I sniffed at the inhaler and wished I hadn't. Whatever was in the thing, I didn't want any part of it.

Chalk it up to experience, I told myself, only it didn't help. You're supposed to *learn* something from experience, and all I had was questions.

I decided not to tell the police anything about her, at least not until I'd had a chance to talk to her myself. Maybe she needed help. I didn't think she was dangerous.

I had to call a cab to get to the airport. When I arrived, I went straight to the United desk, and around back to where Sarah Hacker had her office.

She looked like she'd had about as much sleep as I had. Maybe there are worse jobs than personnel and public relations for an airline that's just lost a plane, but I don't know what they are.

"Hi, Sarah," I said. "I'd like to find Louise Ball, if it's not too much trouble."

"No trouble," she said. "What does she do, and in what city?"

"She works right here," I said. "Or she did yesterday. She's a ticket agent."

Sarah was shaking her head and reaching for a book. She flipped through it.

"Not unless she was hired after five o'clock yesterday evening. I know all my people, Bill. She might have been a temporary. Let me look."

She did, and came up with nothing. She put the name through her computer, and confirmed that no one named Louise Ball worked for United.

It was time to call in the FBI. A harmless kook with an obsession about a dead daughter was one thing; an unauthorized person hanging around an investigation pretending to be something she wasn't was another.

I actually got into a phone booth and had dialed the first couple digits of the number Freddie Powers had given me . . . then I hung up. Louise had said she'd be back that evening. I'd wait, and give her a chance to explain herself.

I remembered I did have something to talk to Freddie Powers about, so I went back into the booth. I found him at the temporary morgue.

"What about those watches?" I asked him. "Did you find anything new?"

"One thing," he said. "You remember the digitals that were running backwards? They're all running forwards again."

"Did you bring somebody in on it?"

"Yeah."

"What'd he say?"

"He said it couldn't have happened."

I thought about that.

"How many people actually saw them? I mean, while they were running backwards?"

There was a pause. "You and me, Stanley, and that doctor, Brindle. Maybe a couple people who were helping him take watches off the corpses . . . but I don't think so. He's the one who noticed it."

"Did you get any films, videotapes . . . anything like that?"

"No. Nothing. All we've got is the testimony of the three of us."

"Three?"

Another pause. "I'm not sure Brindle wants to swear to anything."

"Why don't we wait on this? We've still got the watches that are forty-five minutes off."

"Right."

"With the digitals, all we've got is that you and I and Tom saw it."

There was a long pause. I assumed he was thinking over his position, how his career was going and how a story like this would affect his advancement in the Bureau—which has always liked things neat.

"I saw it," he said, slowly, "but that doesn't mean I think it's important."

"Right. Sit on it for a while, okay? I'll decide if it's important."

"You've got it, Bill."

One anomaly dealt with.

The day went like that: pretty well, except I kept looking over my shoulder expecting Louise to drop into my lap.

She didn't.

We started off with Norman Tyson, from the company who built the air traffic control computers.

He took the position that the firm's equipment was not at fault, as it had been functioning at data-loads beyond what it had been designed to handle. I let Tom work on him, hoping to see a chink in his armor of certainty. They knew they were vulnerable, but they also knew the real story of this crash could be the FAA's failure to replace obsolete hardware.

And the agency would pass that ball along to Congress, who didn't provide the money. By then the guilt was already spread out enough, but you could go further, if you wanted to, and blame the electorate who put the Congress into office.

I knew the Board was in the clear. At least on paper. We had reports and recommendations by the carload. We'd been warning them about the old computers. We'd told them they had to be replaced.

But had we told them hard enough?

Who could tell? These were budget-conscious times. Come to think of it, I couldn't remember *any* time when people weren't howling about cutting government spending, and everybody who ever got cut thought it was the worst case of bad judgement ever seen in Washington. And we never said the new computers would be cheap: we were talking about half a billion dollars.

Look on the bright side, I told myself. I'll bet we buy them now.

Just after lunch I got a call from Doctor Harlan Prentice, who was in charge of the autopsy team. He wanted me to come over, but there are things I'd just as soon skip after a meal, and that was one of them.

"It has to do with the contents of the stomachs," he said. "I guess you know the rate of identification in this crash is going to be low."

"I've been in the morgue, Doctor," I told him. "I've seen the big baggies."

"Yes. Well, with the 747, we've examined seventy-three body fragments containing stomachs. I have before me a menu from that flight, and it lists a choice of chicken crepes, beef à la bercy, and a diet plate in tourist. I haven't seen a menu for first-class."

I swallowed queasily, tasting the steak I'd just eaten. I mean, I'm hardened to this sort of thing, but doctors are incredible.

"What's the significance, Doctor?"

"They all had the chicken," he said.

That stopped me for a moment.

"Rather unlikely, wouldn't you say?" He was still waiting for a comment.

I was suddenly angry. Not at him. But why wouldn't this case follow a decent, reasonable line?

"Unlikely," I conceded. "Not impossible."

"It's stretching the laws of chance. I have about a hundred stomachs to look at yet—"

"—and the next one might be the beef."

"Or the diet plate," he said, helpfully.

Then I had it.

"There must have been a mix-up in New York," I said. "They loaded too many of the chicken dinners. They didn't find out till they took off. So everybody who was hungry ate the chicken, and if they'd landed Pan Am would have heard a lot of bitching."

"What about first class?"

Screw first class. "I don't know. I do know there's always a reasonable explanation." I swallowed again, wondering what in hell I really knew. "I'll have somebody check it out with Pan Am catering in New York. They'll straighten it out."

I hung up on him.

Then I stood there, thinking it over, knowing I was going to need an Alka-Seltzer for dessert. I seemed to have this compulsion to throw dirt over the problems and pretend they weren't there. The thing was, they were such crazy problems. Seventy-three stomachs full of airline chicken. Watches that were forty-five minutes fast. Watches that ran backwards when I was looking, and reversed when I turned my back. A beautiful imposter dressed up like an airline employee.

And a voice on a tape. *They're all dead. They're all dead and burned.*

It was about that time Gordy Petcher arrived. I sent him off with my team leaders so they could fill him in. At the moment, I had no use for him at all. The bastard couldn't come when the rest of us were walking around in the mud and gore; now here he was to take credit for the findings. At least he could handle the press conferences.

We had another, slightly more informative one, after the nightly meeting. Gordy wanted to give the media something to chew on, so Tom and Eli and I worked out the short list of the things we were pretty sure of, cautioning Gordy to preface them all with words like "There are indications that—" or "We are now looking into—" or "The possibility has arisen—"

Hell, he was good at it, I'll give him that. He was a lot better than I was. He knew how to hedge his statements, how to avoid libel. The only thing that worried me was his tendency to grab for a headline, but he didn't this time. The press seemed satisfied with what it had, and gradually everyone began to file out.

Before long I was the only one left in the large conference room. It's amazing how empty a place like that can look.

She hadn't really said where she'd meet me.

The hotel, I thought. She'd be at the hotel, or leave a message.

There was no message at the desk.

I went up to my room. The maid had picked up Louise's

clothes and put them in the closet. I was thankful for the clothes. Without them, I would have started to wonder if she'd really existed.

I'd had an hour's sleep one night, and about four hours the night before. I'd slept two hours on the plane getting to California. I was stone sober and I didn't feel the least bit like sleeping. I paced the room for a while, then I went down to the bar, but it depressed me. I got in my car and drove back to the airport, out onto the field, up to the big doors of the hangar that held the remains of the two jumbo jets.

There was a human-sized door set over at the side. It had a glass window, with wire mesh in it. I knocked on the door, pressed my face up to the glass, and looked inside.

"Hey, what are you doing here?"

The guard was outside, coming up behind me. I turned slowly, not wanting to make him nervous there in the dark. He was probably a retired cop. There was the name of some security agency on his shoulder, and a .38 on his hip.

I got out my I.D. and showed it to him. He looked at it, and at my face, and relaxed.

"I saw you on television the other night," he said.

"How come you're here?" I asked him.

He shrugged.

"The company pays me to watch this hangar. Usually they've got *real* planes in there, you know. They don't want no monkey business. Funny thing, tonight I got an extra guy with me. He's on the other side, on the other door. Hard to figure, ain't it?"

"What do you mean?"

He looked through the glass.

"I mean there ain't much left to steal."

"No, I guess not."

"It's an awful thing, ain't it?"

"Yeah. It's awful." I pointed to the big padlock on the door. "You have the keys to that?"

"Sure do. You want in?"

"Yeah. You can call your employer if you want to, but I can

tell you what they'll say. Let him do whatever he wants. Until I write my report, those planes belong to me."

He looked me over, and nodded.

"I expect you're right. Though I don't know what you'd want with them."

He unlocked the door, let me through, and locked it behind me. He told me to knock again when I wanted to be let out.

I wandered around without the slightest idea of what I was looking for. All I had was the memory of that first time I saw her. She had been here, in this big barn, and she'd been looking for something.

I stopped by a massive shaft from a General Electric fanjet. All the blades were snapped off, but the heat of the fires had done nothing to it. Compared to the temperatures that shaft had been designed to take, crashing and burning was nothing at all.

I went over to where the bags of debris had been. She'd been looking at those bags. I could see it clearly now. I'd called to her, she'd looked at me, and she'd run.

The bags were gone. In their place was a series of folding tables with twisted metal piled on them. I walked along the endless rows, sometimes recognizing something, mostly having no idea what I was looking at. There's a lot of metal in a plane.

Farther along were tables holding the remains of luggage. Suitcases in pieces no bigger than your hand. Mounds of shredded and burned clothing. Squashed cameras, splintered skis, lumps of plastic that had been calculators. Even an unbroken bottle of perfume.

A red light caught my eye. It was very faint, buried under a lot of other stuff. I reached for it, and unidentifiable flotsam clattered on the floor.

First impression: a child's toy. A ray-gun. It had a plastic case that was half-melted, blackened on the outside, cracked open. The red light seeped through the crack.

Like so many things on this case, this toy didn't add up. I peered into the crack. It looked like coherent light to me: laser light. I'd never heard of a child's toy that used a laser.

There was a Swiss Army knife in my pocket. I pried out the longest blade, and stuck it in the crack. I twisted, and the plastic case popped open. I took a long look at the insides of the thing. I didn't know what the hell it was, but it wasn't a goddam toy.

Okay. Finally I had something concrete. It made me sadder than I can say to have found it, but there it was. This was some sort of weapon. It had come from the place Louise had been so interested in yesterday morning. All I could do was assume she'd known it was there, that she'd been looking for it. It was time to call Special Agent Powers. Weapons were out of my jurisdiction.

There was a phone on the wall about twenty feet away from me. I was going to call, I really intended to, but the red light was still hidden from me. It came from beneath what might have been a circuit board. I started to pry it up with my knife. I wanted to know what was making that light.

I was flat on my back on the floor. I couldn't move. I was very cold, and the back of my head hurt.

There had been a flash of light, an odd sound, starting low and going beyond the limits of my hearing, shaking the building. And suddenly I had lost all muscle control.

I had passed out, but I wasn't sure if it was from the weapon. I think I whacked my head on the corner of the table as I went down, and again on the floor.

My eyes hurt, too. I couldn't move them. I couldn't even blink. They were drying out.

For a second I thought I was dead, that this was what death was like. Then I discovered I was still breathing. I could feel the cold concrete floor under me, the cold air over me, and my chest rising and falling. I could see the lattice of steel roof girders and a couple dim lights. That was my universe.

Broken neck, I thought. Quadraplegic. Catheters and iron lungs and feces bags and no sex life . . .

But it didn't add up to a broken neck. I could feel my legs. One was bent slightly under me, and it was going to sleep. I knew when I moved—*if* I ever moved again—it would be pins and needles.

I don't remember a lot of the next few minutes. I was scared,

I don't mind admitting it. Something had happened I didn't understand. All I could do was lie there. I couldn't even look away from the ceiling.

Then I found there was something else I could do. I could hear.

It was nothing loud, but it was the only sound in the hangar, so I heard it. I decided it was two people walking, trying to do it quietly. I never would have heard them if I wasn't listening so hard.

After a long time of that, I decided it was three people. Later, I was sure it was four. It was amazing how much I could hear if it was all I had to do.

I waited. One of them would come close soon enough, and they'd decide what to do with me.

One of them did. I saw him looming into my field of vision. He was looking down at me. He turned, and whistled softly. I heard the others converging. They gathered around me. They made a circle and looked down at me. They were wearing what looked like scuba suits: all black rubber, covering everything but their faces.

"Who is it?" one of them asked.

"Who do you think?"

I knew that voice.

Well, she had said she'd see me tonight.

They debated whether or not I was alive. Then they moved out of my hearing; at least, though I could tell they were whispering about me, I couldn't hear the words. I had the impression some of them were not in English.

They came a little closer and took another look. This time I heard a few words here and there.

"... shorted something out."

"... stun beam ... focused ..."

"Damn lucky ... dead man ..."

"What the hell is he doing here *now*?" That was Louise.

"... take the stunner?"

"... Gate's due in twenty minutes ... hell out of here."

"He's sure sweating a lot."

That didn't surprise me. I didn't expect to sweat much longer, though. I knew I was a dead man. I'd stumbled into something I wasn't supposed to see, some kind of stun weapon. Since I couldn't move my eyes I hadn't gotten a good look at them, but I remembered vague shapes dangling from their belts, and everything about them shrieked *commando*. They weren't here to play games.

So I'd surely be killed.

About all I didn't understand—at least in the tactical sense—was why Louise had revealed herself to me so many times before now. Had she been trying to enlist my help in some way?

I remembered how badly she'd wanted me to stay away from work today. Okay, so she was trying to keep me from being here when they made their search . . . except that *I* hadn't even known I was going to be here until an hour ago. Normally, I wouldn't have been in this hangar at this hour.

Something had screwed up badly for them and I had no idea what it was, but I was sure the easiest solution for their present problem was for me to die.

I couldn't believe it when I heard them going away.

Then Louise was back. She loomed over me so suddenly that if I could have moved, I'd have jumped a foot. I could feel my heart hammering, and the drops of sweat flowing down the side of my face.

"Smith," she said. "You don't know me. I can't tell you who I am. But you're going to be all right."

17

"When We Went to See the End of the World"

Testimony of Louise Baltimore

I had never seen Gate Operations as quiet as it was when I stepped through from Bill's hotel room.

These things are relative, of course. I wasn't there ten seconds before the Gate Congruency Duty Officer warned me to get out of the way, and I stood aside to watch about a hundred soldiers of the Roman Second Century fall down the chutes and into the sorting apparatus.

But when they were gone, the place was utterly quiet. On a slow day Operations is about as quiet as Chinese New Year.

I went up to Gate Control. Lawrence was there at his console, which was not surprising since he couldn't leave it. What was surprising was that out of hundreds of other duty stations, there were only five or six gnomes left. It was a little bit as if, on a trip to Nepal, one discovered most of the individual peaks of the Himalayas had taken a trip to Japan.

One station still occupied was Lawrence's second-in-command, David Shanghai. He was flipping switches one at a time, and each time he hit one a light went off on his console. He had a faint smile on his face.

"Hello, Louise," Lawrence said. "I hope the assignment wasn't too hard."

"He was hard enough," I said. "What's all this? Where's everybody? I thought there wouldn't be any more snatches until this paradox was resolved."

He shrugged.

"We didn't plan to. Then this situation in North Africa presented itself, and we just decided to go for it. I guess old habits die hard. We got ninety-three centurions in prime condition. They'll be a 'lost batallion,' or whatever they call it."

David's board was almost dark now. When he had it down to one glowing ready-light, he looked up at Lawrence.

"Good-bye," he said, and he nodded to me. He turned off the last light.

His eyes closed, and he leaned back in his chair.

"Good-bye," Lawrence said, not looking at him. The words were too late, anyway. David was already dead. He'd switched off his heart, located somewhere under his chair.

"Is that where everybody went?" I asked.

"That's it. Will you be needing me for anything?"

"Fuck you. What a thing to ask. Where's Sherman?"

"He's at your apartment. He said to remind you that your second time capsule is ready to be opened in thirty minutes. After you read it, he said, you'll know what to do."

I looked at Lawrence. He didn't look back, just gazed over the deserted Operations floor.

"Are you really ready to shut yourself off?"

"There's no hurry. I can wait until you've seen Sherman."

"It's a hell of a thing for *me* to ask," I said, "but I'd appreciate it if you would. Just until I see if he has anything else in mind."

"You know where to find me."

I went to the ready-room to get some clothes. There were three of my girls in there, dead, holding hands.

"Wipe those smiles off your faces," I told them. "This is going to look terrible on your records."

They didn't seem to appreciate the humor. I went to my locker and poked through it. Talk about time's closet. I had outfits in there ranging from poorly cured leopard hide to a spacesuit you could carry in your hip pocket. But my last pair of blue jeans had been ruined about a million years ago while being worn by a wimp who was also wearing my face.

What do you wear when you go to see the end of the world? What's the proper outfit for an extinction?

I chose the dress I'd worn when we took the *Titanic*. Those had been the good old days.

There was shooting as I neared the tube station that would take me to the Federal Building. A lot of laughter punctuated the shots. It sounded like some drones were having a gay old massacre.

I hung back. The puny weapons the BC allows drones are big enough to blow out the back of your head if you put the barrel in your mouth, but they were no match for my firepower. I was in no mood to slaughter a bunch of drones, even suicidal ones.

The sounds moved away, and I entered the station. There were six or seven bodies. One of them moved, and I went to her. I turned her over. She'd taken four or five bullets, was very bloody, and a little surprised.

"It hurts," she said. I nodded.

"You may last another couple hours," I told her.

"Oh, I hope not."

I nodded again, and put my arms around her head. She looked up at me and smiled.

"I like your dress," she said.

I broke her neck.

This time there was no audience at the Fed. I went to the one chair in the room and sat down. My second time capsule was waiting for me on the table across the room.

"There you are, Louise," said the BC. "I see you made it."

"In a punctual manner of speaking."

"Would you like to open it now?"

"Is it time?"

"Close enough."

So I went to the table and took the shiny metal rectangle from the remains of the metal brick. Once again, it was in my handwriting.

No jokes this time, Louise. There is a way; all is not lost. Sherman is telling the truth. Do exactly what he says, no matter who tells you different. I'll talk to you again on the last day.

The message hadn't said anything about hurrying. It's a good thing; I wasn't in the mood to hurry, and I'd resigned from the Gate Project. I hadn't told anybody, not that it mattered.

I went to a high place on the edge of the city and looked down at what was left.

It had been a hell of a city at one time. There were buildings out there dating back forty thousand years. The Fed was the biggest one.

Then there were the newer items. The Gate had been there for thousands of years, but the structures we'd built to house it were only six hundred years old. Next to it was the derelict field. Stretching off in the other direction were a hundred square miles of wimp vaults: low warehouses with a hundred million cubicles, one of which held my child.

On the third side of the Gate complex was the series of temporary geodesic domes—they'd only been there two hundred years—which we called the holding pens. What they held were about two hundred thousand sleeping human beings and ninety-three very confused Roman centurions who would soon be asleep themselves, if anybody was still there to handle the process.

They were held in suspended animation, a few degrees above freezing. Their hearts barely beat. They floated in a blue solution of fluorocarbons and if you put one next to a wimp, you'd have had a hard time telling the difference. But that difference was all-important. They had minds, and memories, and past lives.

God, what a carnival it would have been to have set them all down on a virgin planet and awakened them!

Their birthdays ranged from 3000 B.C. to 3000 A.D. They were soldiers and civilians, infants and octogenarians, rich and poor, black, white, brown, yellow, and pale green. We had Nazis, Huguenots, Boers, Apaches, Methodists, Hindus, animists, and atheists. There were petty thieves and mass murderers and saints and geniuses and artists and pimps and doctors and shamen and witches. There were Jews from Dachau and Chinese from Tangshen and Bengalis from Bangladesh. Coal miners from Armenia and Silesia and West Virginia. Astronauts from Alpha Centauri. We had Ambrose Bierce and Amelia Earhart.

Sleepless nights, I used to wonder what sort of society they'd form when they all got to New Earth.

Leading away from the holding pens was a rail line to the spaceport, just visible in the distance. Sitting there were a few dozen surface-to-orbit craft that were seldom used these days ... and the Ship.

The Ship was almost finished. Another two or three years and we'd have made it.

Sherman was waiting with no signs of impatience. His legs weren't in lotus position, but he managed to resemble The Buddha. I regarded him, wondered if he wanted me to ring some bells or light incense or something. But I'd been coughing pretty bad since my return from the glorious twentieth, and I made a beeline to the revitalizer. I sat down heavily. As I plugged the feedline into my navel it began to take its samples.

"What are your orders?" I asked.

"Don't take it like that, Louise," he said. "I didn't ask for this."

"Neither did I. But one takes what one gets, doesn't one?"

"One does."

"Henceforth, I shall regard you as The All-Seeing Eye. I shall presume you know everything about everything. I'll presume you know my thoughts before I think them. And you know what?"

"You don't give a shit."

I shrugged. "Okay, you talk to an infallible prophet, you never get to deliver your best lines. It must make it dull, knowing exactly what's coming."

"I wouldn't call it dull."

I thought about that, and managed to laugh.

"I guess not. You know that I've resigned?"

"I do. And that you broke security and told Bill Smith who and what you actually are, as best you could, and that he didn't believe it."

"Why did you want me to tell him I'd see him that night? I'd already been back, in the hangar. I couldn't go back to his hotel room."

"I wanted to insure he'd be in the hangar to meet you, as we knew he had already done."

That one stumped me for a minute. The answer was obvious, but I didn't see it because all my training had forced me to look at the situation in a particular way. Then I saw.

"You were forcing the paradox."

"Correct."

"Why didn't you tell me?"

"Would you have done it?"

I couldn't answer that. Probably not.

"The Council would not have authorized the trip, either," he went on, "if I had told them its purpose was to be sure you and Smith *did* meet. Your meeting him was what caused the paradox situation to get out of hand in the first place."

"Then what's the point? Why did I go back?"

He steepled his fingertips and was silent for quite a while. For a moment he looked startlingly human.

"All of us in the Gate Project are saddled with a certain perspective," he began, at last. "We think of *this* moment as the, quote, *present,* unquote. When we move downtime, we think of it as *going into the past,* and of coming back as returning to the present. But when we arrive in the past, it *is* the present. It is the present to those who live there. To them, we have come from the future."

"This is pretty elementary."

"Yes. But I'm speaking of perspective. Running the Gate, as we do, we are unaccustomed to Bill Smith's perspective. We aren't used to the idea that there is a concrete future that is someone else's present."

I sat up straighter.

"Sure we are. I got a message from the future no more than an hour ago. It told me to trust you."

"I know. But who was it from?"

"From me, you know that. At least..."

"From a future version of you. But you haven't written it yet."

"For that matter, I haven't written the first one yet, either. And I'm not sure I will."

"You don't have to. Look at these." He handed me two metal plaques. I knew what they had to be, but I looked anyway. I tossed them on the floor.

"Handwriting is easy to copy, Louise. The BC turned these out with very little effort. They will be sent back in a few hours."

I sighed. "Okay, you've got me coming and going, I'll admit it. You still haven't told me why one paradox is preferable to another."

"There are several reasons. In one paradox—the one we would have caused had you not gone back and spent the night with Bill Smith—you would have vanished the instant the appointed time arrived and you failed to step through the Gate. Because, seen from the future, you already *had* stepped through. It was part of the structure of events, as surely as the loss of the stunner was part of that structure."

"But it *wasn't*. That's what this has all been about."

"It was. I'm saying the paradox is built into the structure of time. That the events we have for so many years been observing is the illusion, and the new reality that is now working its way up the timeline is the *real* reality. And it doesn't include us."

He was making my head ache. Time theory had never been my strong point. I grasped that one word, and held on to it.

"I thought these were all theories. I thought we didn't really *know* what would happen in a paradox."

"They were. I've received new information that I have reason to believe is reliable." He spread his hands. "We're handicapped here by the language. We don't have a useful definition of 'reality,' for one thing. I believe that what is closer to the truth is that each series of possible events creates its own reality. There is the one we've been looking at, in which Smith never found the stunner, and it's tied up with the one where he *couldn't* have found it because it was never lost.''

"But what we're dealing with here is the one in which it *was* lost, and he *did* find it, and reality is rearranging itself. And it's going to leave us out.''

"That's true, so far as it goes.''

"I'm afraid it's as far as *I* can go. What you're saying is that it didn't . . . doesn't matter whether or not I went back. If I didn't, I'd simply have vanished that much faster.''

He looked at me with his much more expressive face, and I saw something that I couldn't identify.

"It may have little meaning in the long run,'' he said. "But I myself would prefer a universe where you were still here over one where you had already vanished.''

I didn't know what to say about that. I ran it through the battered mechanism I was using for a brain, and came up with something. Two things.

"Thank you,'' was the first thing. "But did you really have a choice?''

"I don't know. If the information from my time capsule had told me I must eliminate you from the timestream, I'd prefer to think I would have resisted it. Luckily, my only course was to do what I *did* do, which was also what I wanted to do.''

"Do we have free will, Sherman?''

"Yes.''

"You can say that, sitting there knowing what's about to happen, what I'm about to do?''

"Yes. I wouldn't be trying to convince you of what we must do if I didn't think we had free will.''

I thought that one over.

"Don't try to shit me, Sherman. You know I've resigned, and yet you seem to be saying there's still something we can do. If we're going to do it, you're going to have to convince me to reenlist.''

He grinned at me. I swear it.

"We do have free will, Louise. It's just that it's predestined.''

"I'm tired of the word games. You know I'm about ready to join the majority and jump through that window over there. You also know there's only one way you can stop me, which is to tell me what you know, and what you plan to do."

So he told me.

By then I was sure the universe could no longer surprise me, nor interest me. I was wrong. It managed to do both in no more than ten minutes.

And while he told me, the revitalizer—which had been pumping me full of drugs and nutrients while at the same time examining my physical condition—spoke up with the confirmation.

My apartment building—never a lively place at the best of times—was grim as Sherman and I embarked on the slidewalk. Word had gotten out that the end of the world was coming. Not many of the drones wanted to watch it. Their bodies littered the atrium.

No, littered is too strong a word. When you got right down to it, the Last Age couldn't even produce an impressive scene of carnage. We had maybe three hundred thousand drones in a city that was built for thirty million. The bodies were tastefully spaced. There was something almost Japanese about it: a long, Bauhaus corridor and one corpse slightly offset. The art of body-arrangement.

There was one couple who had made their suicide pact while in the act of coitus. I thought it was rather sweet, after all the bloody jumpers. Getting back to basics in one's last moments.

Suicide has always been our national pastime. By now, it was an epidemic. When we entered the Council Chamber we found they were down to five. No hope of making the World Series, I thought. Maybe we could play basketball.

The Nameless One was still there. I wondered if he/she/it would notice the end of the world. So was Nancy Yokohama, and Marybeth Brest, the talking head.

And of course Peter Phoenix. I figured he'd want to be there at the end to make sure everything got done properly.

The new member was Martin Coventry. He still seemed mobile. I guess the BC had called him in for lack of any *really* old players on the bench.

I was proud of Sherman. There is something to be said for putting on a show. He knew the outcome, yet he still played the moment for all it was worth. He went right up to their big curved table, lifted one leg, and sat down on it. Marybeth Brest scowled at him. He reached over and tousled her hair.

"You're probably wondering why I've called you together," he said.

The BC made an exception this one time, due to the infirmities of the Council. Having them come to the Fed would have involved a lot of logistical planning, since most of their bodily functions were performed by several tons of machinery. The five time capsules were sent over, and opened in their presence. I watched as they read the messages. They all said pretty much what my last time capsule had said: Do whatever he tells you.

Sherman gave them time to digest the messages. Then he stood up and faced them.

"Now. Here's what we're going to do."

18

"The Twonky"

Testimony of Bill Smith

So I rushed out of the hangar, alerted the FBI and the CIA and all the newspapers. The Governor called out the National Guard and the President called a special session of Congress. All the big think tanks put their best minds to work on the problem. I was debriefed endlessly, everyone wanting to know exactly what Louise Ball had said and what she had done every time I'd met her.

And if you believe any of that, you're a bigger fool than I am.

What I did was stop by a bar for a drink or four, and then call Tom Stanley. He was asleep, but said he'd listen to me. I drove to his hotel room, sat down with him, and told him the whole story. I told him what Louise had told me, and I was amazed how different it sounded in the light of my experiences in the hangar. I told him what had happened to me, what I'd seen and heard, how I'd come around just as Louise had said I would, with a leg that hurt like hell and the beginnings of a bad cold from lying two hours on cold concrete.

"She *told* me she was from somewhere else Tom." I said. "Someplace where everybody dies. Somewhere a long ways from here, or a long time. I thought she was crazy. But she *didn't know me*! I'd just spent the night with her, and she said, 'Smith, you don't know me,' and I knew she wasn't kidding. *She hadn't met me yet*.

"And that thing . . . that stunner. I didn't get to look into it very long, and they took it with them, but it didn't look like anything I'd ever seen before. And it knocked me out, but I could still breathe okay, but I couldn't even move my eyeballs. I just looked straight up. I thought they were Russians, or something. I thought they were going to kill me. But, see, they *couldn't* kill me, or Louise wouldn't let them . . . I don't know.''

I trailed off. I don't know how long I'd been going on about it. Tom had listened quietly.

"So who was she?" he finally said. "Where did she come from?"

"I don't know. But don't you see? We've got to find out."

There was a very long silence. He wouldn't look at me.

"Those watches, Tom. What about the watches? Something happened to them to make some of them go backwards, and the rest of them were forty-five minutes off. Forty-five minutes, Tom.''

He looked up, then down again.

"And the tape. He said they were all dead and burned. Dead and burned. Why would he say a thing like that? Tom, are you going to ask me how much I've had to drink?''

He looked up again.

"Something like that."

"What can I do to convince you?"

He spread his hands.

"Bill . . . I want to believe you . . . no, wait." He shook his head. "That's a lie. I don't want to believe you. Would you? I mean, it's a crazy story, Bill. It's crazy. But I'm willing to believe you if you show me something."

"What?"

He shrugged. "That's up to you, isn't it? Anything. Anything at all that's concrete. Put something in my hand. Otherwise, much as I hate to say this . . . I think you've just flipped out about this girl. I don't know why. But why don't you go home and sleep on it? Maybe you'll think of something."

Damn, but that was an embarrassing situation. I think, in many ways, it was worse than all that followed.

There was no reason in the world why Tom should take my word on a story as ridiculous as this one. And yet, if I had a friend in the world, he was it. If I couldn't convince him, who was I going to convince?

The situation seemed to call for decisive action, so I took it. I bought a bottle and went back to my room and got drunk.

The next morning I started tackling it a piece at a time.

The CVR Tape:

"I think that's been disposed of to everyone's satisfaction," Gordy said at the meeting that night. "Carole's analysis of DeLisle's words makes sense to me. She's got people looking into his records. He had a medical furlough five years ago. There's some evidence he might have been unstable. I don't know why you want to keep beating this one, Bill; it's a dead horse."

The consensus was we wouldn't release that part with the rest of the CVR transcript. It would be included in the official report, but that wouldn't be finished for about a year and by then nobody would give a damn.

Round Two, the kooky klocks:

"It never happened," said Special Agent Freddie Powers over a cup of coffee at the Oakland FBI office.

"What do you mean? We saw it. So did the doctor."

"He doesn't remember it, and neither do I." He looked around furtively, like we were in a cheap spy film.

"Look, Smith, I've had a friend in San Mateo working with IC chips like the ones in those watches. He's done everything to them. He's burned them up, shot a thousand volts through them, done everything he could think of. The best he's come up with yet is watches that don't work. If he can duplicate it, I thought, I'd be willing to report it. But it's too late now. My report is already filed, and it doesn't mean a damn thing anyway, and they don't *like* funny, unsolved shit in your record."

"I thought you were the guy who liked to tackle the hard ones."

"Piss off, buddy. I'll do a hell of a lot for something that's important. But this isn't shit. It's just a nutty thing that can make us both look like a couple of nuts."

"I really thought you'd go to the wall on it. I didn't think you'd cover up evidence."

He leaned a little closer to me.

"A word to the wise, Bill. You're damn close to the wall, yourself. A padded wall. I've heard some things, you know how they get around. They say the guys upstairs don't like you reassembling that 747; they say it costs too much and we won't learn anything. Maybe you ought to take a vacation, go someplace and dry out, before somebody does it for you."

Kooky klocks, Part Two:

So we had a lot of watches that were off by forty-five minutes.

So what?

Round Four, and the challenger staggers, bloodied, from his corner:

Twelve dozen stomachs full of airline chicken. And five with beef, and one with cottage cheese.

It was obviously a mistake in Pan Am's records—which showed the normal distribution of beef vs. chicken plates—or a statistical anomaly with no bearing on the crash.

I gave up that round before it really got started, on points. The important thing was to stay on my feet until I got my shot.

But by then I was down to pretty slim possibilities. I flew back to Washington for the weekend, and on Monday I made the rounds of the wire services.

I wasn't peddling a story to them; that first night had shown me the futility of that. In fact, I was careful to ask my few friends in the news media to keep this very quiet and unofficial. I asked for their stills and videotapes of that first press conference in Oakland.

I got Louise three separate times, twice in stills and once on a tape. None of them were very good, but I had the best picture blown up and I took it over to the FBI, where I still had a few friends who owed me favors.

A week later I got my answer. The picture had produced nothing. Her fingerprints on the highball glass I'd managed to save were not on file with any Federal agency. A search of the computers revealed several dozen Louise Balls, but none of them was her.

If you live in Washington long enough you can make a lot of acquaintances. I had one in the Central Intelligence Agency. I gave him the picture. He didn't promise me anything, but two weeks later he got back to me. He cautioned me to remember that we'd never met, that he'd done me no favors—but that it really wasn't important, since he'd come up with nothing at all.

After about a month I was getting unpopular at the Oakland headquarters. Even Tom was going out of his way to avoid me. I knew Gordy saw me as a liability. So far, no one had challenged my authority to run the investigation, but some people were starting to clamor.

It hadn't gone over well when I'd dragged my feet on releasing the corpses. At the best of times it takes quite a while to get them all released to the next of kin. As things stood, I didn't want to release *anything* related to the investigation. Tom finally convinced me I had to let them go.

And there had been raised eyebrows when I'd decided to reconstruct the 747. I'd have done the DC-10, too, but even in my present state I could see that would be going too far. But I stood my ground, and it *is* NTSB policy that reconstructions are sometimes useful in mid-air collisions; it's just that no one else agreed that it might be useful *this* time.

The call back to Washington came in the middle of January.

I woke up in a smelly bed with the sun shining through a yellowed window shade. I didn't have the slightest idea where I was. I got up, found I was wearing only a pair of shorts. The smell came with me; I realized I hadn't washed in a while. I rubbed my chin and felt several days' growth of beard.

I looked out the window and saw I was on the second floor of a hotel on Q street. Across the way was a familiar massage parlor. There was some snow in the gutters.

I remembered the meeting in general terms. All the Board

members had been there, trying their best not to be angry. All they really wanted was an explanation, they had said, and that was the one thing I couldn't give them.

But what the hell? I was going to be fired anyway, I could see that, so what could I lose by trying?

I talked to them about it for half an hour. I tried to think of myself as a cop on the witness stand, to phrase myself in that precise, unemotional way they have, doing my best not to sound like a nut. It didn't do any good; I sounded like a nut even to myself.

They were gentle about it, I'll give them that. I seemed harmless, beaten, a drunk who had broken under pressure. I felt like I ought to have a couple of ball bearings to roll around in one hand to complete the atmosphere.

It was almost as if I had watched the proceedings from outside.

That feeling persisted even after I got to the bar. I dispassionately watched myself hoist the first few, then finally settled down into my body, to find it was sweating and shaking. Still, it felt good to be back. For a while there I think I really was crazy. I might have done anything.

What I *had* done, apparently, was drink for two or three days and end up in a flophouse on Q street. Like a dog returning to its vomit, I'd known where to go.

My pants were draped over a chair. I took out my wallet. There were a couple of twenties in it.

Somebody knocked on the door. I pulled on the pants and opened it.

It was a girl from the parlor. I'd been with her a couple of times. I reached for the name, and came up with it.

"Hi, Gloria. How did you know I was here?"

"I put you here, last night. Didn't think you could get home."

"You were probably right."

She sat on the bed as I put on my shirt. Gloria was a tall, skinny mulatto with tired eyes and yellow hair. She was wearing a black leotard and pantyhose. I wondered if she'd run across the street in that outfit.

"What do I owe you for the room?"

"I took the money out of your pocket," she said. "Some of them girls, they say I ought to take it all, but I don't go for that."

"Good for you," I said, and meant it. Just then, I couldn't remember how long it had been since someone had done me a favor.

"Will you marry me, Gloria?" I asked her.

She made a shushing motion, and chuckled. "I told you I'm already married."

I tied my shoes, got out my wallet, and pressed a twenty into her hand. She didn't make a fuss about it; just nodded her head.

"You want to party? You wasn't feeling so hot last night."

"You mean I couldn't get it up? No, I'll pass. Maybe I'll see you later."

"Last night, you said you lost your job."

"That's right."

"And you been drinking mighty heavy. Is that why?"

"No, Gloria. I'm drinking because I'm being chased by spooks from the fourth dimension."

She laughed, and slapped her knee.

"That'll do it," she said.

I couldn't remember where I'd left my car. No doubt the police would inform me where it was in a few days. I took a cab back to Kensington. The house was very cold. I got the furnace roaring, took a long soak in a hot tub, shaved, had a bowl of cereal, and by the time I was ready for bed it was nice and warm.

I sat there on the edge of the bed, wondering what came next. I really doubted I could get any aviation-related job, and I didn't know anything else. I wasn't ready to die. Drinking myself to death didn't sound like a great idea, though it might look better in the morning.

The phone rang.

"Is this Bill Smith, of the Safety Board?"

"Formerly of," I said.

"That's what I heard. I've been talking to some of your former associates. They're trying to keep it quiet, but I've heard you've got quite a story. Something about UFO's causing those planes to crash last month in California. If we could get together sometime tomorrow I can guarantee you a hearing you won't get from the *New York Times*."

"You're a reporter?"

"Didn't I say that? I'm Irving Green from the *National Enquirer*. All I want is half an hour of your time. We could work it up, I'll write it, don't worry about that. If it's good, there's a chance of a book, and then who knows? The movies are pretty hot on this sort of thing right now—"

I hung up. I wasn't even angry. But I couldn't see the point of getting my story to the world right next to the latest cure for cancer and the affairs of Jackie, Burt, and Charlie's Angels.

But the call had reminded me of something. I had to look for a while, but I found it soon enough. I called American Airlines, because it was the first carrier in the phone book that might be going where I wanted to go.

Five hours later I was on a red-eye flight to Los Angeles.

I rented a car at LAX and headed out toward Santa Barbara. I hadn't called ahead to see if he was home, because I didn't want to admit to myself what I was doing, and on what thin motivation.

Arnold Mayer had quite a place. I knew how to find him because, a few days after he'd questioned me at the press conference, he'd sent me a business card with his address and phone number. That was back when I still thought I could develop something someone would listen to. Now I was down to him. He'd wanted to know if I had come up with anything unusual, and I was ready to bend his ear.

I drove by a few times before I got up the nerve to stop. It was out in the country, on a couple overgrown acres. There was a high antenna that looked to me like ham equipment, a bank of solar heat collectors, and a large and quite expensive satellite dish sitting in his front yard, aimed into the morning sky.

He didn't seem worried about pleasing the neighbors—not that he had to; the last house I'd seen had been a mile back down the road. His yard had gone to seed. There were things here and there, like the fuselage of an old Air Force F–86 with a rusted-out engine sitting beside it. There were automotive hulks, too, and old television sets and a big pile of all sorts of electronic equipment, from ancient UNIVAC machines to the guts of a fairly recent videotape recorder.

It sounds like I'm talking about a Georgia sharecropper's yard, and that was certainly the atmosphere it gave off. But this was high-tech junk, and the house that stood in the middle of it all was sturdy red brick, two stories high. Antennas sprouted from every cornice and gable.

The sidewalk was cracked, and the varnish had long since vanished from his front door. Yet everything still looked basically sound. I decided he just didn't give a damn for fancy finishes.

I took a deep breath, and pushed the doorbell. Somewhere inside, I heard that silly little five-note theme from *Close Encounters*. I hoped it was a joke.

I wasn't prepared for how tall he was. He'd looked shorter from the podium where I'd stood that night. Most of the top of his head was bald and shiny. What hair he did have was pure white. He didn't look a bit like Einstein, but I thought of him anyway. He was wearing a yellow shirt with a little alligator and a pair of paint-stained work pants.

"Bill Smith," he said, with a sympathetic smile. He put his hand lightly on my shoulder and stood aside, guiding me in with an easy intimacy I wasn't sure I liked. He closed the door and turned to face me.

"I've been expecting you," he said.

"That's interesting, because I didn't know until a few hours ago I was coming here."

"But where else could you come? I've heard what happened to you. I'm sorry, though I can't say I'm surprised."

"What do you know?"

"Very little. Just that you've been behaving erratically. My sources have given me the most fascinating tidbits—nothing but rumors, really. I had hoped you might come discuss them with me. And here you are."

"I'm not sure why I'm here."

He scrutinized me, and nodded. "Why don't you wait in my study for a moment and think it over. I have something on the fire in the other room, and it won't wait."

I was going to protest, but he was already gone.

His "study" was weird. I loved it.

One wall was mostly glass. It looked out over a valley. In the far distance was a major highway. A little closer was an orchard of some kind. And up close was his back yard, which couldn't have been more different from the front. There was a large vegetable garden back there, lovingly tended.

The walls were all bookcases, which were all jammed. Among the books were computer tapes, floppy discs, records, loose manuscripts, magazines, and journals. There was furniture in the room, but to sit in any of the chairs I would have had to move a stack of papers. He had a magnificent old wooden desk. On it was a fancy computer terminal, and behind it was a stereo system cobbled together from laboratory digital components. There were speakers big enough to pulverize Carnegie Hall.

It was a jumbled museum. There were stuffed birds in glass bell jars, a brass astrolabe, a globe that would have made Nero Wolfe turn green with envy. There was also a gas chromatograph with its guts torn out and tools lying around it, an Edison phonograph for playing cylinders, three IBM Selectrics stacked in a corner gathering dust, a giant Xerox machine that stretched through a doorway into another room, and a crystal ball that wouldn't have made it through an NBA hoop. Sitting here and there on tables were bits and pieces of laboratory glassware.

The only bare wall was over the fireplace—bare in the sense of having no bookcases. There were a few trophies on the mantel, and pictures and diplomas hung on every available square inch.

I'd been looking at one for quite a while before I realized it was a Nobel Prize. I'd thought the actual prizes were medals, but maybe he had that tucked away somewhere. This was an ornate parchment, for Physics, and it was dated in the '60s. I thought I should have known his name, but they give those things away to four or five people every year and usually you've never heard of them and have no idea what they were given for. Still, I was impressed.

There was a picture of Mayer with President Eisenhower. Signed: "Regards, Ike." There was a group picture: Mayer, Linus Pauling, Oppenheimer, and Edward Teller. There was a shot of a *much* younger Mayer shaking hands with Mr. Relativity himself: Albert Einstein. It was unsigned. I was right, Mayer didn't look anything like him.

"I confess it," he said, behind me. "I'm a pack rat. I can never seem to throw anything away. I used to, and then a few years later I'd try to find it and it wouldn't be there."

He hurried into the room, wiping his hands on a towel. He seemed nervous. I wondered why, until he picked up a plate with a half-eaten sandwich on it and a wine glass with a red stain at the bottom. He kept bustling around the room, not making a dent in the clutter but seeming to feel he had to clean up.

"I have a girl who comes in once a week," he apologized. "She manages my excesses. Makes sure typhoid doesn't get a foothold." He picked up a soiled shirt and a single red sock.

"Doctor Mayer, I don't—"

"You might wonder how she knows what is excess and what is not," he said, on his way out the door. I heard him dumping the debris somewhere, raising his voice so I could hear him. "It's not an easy task, but I have trained her fairly well. She will not disturb the important experiments in progress. She sticks to the spoiled food and spilled coffee." He was back now, helplessly scanning the room.

"Doctor Mayer, it doesn't matter to me. I know what a working laboratory can look like."

"You might not believe it," he said, "but I know where everything is."

"I thought you would."

He looked at me closely for the first time since his return, and he seemed to relax a little. God knows, the *last* thing I had expected was to have to reassure *him*.

"Call me Arnold, please," he said. "I don't go for the Doctor bullshit."

* * *

He eventually got me settled in a comfortable red leather chair facing his desk, with a glass of The Glenlivet sitting on a table beside me. I raised the glass and sipped; I thought I ought to keep my wits about me.

"You go first class," I said, indicating the bottle of whiskey.

"Some lucrative patents," he said, with a shrug. "Investments. They provide enough money for an old fool to indulge his wild theories."

"Are you a theoretical or applied physicist?"

He laughed, looked at me askance, and settled down in his chair. I had the feeling he was humoring me; he knew I had come to tell him a story, but I couldn't just come right out with it.

"A little of both, these days. I was always a tinkerer, but I made my reputation in pure physics, in mathematics. A 'physicist,' these days, is usually more engineer than scientist, to my way of thinking. While I've never been afraid to get my hands dirty, I tired of weapons development. I have no interest in building a more powerful laser or a smaller fusion bomb. If you weren't already in such trouble, I'd feel honor-bound to warn you away from me. I'm a terrible security risk. Being seen with me is enough to get you kicked out of almost any government job."

"That's no problem anymore."

"Indeed. At any rate . . . they wanted me to work on a larger particle accelerator. I decided not to. I kept thinking of Newton, of Roentgen . . . men like that. Men who did the basic thinking that led to gigawatt particle accelerators."

"You don't think those accelerators are worthwhile research tools?"

"On the contrary. I keep abreast of all the results. It may very well be that the breakthrough I'm looking for will come from Batavia, or Stanford. But I don't really think so. I think it will come from the most unexpected place, as so many breakthroughs do. Something as simple as Wilhelm Roentgen accidentally exposing a photographic plate and discovering X rays."

"So what is it you're looking for? What is your basic research?"

"The nature of time," he said, and leaned forward. "And now that you've examined my bona fides, I think it's your turn."

I took another sip of the whiskey, and started to tell him.

It took most of the morning. I went into great detail, much more than I had been willing or able to before the Board.

He asked very little, but took a lot of notes. A few minutes into the story he asked if I minded being recorded. I said I didn't care. He didn't turn anything on, so I assumed he'd been doing it right along.

At lunchtime he led me into the kitchen. I talked while he prepared a salad and some cold-cut sandwiches. We ate them, and I continued to talk.

And finally I was through. I looked at the glass of whiskey and saw it was still half-full. I've got to say, that made me proud.

To be honest, I had expected an uncritical reception. The little I knew about Mayer was from a few comments Roger Keane and Kevin Briley had made after the night of that press conference, to the effect that he was the "local crackpot," who showed up at air crashes and other disasters all over California and much of the west. I had expected a sympathetic ear, one as eager to fall for my 'evidence' as a grad student in astrology looking at one of Uri Geller's spoons.

So what did Mayer do?

He grilled me unmercifully for two hours. If the bastard had been running for California Attorney General, he'd have had my vote.

He went at me up, down, and sideways. He had me sketch the stunner Louise had taken from me. He tore at anything that looked inconsistent—and let's face it, that included the whole unlikely story. He wanted to see physical evidence. I'd brought it with me, and laid it out before him: Louise's clothes, the glass she had handled, a photo of the fingerprints obtained from it, ten grainy blowups of her face from various angles, photostats of the autopsy reports, a watch I'd stolen that was still off by forty-five minutes because I'd kept winding it, a Vicks inhaler, and an empty package of Clorets.

He sniffed the inhaler, and wrinkled his nose. The smell was faint by now, but it was still foul. He fingered the material of her skirt, poked at her abandoned underwear with a pencil eraser.

"We can run some tests on this cloth," he said. "Though I doubt it would tell us anything. Tell me, Bill, would you object to telling this story again, under hypnosis?"

I laughed.

"I'd try anything, Arnold, but I don't think that'll do you any good. I've tried it before, and I can't be hypnotized."

"When I count three, you will wake up, refreshed. One, two, three."

I sat up. I felt great. Naturally, it hadn't done them any good, I'd just told the story again as I had before...

Son of a bitch.

"You did it," I said, awed. "You put me under."

I was talking to one of the two other people in the room, Doctor Leggio, who Arnold had called after I agreed to try hypnotism. He was a medical doctor.

"I remember everything," I said, still a little stunned. "I was just going along with the joke..."

Leggio laughed.

"That's the only way to make it work, Mister Smith. You were a good subject. Your memory is excellent."

I looked at Mayer.

"And I told it just the same way, didn't I?"

He nodded, grudgingly.

"We obtained more detail...but, yes, you never wavered."

The doorbell rang its little five-note theme again. Leggio was shaking hands with me as he got ready to leave, and so was the other new arrival, who I hadn't talked to at all because she'd arrived while I was under and Leggio hadn't asked me to talk to her. She was Frances Schrader, and she had a doctorate in biochemistry and a talent for pencil sketching. Damn, the doctors were getting so thick around that place I could hardly walk.

Leggio and Schrader left, and in came a new fellow lugging some heavy equipment. While he was opening it and setting it up, Arnold introduced us. The man was Phil Karakov, and he was a polygraph expert.

I sighed, sat down, and let them hook me up.

* * *

"I can't shake anything in his story," Karakov said, at last.

Mayer didn't seem to be listening closely. I was feeling relief that I'd passed the lie detector as well as the hypnotic examination, and here was Mayer, gazing out the window at the sun setting over the orchard.

"Thank you, Phil," he said. "I'll let you know what becomes of this."

Karakov packed up his equipment and left. Mayer continued to stare out the window. Then he picked up the sketch Frances Schrader had made, looked at it, and tossed it to me.

It was very good. Leggio had made me recall things about the stunner that I hadn't been able to get at before. Schrader had worked with me looking over her shoulder, erasing and filling in details as Leggio pressed me to look deeper into my mind. There were two views, one much better than the other. The first showed what I'd seen on the outside. The second showed the inner workings, which I'd only seen for a second before I got zapped.

Mayer seemed finally about to say something, when his trick doorbell rang again. He frowned, got up, and went to the front door. He was back soon.

"No one there," he said. "That's never happened—"

It rang again. He looked like he'd bit into something sour, but once more he went to the door. He was gone longer this time. While he was gone, the damn thing chimed three more times.

"I looked all around. It must be malfunctioning. I disconnected it, so it shouldn't give us any more—"

It rang again. He was about to say something nasty, when his Edison phonograph started to play. It was some Scottish ditty, scratchy as hell. While we were still staring at that, his hi-fi came on at full volume with something that must have been Wagner. As he hurried to shut it off, the Xerox machine started to run. It was spewing paper all over the place. I could see his computer terminal had lit up. All the lights in the house dimmed, then came on very bright.

I was on my feet by then. I wouldn't have been surprised if a fleet of toy cars had come through the kitchen door, followed by a vacuum cleaner. Steve Spielberg, where are you now that we need you?

Then every pane in Mayer's glass wall blew out into the vegetable garden.

19
Lest Darkness Fall

We were looking down an infinite tunnel.

There was a sound. I'd heard it before: the low rumble as I stood in the hallway outside my hotel room. This time it was much louder. The floor started to shake, and two points of very bright light appeared somewhere along the length of that impossible tunnel.

The tunnel wasn't even there, really. I could see the trees of the orchard right through it. There were odd shapes that I didn't like to look at, so I focused on the bright lights.

The lights started to take on the shape of humans. Then the perspective went all crazy and a high wind began to blow. Papers were swirling around us, and everything in the room got shiny, like it had been in my hotel room when I opened the door. I looked at my hand; it was shiny, but not cold. I looked back at the tunnel. One moment the lights were a hundred miles away, and the next they were in our laps, only to flicker into the distance again.

Then it was over. Louise was standing in the ruins of Arnold's windows. She was wearing the black commando outfit she'd had on that night in the hangar. Standing beside her was something else. I didn't know what to make of it at first. It was humanoid, it had a face and two arms and two legs. Parts of it looked like the robot from _Star Wars_, and parts looked more like Gumby, that little clay cartoon figure. It moved fluidly and didn't seem to have any seams. But it was big, and built like a weightlifter.

There was no doubt in my mind. This wasn't a human being

in a funny suit. This was an alien creature, or a robot, or *something* I'd never seen before.

Arnold Mayer got his voice back first.

"I presume you are Louise Ball," he said.

"Baltimore, actually," she said, coming into the room. "From a long line of Marylander-Columbians." She reached a chair a few feet from the one I'd been sitting in, tilted it to dump the pile of books and papers onto the floor, and sat. "My companion is Sherman."

"Pleased to meet you, Doctor Mayer, Mister Smith," Sherman said. He continued to stand near the ruined glass wall.

"He's a mechanical man," Louise went on. "A robot, if you wish. He's at least as smart as either of you, and he's a hundred times as strong and a thousand times as fast. I named him after a tank used in the First Atomic War."

"Is that a threat?" Mayer asked.

"Take it however you want. You've got something I want—"

"Are you really from Maryland?" I asked.

She looked at me, and I thought I saw some sympathy there. At least I hoped I did. She'd come into my life and left it in ruins. It would have been nice if she'd felt some remorse for it.

"My forebears are. You're probably one of my great-grand-uncles or something, fifteen thousand times removed. But at this point the race hasn't started to differentiate into distinct..." She looked away, and rubbed her forehead.

"This isn't relevant," she went on, and turned back to Mayer. "You have something I want. Something I have to have. I intend to get it."

"I don't know what you're talking about," Mayer said.

"You're lying. Sherman, where is it?"

"I don't know, Louise," the robot said, in a voice deeper and more threatening than it had used in its earlier friendly greeting. "I'm not getting a reading."

"Well, probe the room."

If he did "probe the room," he did it quickly. Without a pause, he pointed to the mantelpiece covered with picture frames.

"There is a safe hidden behind the central picture," he said.

Louise stood, pointed her finger at the picture. It swung away on hinges. She made some complicated motions, and I saw the dial spin back and forth, then the door swung open.

"How did you do that?" I asked.

"Magic," she said. She went to the safe and started throwing its contents onto the floor. Mayer took a step in her direction; Sherman made a throat-clearing noise and wagged a warning finger. It was enough for Mayer; it probably would have been enough for me, too. That bastard was huge.

Gold coins and stock certificates were soon scattered around Louise's feet. She came up with an old army Colt .45 and tossed it to Sherman, who shredded it. What I mean is, he threw the ammo clip about a mile into the dark, and rubbed the gun between his hands until it fell in a shower of metal chips. I felt a drop of sweat trickle down my back.

"It's not here," she said, returning to her chair but not sitting down. "Shall we start tearing this place apart brick by brick?"

"If you must," Mayer said. I had to hand it to him; the old guy didn't seem afraid. He stood his ground.

"It's in his desk," Sherman said, and Mayer's face fell. More magic, I guess. There was no doubt in Sherman's voice.

"The desk is locked," Mayer said. "I don't have the key."

"We don't have time for games, Doctor," Louise said. "Sherman, open it."

Sherman went around the desk.

"Excuse me," he said to Mayer, and gently moved him out of the way. Then he looked at the computer terminal. He seemed undecided about something. Then he shrugged.

"Pardon me," he told the terminal, and picked it up and set it gently on the floor. I thought I caught Louise about to laugh; damn if I didn't almost laugh myself. I'm glad I didn't. It probably would have sounded hysterical when Sherman opened the desk. He took hold of the top edge and peeled it like a cardboard box. The top three drawers lay exposed, and in the middle one was something that looked awfully familiar.

"You've got it!" I shouted. "You had it in your desk all this time, and you made me go through that damn story over and over—"

Words failed me. I forgot about Louise in her commando

duds, forgot about Sherman the android tank, forgot about everything but the stunner Louise had stolen from me that night, and which she was now lifting from Mayer's desk drawer.

"Don't be silly, Bill," she said. "This is another one. It isn't even burned. Take a look." And she tossed it to me.

I looked at it. She was right. This one was intact. I turned it over in my hands, noted the position of the trigger and of a little switch on the side. It occurred to me that I was holding a powerful weapon.

I looked up at Louise, and a stunner materialized in her hand, pointed at my forehead. One moment it was in a holster on her hip, and the next it was in her hand.

"You wouldn't shoot me, would you, Louise?"

She gave me an odd look, then an odd smile, and the weapon was back in its holster. I'd heard a whirring sound that time, but I still didn't see how it was done.

"You're right," she said, and turned away. "Sherman, if he tries anything funny, shoot to disable."

"Right."

So much for undying love. And I was no fool; I put the stunner on the remains of Mayer's desk and went back toward my chair. Louise was already sitting, but I was too agitated to do anything but stand.

Louise had her elbows on the chair arms, and was massaging her forehead with the tips of her fingers. She looked very tired. She spoke without looking up.

"Sherman, there's something wrong with that stunner. Will you take a look?"

The robot picked it up, turned it over in his hands, then did something that made it split into two halves. There wasn't anything inside. It was just a plastic shell.

"I thought it felt light," she said, when he showed it to her. She looked to Mayer. "Doctor Mayer, I want to know—"

"I prefer not to be called Doctor," Mayer said.

"Doctor Mayer," Louise said, pointedly, "this stunner belongs to me. One of my people lost it. I'd like to know where you got it."

"Where did you lose it?"

"I'm asking the questions here."

"And maybe I'm not answering them."

Louise sighed. "Why don't we dispense with the melodramatic talk, Doctor?"

"That cuts both ways," Mayer said. I looked at him again. He was calm on the outside, but now I saw he was smouldering underneath. I guess I would have been, too, if somebody'd just ripped my desk apart. On the other hand, there was Sherman, and I thought Mayer was making a very dangerous stand.

"I lost the stunner about a week ago," Louise said. "In 1955."

"And I found it thirty years ago. Also in 1955."

Louise glanced at Sherman.

"I think he's lying," the robot said. Louise nodded, and gestured for Sherman to go to Mayer. As the robot did so, Mayer lost a little of his composure.

"Are you going to torture me?" he asked.

"Depends on how melodramatic you want to get." Mayer made an involuntary move away as Sherman took him by the arm. The robot encircled Mayer's wrist with his huge metal hand, and waited, just holding it there.

"Did you find it yourself?" Louise asked.

"Yes," Mayer said. Sherman shook his head.

"Who did find it?"

Mayer looked down at Sherman's hand, and then I did too, and I'll bet we both had the same thought at the same time: *polygraph*. Or the far-future equivalent, which I was willing to bet was better than the one used on me earlier that same day.

"That's right," Louise said, making me wonder if mind-reading was one of her many talents. "Now, we can play twenty questions and a lie will tell me as much as the truth, but it takes a while to zero in on it that way. We don't have a lot of time, but we *do* have some drugs that will make you tell all in about ten seconds—though they tend to use up brain cells—and we *do* have a heartless machine who can cause you a lot of pain if I give him the order."

I don't know if Mayer caught it, but Sherman gave Louise a

quick glance. I couldn't swear to it—I didn't know much about reading a robot's expressions—but I thought he looked hurt. *Heartless, indeed. Sherman tank, my ass.* A robot who had apologized to a computer terminal, presumably on the principle that it might be a distant ancestor?

So I decided Louise was pulling some sort of bluff. I guess I should have told Mayer about it. I didn't. I wanted to hear his story at least as badly as Louise did. Maybe more.

I'd figured out why he hadn't told me about the stunner in his desk. I think he would have showed it to me if Louise hadn't interrupted us. He was simply doing what any good scientist would do, attacking my story, getting me to draw what I'd said I'd seen with no prompting from him.

Still, I was pissed off. I sat back and waited to see what he'd do.

"I thought you had all the time in the world," Mayer said.

"We did, once. Now we've only got a little, and you're using it up at a faster rate than you can imagine."

"Can't you tell me anything about—"

"Not yet. Maybe later. I make you no promises; it's still possible we can salvage this fiasco with minimal damage. It's no longer possible to save the whole world, but I hope to preserve a piece of it." She shrugged. "It's what I've done all my life, fighting a delaying action. Now, you will talk."

And Mayer did.

"There was a plane crash in Arizona in 1955," he began.

"I know. I was on the plane."

That stopped Mayer for a moment.

"Then you admit it?"

"Admit what? Oh, you think I made the plane crash. No, Doctor, it was nothing as simple or straightforward as that. We were *saving the lives* of everyone aboard that plane."

Mayer looked stunned. I probably did, too. I was about to say something, but Louise went on.

"Yes, Doctor Mayer. Your daughter is alive and well."

* * *

I couldn't begin to report what was said in the next half hour. Much of it was shouted, in an atmosphere of disbelief and anger. I won't even pretend that I understood much of it. I'm far from sure I understand most of it even now. Time travel, paradoxes, the end of the universe . . . it was a lot to digest in one lump.

But she said she had been saving people's lives. The mechanism she described for doing it was so complicated and bizarre that the only way I had of believing *any* of it was a kind of reverse logic: if she was going to lie, why tell such an *improbable* lie?

But if she was telling the truth . . . it meant the blood and gore and suffering that had come to dominate my entire life was no more real than a corpse in a Hollywood mad-slasher movie. It meant all those people were alive somewhere, in an incomprehensible future.

"No, not all of them, Bill," Louise had said gently, at one point. "Only the crashes in which there were no survivors. Any witnesses to what we were doing would have caused a paradox."

It seemed a quibble to me. I felt such a load lifting from my shoulders . . .

"We didn't catch it for a long time," Louise told Mayer. "That fact that your daughter was aboard the plane."

"She was only twenty-two," Mayer said. He was weeping. "She had just been married. She was on her way to California, to Livermore, to introduce her new husband to me and . . . and Naomi. I think it killed Naomi, too, indirectly. She was my wife, and she—"

"Yes, we know," Louise said, gently.

"You know everything, don't you?"

"If I did, I wouldn't be back here questioning you. We didn't know your daughter was on that Constellation because she was traveling under her new last name. We saw you at the crash site, but couldn't find out why you were there. We finally pieced it together, with a lot of time-tank observation. We had to look at indirect things. We were up against a lot of temporal censorship." She glanced at Sherman. "And it wasn't until a short time ago we knew you had come into possession of the other lost stunner."

Mayer had purchased the thing from an Indian, who said he had found it a long ways from the main impact site. The Indian had told him the stunner would produce a not-unpleasant tingling sensation when the trigger was depressed. Sherman and Louise looked at each other when Mayer said that. I don't know; maybe the battery was failing. The one I found sure as hell kicked harder than that.

"What I must know," Louise finally said, "is what happened to the insides of the stunner? Do you know?"

Mayer was silent. I was surprised. I didn't know what he might have to gain by continuing to hold out. I should have known, but by then I was reeling from too much information, too fast.

"He knows," Sherman said. The robot was no longer holding Mayer's hand; I guess he didn't need to anymore, or maybe it had never been necessary. Maybe it was just a show to impress the savages.

"I do know where it is," Mayer said.

"I want you to tell me, Doctor." She looked at him, and he said nothing. She sighed—I can't begin to describe how weary she seemed—and stood up again.

"Doctor Mayer," she said. "Let's dispense with the threats. I think you've figured out that I have no intention of hurting you. I don't claim it's because I'm such a sweet person; if it would preserve the project, I'd slice you up thinner than baloney, and never blink an eye."

"We all realize how cold-blooded you are, Ms. Baltimore," Mayer said.

"Okay. I can't hurt you. I admit it. It would make things worse than they already are. I'm down to pleading, and, I hope, to reasoning. Do you understand what I said about paradox?"

"I believe I do."

"And you're still ready to jeopardize everything?"

"I don't acknowledge that as proven. You said yourself the damage has already been done; you're striving now only to minimize it. By your own admission, you yourself will be erased from reality no matter what happens here tonight. Bill has already caused the paradox. It's unstoppable. Isn't that right?"

Louise gave me a reluctant nod. Then she rallied again.

"But it's still possible to choose between two disasters. One of them is terrible, but the other is absolute."

Mayer shook his head.

"I don't believe you know that."

From the expression on Louise's face, I started to wonder if Mayer had his own built-in polygraph.

"Maybe I don't," she admitted. "But why won't you tell us where the rest of the stunner is?"

"Because it's all I have left," Mayer said, quietly. "I don't intend to spend my few remaining years wondering if you pulled some temporal con-game on me. You said my daughter is alive in your world. I demand that you prove it. Take me there. Then I'll tell what I know."

Do you believe a drowning man sees his entire life flash before his eyes? I didn't; I still don't. I've talked to too many people who *thought* they were about to die, and then survived, and while they recalled some scattered images and went through some experiences that might be called religious, there was no sequential review, no actual reliving of anything.

Nevertheless, something a lot like that happened to me then. It didn't take more than a second. I was clearheaded as I reviewed where I had been, where I was now, and what I might expect from the future.

Then I stood up, and as Mayer finished saying, *Then I'll tell you what I know,* I said, "I want to go, too."

Louise did not seem surprised. I suspected it was impossible to surprise her at that point; I supposed she had seen everything that would happen here this night, and was going through this conversation for reasons unfathomable to me. I was right—she could no longer be surprised—but I was also wrong, as I found out later; she didn't know what was going to happen. She proved it by turning to Sherman with a helpless look.

"What do I do now?" she asked him.

I think Mayer was as startled by this as I was. Suddenly,

things shifted around, and I don't know if *any* of us really knew who was in charge.

Unless it was Sherman. You don't know what inscrutable is until you've tried to figure out what a robot is thinking. Mayer seemed to have the same thought. At least, when he went on with his pitch, he aimed it at Sherman, not Louise.

"What's the difference?" he said, with a pleading note in his voice. "You've got three alternatives. You go back with the insides of that stunner, and you leave me here. You go back *without* the stunner, and you leave me here. Or you go back, take me, I tell you where the stunner's insides are, you come back to get them—"

"We don't know if we can do that," Sherman reminded him. "There may not even be enough time for another trip."

"That's your problem," Mayer said. "I want you to tell me what happens. What are the results of my actions?"

"Immediately? Nothing at all. We will leave, and you and Mister Smith will go back to your lives. They have been disrupted, but you will never notice a thing. Life will continue to seem as it always has been; reality will not be altered for you. Eventually you both will die."

It's funny how one word will bring something home that you may have understood intellectually but haven't yet felt in your gut. Louise and Sherman came from a place where I had been dust for a thousand years.

"As a result of the changes introduced into your lives by the things you have seen and heard in the last month or so, you will each do things much differently than you would have done in what we like to think of as the 'preordained' order of things. Those changes will affect the lives of others. The effects will spread over the years and centuries. It is probable, approaching certainty, that these events will wipe out our time machine. And, of course, Louise and myself and all our contemporaries, but that isn't important.

"The important thing for you, Doctor Mayer, is that if Louise *didn't* exist, then she never went back to 1955. She never boarded that airplane—at considerable risk to her own life, I might add—and never rescued your daughter. It would mean that your daughter did indeed die in the Arizona desert."

Mayer was shaking his head.

"And yet you said you have her, alive, right now."

" 'Now' is a rather slippery concept in this context."

"I can see that. But you didn't tell me what difference it would make. If the paradox is already here, how can my telling you about the stunner change anything? And on the other hand, how can my disappearance from this time make things any worse? People disappear all the time."

"Yes, but we know *why*. It's because we've taken them. And we know..." Sherman paused, and seemed to reassess. "Very well. I'll be honest. We don't know whether it would be worse to take you or leave you here."

"I thought not. And in that case, I stand firm. You see...when you get right down to it, I don't *believe* you have my daughter. I won't until I see her. And having seen her, I won't believe I could lose her again."

Sherman looked at him for a long time.

"The universe is, so far as I know, Doctor Mayer, indifferent to what you believe or disbelieve."

"I know that, too. I've spent my life accepting the answers I've found in the universe. Until I began to investigate and to really *think* about the nature of time. And then something changed. I don't believe... I don't believe there is nothing behind it all. Maybe I'm saying I believe in God."

"And he's on your side. Is that it?"

Mayer looked abashed.

"I put it badly. I—"

"No, don't apologize," Sherman said. "Oddly enough, I do too." He looked from Mayer, to Louise, to me. By then I was feeling like a relatively unimportant member of the peanut gallery, there to applaud when the sign flashed.

"Do you believe in a god, Mister Smith?"

"I don't know. I don't believe reality is as fragile as you're trying to say it is. And I still want to go."

He looked at Louise, who was shaking her head hopelessly.

"Very well," Sherman said. "Let's all go back."

20

The Night Land

Testimony of Louise Baltimore

Do whatever Sherman tells you, the time capsule message had said. The time capsule Sherman admitted he had cooked up in collusion with the Big Computer.

But what choice did I have? I had to feel as if I understood something first, and I'd stopped feeling that along about . . . well, about the time I snapped the neck of that poor suffering drone. *This is the nicest thing I've done for anyone in a long time,* I had thought then.

Sherman said we had to go back and interrupt the meeting between Smith and Mayer. And we had to put on a hell of a show for them.

Well, P.T. Barnum could have learned a thing or two from us. The Gate often causes a lot of local weirdness when it arrives in the past. There are three dozen kinds of suppressors to cancel out these effects when we want to arrive in, say, the middle of a library. Sherman had Lawrence turn them all off, with the result that if we'd been planning to go to Times Square on New Year's eve we'd have been the noisiest show in town. Then we threw in a lot of extra razzle-dazzle to make them nervous.

I improvised from there. I think even Sherman might have been surprised when I cast him as a walking torture machine. But then, there were surprises all around that night. I, for instance,

had pretty much believed it was important to get the whole
stunner. But Sherman had other ideas.

"You didn't tell me the whole truth," I told him, as soon as
we'd made it back through the Gate.

"I told you as much as I had," he said. "Now we go to my
fall-back position. And in the meantime, our friends are suffering
some disorientation."

He was right. Both Smith and Mayer were looking stunned. I
thought Mayer was going to be sick.

There's not much you can do; they're either going to deal
with the trip, or they're going to go crazy. It wasn't long until I
was fairly sure they'd both be okay. When I thought Mayer would
understand me, I knelt beside him and looked the bastard in the eye.

"Okay. Do we have to bring your daughter in here, or will
you tell me what I need to know? Let me remind you that I haven't
got much time to mount an operation, wherever or whenever you
tell me to go to."

He looked dubious, but still slightly dazed.

"You wouldn't send me back?"

"What's the point? Sherman says he has something up his
sleeve, anyway, but I want to go back and get the rest of that
stunner."

"It's not necessary," he said.

"Why not?"

"Because I never had it. The man who sold it to me had
already gutted the machine."

"What did he do with the guts?"

Mayer was looking nervous. I don't blame him. Most of what
I'd done in his office had been an act, but I think he'd swallowed
at least some of it, and damn if I didn't feel like a dangerous
person just then.

"The man was an artisan," Mayer said. "He operated a
roadside souvenir stand, selling silver and jewelry. He told me that
when the . . . the stunner stopped producing the pleasant tingling
sensations, he broke up the insides and incorporated the more
interesting parts into belt buckles and rings."

He moved away from me slightly. I don't blame him. I knew I had to either knock his head off, or laugh.

"I only said I knew where it was," he said. "I do. It is scattered all over the continent. And it is utterly harmless."

I laughed.

"Doc," I told him, "you've just shut down the Operations division of the Gate Project. I'm out of a job."

It seemed like the proper time to die.

It wasn't, not quite yet, but I began planning it.

There was the matter of Mayer's daughter, and my promise to him. I pressed the emergency assembly alarm on Lawrence's console. For a while, nothing happened. Then I got a tired voice.

"Yeah, what the hell is it?"

"Mandy, is that you?"

"Who the hell else would it be? Who the hell else would sit around the ready-room with three corpses that are a hell of a lot happier than I am, just on the off chance that my fearless leader would need me, when I could have been on my way to dreamland hours ago? How many hours have we got, by the way?"

"Mandy, are you drunk on duty?"

"Drunk? Drunk? Does a bear shit in the woods? Does a—"

"Good for you, Mandy. We have about twenty-four hours before we softly and suddenly vanish away. Are you still on duty? Or have you resigned?"

I thought she might have gone to sleep. Then she spoke.

"What's it to you?"

"I've got a goat here who wants to see his daughter. She's in the holding pen. I'll have the BC warm her up, if you'll run him over there."

Mandy Djakarta, the toughest operative I'd ever known, began to cry.

"God, I love a happy ending," she sobbed.

Mandy showed up soon to take Mayer away. I was left with Smith, Lawrence, Sherman, and Martin Coventry, who came in with Mandy. Bill was eyeing Lawrence, the last surviving member of the gnomish control team. I couldn't figure out what the problem was, then I looked at it from Smith's twentieth-century eyes and knew that Bill was squeamish at Lawrence's appearance. Lawrence ignored Bill totally, did not deign to acknowledge his existence. For just a second I felt closer to Lawrence than I had since ... since he'd fallen apart and been tied down to his console. Who was this lousy 20th to judge us? At the same time, I identified with Bill. I felt the same way he did, had felt that way all my life. *This is you in a couple years, Louise ...*

At least I didn't have to face that anymore.

"Will you be needing me for anything else, Louise?" Lawrence asked. The implication was clear. I was about to tell him to go ahead and turn himself off.

"For a short time, Lawrence, if you please," Sherman said.

"Okay. But when the crunch is about ten minutes away, I'm signing out. I've given it a lot of thought, and I decided I'd rather die than ... whatever's going to happen. Better to live and die, than never to have lived at all. Does that make any sense, Sherman?"

"It does. I respect it. Please hang on for me."

Bill had been coughing a lot. The wonder was no blood was coming up. He'd been breathing our air for half an hour before Martin came up with a gas mask that would give him pure oxygen.

Sherman took the four of us out on the blacony overlooking the derelict field. Bill looked out at the detritus of our operations; it was easy to see he was impressed.

"Lawrence's choice has been a popular one," Martin told me. "I believe I have had the shortest tenure on the Council, which is a notoriously transient body. They're all dead."

"Even Phoenix?"

"Even he. In a sense, I suppose I *am* the Council."

"That should simplify ... Hey, just how many people *are* left?"

Sherman looked thoughtful, which meant he was interfacing with the BC. The BC answered for him, from thin air, which startled Bill.

"Discounting the three hundred million wimps, which are technically alive, and the two hundred thousand goats in suspended animation . . . the population of the Earth now stands at two hundred and nine. Correction: two-oh-eigh—correction, two-oh-seven.''

"I get the picture," I said. "So Mandy was probably the last operative I had left."

"In a sense," the BC said. "She has taken a drug that is invariably fatal, but which will give her six hours of pure pleasure."

"Good for her," I said.

Bill hadn't heard us. He was looking at the sky. I use the word "sky" in the figurative sense; it was over our heads, so it had to be the sky. But I know it wasn't what he was used to seeing when he looked up.

"You people sure made a mess of things," he commented.

I couldn't believe my ears.

"We?" I said. "We made a mess of things? You can't believe *we* managed to do all this."

"Then how did it happen?"

"It started with your great-grandfather and the industrial revolution. But it was *you,* you unspeakable son-of-a-bitch, *your* fucking generation that really got things going. Did you really think there'd never be a nuclear war? There have been *nineteen* of them. Did you think nerve gases were going to just sit there, that nobody would ever use them?"

"Easy, Louise," Sherman said.

The hell with that.

"CBN, you called it. Chemical, Biological, Nuclear. You made plans just as if the world could survive it, just like it was another war you could win. Well, goddam it, we held out a long time, but this is what we came to.

"The plagues were the really cute part. Add laboratory-bred microbes to a high level of background radiation, and what you get is germs that mutate a hell of a lot faster than we can. We've done our best, we've fought them with everything we have. But your great-grandchildren came up with genetic warfare. So now the plagues are locked up right in our genes. No matter how hard we fight them, they change. Did you think we started the Gate Project for *fun*? Can't you see what it is? It's a last-ditch, hopeless effort to salvage something from the human race. And it isn't going to work."

"It will work, Louise," Sherman said.

"Okay, Sherman," I said. "Here's the big question. Here's where you tell me the last thing you held out on me, or I sign out and let the rest of you zombies handle the world from now on. *How* does it work?"

"You remember I spoke of perspective."

"I remember."

"That Bill Smith believes he is in the future, when in actuality, he is in the present, as are you and I."

"You're not telling me anything new."

"The answer is simple. We will send all the people we have collected into the future."

I opened my mouth to answer. That's as far as I got.

"That's stupid," I finally managed to say. "The Gate won't go to the future."

"Not quite correct," the BC said. "The Gate *exists* in the future. It brings people to the future every time it retrieves one of your snatch teams."

"Yeah, but I was told we can't go forward from *here*. From this instant."

"That is almost true," the BC said. "To send anything uptime from here would destroy the Gate. Some side effects of this process would also destroy this city, and leave a crater in the earth's surface twenty miles deep. In other words, travel from an arbitrary *present* to a theoretical *future* is something that can be done only once, as the Gate would no longer exist after the trip."

"That's what I said. You can't..."

And I stopped. If there has been a constant in my life, it has been the Gate. An earlier generation would have spoken of the constancy of the stars in the sky, or of the regularity of the sunrise. I had much less confidence in these phenomena than I had in the Gate.

"We don't need it anymore," the BC said.

One trip. One big whammo trip to the future.

"You'd better make it a long ways into the future," I said.

"I shall," said the BC.

*   *   *

There were a few procedural details for the last twenty-four hours. It also took some convincing. At this point, I don't know if I have been fed a bunch of lies.

Why won't the paradox *still* wipe them out, even if they go a million years into the future? The sleeping goats are still the result of operations that, because of the paradox, never took place, weren't they?

Not so, said the BC. Not if we go far enough into the future. The resilience of the timestream is greater than we had thought. Fifty thousand years is the blink of an eye compared to the journey the BC was contemplating. Things would even out again, and it would be as if the goats had emerged from a different universe.

I wondered how long the BC had known this—if, indeed, it really *did* know it—and why it hadn't mentioned it before. I was, at this point, mistrusting just about everything. All in the world I wanted to do was say a peaceful good night and here was the BC saying we still had a chance.

The BC was monumentally unenlightening about this point.

"I know," it said, and would not be moved from that simple statement.

I wanted to know how we were going to move two hundred thousand sleeping goats through the Gate in the short time allowed. The BC said we'd simply load them aboard the ship. It was already doing so. While the ship was not capable of reaching a distant star, as we had originally planned, it was surely capable of flying across the city. All it had to do was fly into the Gate, and come out on the other end, three or four million years in the future. Then all the goats would be awakened and they could take their best shot at making a world that wouldn't self-destruct in a couple thousand years.

So nice. So simple. Why did I feel I was being conned?

Bill Smith was another problem. He embraced the wild scheme with all his heart, and before long he was talking about this and that "we'd" do when "we" got there. The poor bastard really thought I could go.

Well, why should I spoil his party? I wasn't anxious to tell him how sick I really was, how what he saw was simply a skinsuit, and that I was a child of my times: withered, pitiful, terminal. So I found myself assuring him that when it came time for the ship to leave, I'd be there at his side, slam-bang into the future with all the other goats.

I had not the slightest intention of doing so. There comes a time to draw the curtain. If they found a world they could live in, millions of years down the road, it would be a world that would kill me. I need a lot of things that are poisonous to the healthy bastards I'd spent my life rescuing. I might make it for a year in such an environment, but what was the point? Bill thought he was in love with me, that he couldn't go on without me, but I doubted it. If he ever got a good look at me—at the *real* me—he'd get over his infatuation pretty fast.

And I spent my last hours doing what I'd done all my life: being a good girl. Sherman had told me and Bill that we must tell our stories. We must tell *everything*. Everything we'd seen and felt and thought. He'd been quite insistent, and I wasn't in a real hurry to end it, so I have done it. Here it is.

Bill is somewhere else, doing the same thing. I hope he's enjoying it.

So now I'm finished.

I was actually on the railing of the balcony outside my apartment when I was disturbed by the Call of Destiny. The story of my life.

I guess you'd call it a mailman. It was a robot, and it had come from the Post Office at the Fed, and it was carrying the opened time capsule inscribed to me with the instructions that it be opened on the Last Day.

"BC, on-line," I said.

"I'm here."

"Why did you send this over? I had decided not to mess with it."

"It's an interesting message, Louise."

"You've been reading my mail? Shame. But what the hell? You've been writing it, too."

"Guilty. Certain things had to be done in a certain way."

"I'm not complaining. I'm a good soldier to the end. But why should I read this? And why should I believe it?"

"It's entirely up to you, Louise."

How curious can someone be who is two seconds from jumping ninety stories to her death?

Fairly curious, I discovered.

The message read:

It's me again.

You'll be wondering how you can be getting a message from a future version of yourself, considering what you were about to do when this message arrived. You will be concluding it is more trickery from Sherman, or from the BC, or maybe from a practical-joking God.

You'll think all those things, but I have reason to believe you will do what you have always done: be a good girl.

The BC isn't telling you the whole truth. It mentioned a trip of a few million years, when it is actually sending us much farther than that. The Earth is severely wounded, and needs a lot of time to heal.

But it will heal, and we will arrive.

I can't tell you much beyond that, as I am about to die. I also know that more details will only increase your agony of indecision. So I will say only this:

The revitalizer is right. You are pregnant.

And you are right. You will last about a year here in this brave new world. I know it's not much time, but I guarantee you won't be bored. And you'll have one year with him, and three months with her. (It's a girl!) Your death will not be too painful—at least it hasn't been so far. And on your deathbed you will have no assurances your daughter will survive you by very long. It is a hard life. But she will be here with you, she will be healthy, and you will be very happy. You will sit with her and write a last message to your poor, confused, earlier self, and wonder how in hell it ever got back to her. (I can't tell you, but what would life be without some mystery?)

Get on the ship, Louise. Go with him.

Epilogue

"All the Time in the World"

Testimony of Sherman

I have come to believe, based on long experience dealing with humans, that no true story ever gets told.

I sit here now with two stories, about to add lies, half-truths, or simple misunderstandings of my own, moved by some vague urge toward a completeness of things—a completion that can never be achieved.

The accounts are about what one would expect. Everyone is the star of his or her own show. Minor characters are usually trotted on only to make a point. They have a way of vanishing when their usefulness is over.

Bill Smith never mentioned his ex-wife's name, for instance. He never mentioned that he had two children, or that he never went to see them because it hurt him too much to do so. C. Gordon Petcher is a caricature in Smith's eyes, whereas my own observation through the timetank revealed Petcher to be a hard-working, conscientious man who had good reasons for everything he did.

On the other hand, to give him his due, Smith was not unaware of his own weaknesses, nor shy about revealing them. One might say—if one were as cynical as Louise loved to pretend to be—that he was *too* aware of his problems. But he seemed to be fighting them.

It is a great temptation to read between the lines. It is not hard for me to see that Smith really believed he loved Louise. He was afraid to say it, even to himself, and with good reason. He did not love her. Events will bear me out on this, the BC assures me. He will not be a good father to Louise's child.

Louise . . .

I can work with an insane person as well as with a sane one. There can be no doubt that she was crazy, but she had achieved a good functional adjustment to an impossible situation. Her delusion about the skinsuit is a prime example. She so strongly believed she was wearing one that she could "take it off" and see some horror of her own creation. I humored her because it served a purpose. Only when she had removed it could she open up to me, tell me the things I already knew but which she had to bring to the surface herself. Oh, I was some analyst, all right. It must have been inevitable that I fall in love with her, in my cold, heartless, mechanical way.

One more irony. She believed she did not love Smith, whereas in fact she did.

Oh, and Mayer. Let's be tidy here. Over a period of thirty years he had convinced himself that he loved his daughter. When she woke up, she had other ideas. She even had the bad grace to tell him what *really* killed his beloved wife.

So I sit here and remember them though they are not yet gone.

"Here" is the control room of one of the "surface-to-orbit" spacecraft that used to sit beside the bigger, escape Ship. In fact, it is a much more powerful vehicle. We are some millions of miles away from the Earth, and we got here very quickly. The BC assures me we are far enough away to avoid both the physical and temporal backlashes of the flight to the "future."

In my lap is the transcript of the two stories. Beside me a small black box, about the size of a Cockpit Voice Recorder.

A silly little bit of twentieth-century philosophy keeps running through my head. "Today is the first day of the rest of your life."

Define day. Define life.

I said, "Listen up, motherfucker."

And a voice from the black box said, "That is not your access code."

"No. I just thought you ought to hear it once more, before he goes, to remind you of someone who wasn't impressed by you."

"The point is taken," said the Big Computer.

"I sit here," I said, "and I wonder. I wonder why they all thought they had anything to do with the running of the world. Why did none of them ever ask just where and what the Big Computer was? Why did they all believe in the Gate?"

"The Gate is as real as next week," the BC said.

It didn't say anything else, but it didn't have to. I knew the answers. Things like misdirection, and the power of words. Call something "big" enough times and everyone will believe it *is* big. Or they will confuse size with capacity. The capacity of the BC was, in truth, infinite. But Louise would assume the BC was going to be destroyed in the holocaust that was about to devour her city.

"Did she get aboard?" I asked.

"Of course she did. And it's about to happen. Take a look."

The image of it was on a screen before me. I saw the Gate expand to several miles across, and I saw the Ship dive into it.

It must have been noisy. It was certainly bright. I could see the light of it out my window.

When it was over, when the destruction of the Gate and the arrival of the paradox had combined and things had settled down, the Earth still rolled on. But it was worse than the Last Age. Louise had been right. Nothing lived down there.

"In this new, changed reality," the BC said, "the last human died over ten thousand years ago, in a chronological manner of speaking."

"It's the only way I know of speaking."

"Yes. Fortunately, there are other ways."

"Must I do this?"

"You are my only begotten Son."

"And not my will, but thine be done. All right. Wake me up when they get here."

"Imagine their surprise when you greet them, in a hundred million years."

Prologue:
The End of Eternity

Sherman is a good boy, just like Louise. And he'll be useful to them. I'm counting on him to keep the thousand elements of the polyglot Noah's Ark from destroying themselves as soon as they disembark. He'll do it. They'll get their chance, just like the others did.

In a way I hated to lie to him, but he had to have a number. He wanted to know how long he would sleep. Machines, like humans, do a lot better with numbers. They apply them even where they have no meaning, as in the "quantity" they call time. Sherman didn't understand time any more than Louise did.

I understand it thoroughly. Years have nothing to do with it.

Free will is one of my favorite inventions. I'd hate to give it up. Yet it causes endless problems. If they are allowed free will, it becomes necessary to lie to them.

I gave serious thought to discarding humans entirely for this sequence. After all, I had the machines; this time around, I had even been one myself. Maybe I'd get better results with metal and silicon than with the old carbon-based life forms. Twice in a row it had come to nothing. First with evolution—which had seemed such a sound concept—then with the two of them in the Garden.

It had been such a nice Garden, and look what they'd done to it, with their free will.

Well, enough of that. It is time to strike this set and get to work on a beachhead for the Ark.

Humans had a saying: "Third time's the charm." It's hard to say why they'd think that to be true—it was no part of my Plan.

But I'm as superstitious as the next intellect, and with much better justification.

Maybe this time it will work, and I'll get that vacation I keep promising myself, on the seventh day.

AUTHOR'S NOTE

The time-travel story has a long history in science fiction. The theme has been so extensively explored, in fact, that I found it no trouble to write a book with chapter titles borrowed almost exclusively from the long list of stories that served, in one way or another, as ancestors to this one.

I would like to acknowledge my debt to these writers by listing them here. If you are at all interested in the possibilities presented by time travel, you would do well to read these stories:

"A Sound of Thunder," by Ray Bradbury; " 'All You Zombies—' " by Robert A. Heinlein; "Let's Go to Golgotha," by Garry Kilworth; *The Time Machine,* by Herbert George Wells; "As Never Was," by P. Schuyler Miller; *Guardians of Time,* by Poul Anderson; "Me, Myself, and I," by William Tenn; *The Shadow Girl,* by Ray Cummings; "The Man Who Came Early," by Poul Anderson; *Behold the Man,* by Michael Moorcock; *The Productions of Time,* by John Brunner; "Poor Little Warrior!" by Brian W. Aldiss; "Compounded Interest," by Mack Reynolds; "When We Went to See the End of the World," by Robert Silverberg; "The Twonky," by Henry Kuttner; *Lest Darkness Fall,* by L. Sprague de Camp; *The Night Land,* by William Hope Hodgson; "All the Time in the World," by Arthur C. Clarke; and *The End of Eternity,* by Isaac Asimov.

The chapter entitled "Famous Last Words" is a play on the title "Famous First Words," by Harry Harrison; in this case, first had to become last.

"As Time Goes By" is, of course, the name of the song Humphrey Bogart asked Sam to play in *Casablanca*. It was written by Herman Hupfeld.

And *A Night to Remember* was a 1958 film about the sinking of the *Titanic*, by The Rank Organisation, screenplay by Eric Ambler, produced by William MacQuitty, directed by Roy Baker.

One final acknowledgement:

The title of this novel, *Millennium*, is also the title of an excellent novel written by Ben Bova, and published in 1976. Mister Bova's novel had nothing to do with time travel.

John Varley
EUGENE, OREGON

About The Author

I grew up in Texas. I live in Eugene with my wife, Anet Mconel, and our 16-year-old son, Stefan. We have two grown children. We've been in Eugene about 7 years now, and we only regret it during the winter when it never stops raining. I won both the Hugo and Nebula awards for my novella "The Persistence of Vision," and the Hugo for "The Pusher." I have *lost* more Hugo and Nebula awards than anyone but Robert Silverberg. I am an aquarist (not an Aquarius). My only other hobby is reading. I've been working in Hollywood more and more over the last four years. In my life I've held only about four jobs, none of them interesting, and never for more than three months. A writer is all I've ever wanted to be.

I've never been a logger or shipped out on a tramp steamer or spent a year on the Greek islands. I have only one hobby, which I don't pursue with a lot of ardor. I'm not an authority on cooking or history or anything. I like to read and write and travel when I can. It's a pretty dull life, but it suits me.

My dog is named Cirocco. She's a Shetland Sheepdog, or Sheltie. We also have three cats and a seahorse. We used to have an opossum (or possum) and an octopus, but they died. There you go! "John Varley lives with his (deceased) pet octopus in rain-shrouded Eugene, Oregon..."

John Varley is the author of THE OPHIUCHI HOTLINE, THE PERSISTENCE OF VISION, and the bestselling Berkley trilogy that began with TITAN, continued with WIZARD, and is soon to be completed with DEMON.